MY SKIN IS
MY SIN

MY SKIN IS MY SIN

A novel by

DeJon

Q-Boro Books
WWW.QBOROBOOKS.COM

An Urban Entertainment Company

Published by Q-Boro Books

ISBN 10: 1-933967-20-X
ISBN13: 978-1-933967-20-2
LCCN: 2006936047

First Printing May 2007
Printed in the United States of America

10 9 8 7 6 5 4 3 2 1

Cover Copyright © 2006 by Q-BORO BOOKS all rights reserved
Cover Concept by DeJon
Cover layout/design by www.mariondesigns.com
Editors: Alisha Yvonne, Melissa Forbes, Tiffany Davis, Leah Whitney

Q-BORO BOOKS
Jamaica, Queens NY 11434
WWW.QBOROBOOKS.COM

Dedication

I dedicate *My Skin Is My Sin* to all my family, friends, and fans who supported me on my first book, *Ice Cream For Freaks*.

CHAPTER ONE

"**D**amn, baby, why don't you lift up that short skirt so I can see that fine, yellow pussy of yours?" Mr. Frost asked in a low but horny voice.

"I don't know. What if someone was to come and catch us? I wouldn't want you to get in trouble and lose your job over me," Moet shyly replied while batting perfectly shaped almond eyes.

Mr. Eddie Frost was a short, stocky dwarf-type man with prominent features that resembled a full-grown pug dog. What caused Mr. Frost's heart to race just a little bit faster and his blood to rise a degree or two higher were young, pretty teenage girls who were just beginning to explore the curious world of sex. Being the assistant principal of the local high school was the perfect breeding ground for his warped, twisted, insatiable sexual desires that his highly illegal overseas videotapes failed to satisfy.

"Don't worry, sweetheart. Nobody ever comes back here this time of day," he replied as he looked around and then lightly grabbed Moet's small waist with his thick fingers.

"OK, I guess you're right. Plus nobody would think dat we would ever be doing anything. Let me get it hard first," Moet stated, feeling a little more relaxed now as her delicate fingers reached for the cheap pants suit zipper.

"Yeah, that's a very good idea. Put it in your sweet mouth so it can be good and ready for your tight cunt," Mr. Frost said in a hoarse whisper as he laid his hands on Moet's shoulder, guiding the bashful Moet to the stage floor behind a heavy curtain that concealed their illicit act.

Nah, I don't want to cum in this bitch's mouth. I got to have a piece of that soft tail, Mr. Frost thought as he pumped Moet's wet mouth while her full lips did their thing.

What Mr. Frost was totally unaware of was that Moet was really a twenty-year-old transvestite who happened to be HIV-positive. Moet worked the Red Light District, deceiving middle-aged, lusting men who often got more than they bargained for. On a few occasions, some of Moet's tricks would find out his true gender during the middle of the sex act, but they would be too far gone to put an end to it. After the customer came heavily, he would usually scream out that he was not gay and that this was the first time something like that had ever happened. Moet would console the whimpering and sometimes confused men while handing them his business card, which they eagerly took.

"Yeah, motherfucker, I know you like dis," Moet spat out, his voice now taking on a more manly tone.

Mr. Frost barely had time to open his eyes in surprise when suddenly a group of females rushed the shocked man, tackling him to the hardwood floor. Before the assistant principal could regain his balance, Moet threw him in a dope fiend chokehold as the girls took off his pants and underwear.

"What the fuck is going on? Do you all know who I am?"

Mr. Frost asked as he looked at the five females, who were wearing low baseball caps and bandannas to mask their identities.

"Yeah, nigga, we know who the fuck you are. You a piece-of-shit pervert who likes to prey on young high school girls," one girl said as she stood over the victim.

"Since he likes young pussy so much, let's give him a little taste," a wide-shouldered girl said while laughing. She then stuffed a super absorbent, period-drenched maxi pad in his mouth and tied it firmly in place with a pair of dirty, stained, pink panties.

The assistant principal tried in vain to free himself as the other girls held his arms and legs down, while Moet maintained his vice-like grip around Mr. Frost's neck.

"Now let's get the real party started," a short, brown-skinned girl said while pulling out a couple of cartons of large, white eggs.

"Oh, shit, this nigga's dick done went and got soft. Somebody get it hard again," someone called out.

"I'm not touching his nasty ass," another girl said with disgust.

"Fuck it! I'll do it. Hold his arm," a teenage girl shouted. Soon she was milking Mr. Frost's organ to its full four inches with lightning speed. A couple of seconds later, when the dick was standing straight in the air, each girl took turns smashing egg after egg on the head of the man's sensitive, exposed penis. The sharp eggshells tore into his skin, making his private parts feel like they had been dragged through crushed glass.

"Let's go," the girls all shouted as Moet punched the half-unconscious man a couple of times in the face.

"And we putting in the videotape of you freaking off with a dude on the Internet," a red-boned female spat out with a sly smirk as she held a tiny, handheld camcorder.

Before Pumpkin left the scene, she cruelly stamped on

the man's tender genitals with her Timberland boots, thinking about how this man that she trusted had groped her in his office on the pretense of her so-called failing grades. The last thing the assistant principal heard before he fully passed out was his ex-students giggling as they fled the scene.

Later on that night, all the girls were at one of their friend's houses, celebrating that they had finally made it through high school. After the group finished cracking up on how they finally got back at Mr. Frost for all those years of chills-run-down-your-back stares and "I'm sorries" when he brushed up against them a little too long, they began discussing their future plans.

"I'm going to move out of mom's house to an ill apartment," one girl said.

"My man wants me to move with him to D.C. where his connect is, so he won't have to travel so far," another female said while taking a sip of E&J brandy.

"I'm going to enroll in some college where they give out all kinds of grants and loans, so I can get me a hooked-up ride," Fatima said, despite the fact that she had dropped out of school three months earlier. Pumpkin just sat there smoking, not responding because she had no idea what she planned to do now that she was out of school.

Soon about six guys arrived at the secret, illegal party, bringing with them drinks and weed, with pussy on their minds. Couples soon paired up, going off to different parts of the house.

"So, Pumpkin, what you planning on doing, now that you squeezed your way through school?" Junior asked playfully.

"I wish I had your skills, so they could give me a full-ass scholarship," she replied. Junior was the school's basketball star. He had just accepted a scholarship to Georgetown University. He was six feet two inches tall with brown skin, and he loved his mother and basketball more than anything in the world. Most of the girls from the hood wanted to get with him, but his rigorous schedule of practicing and studying made it hard. He and Pumpkin met a year ago, when they played a friendly game of basketball at the local playground.

Pumpkin and Junior talked for a while about everything from music videos to how he wasn't going to let any college girls trap him. It was a well-known fact that he was destined for the NBA. Junior walked Pumpkin home and they promised to keep in touch with each other, no matter what.

"Pumpkin, you home?" a voice called out. Pumpkin groggily awoke from her sleep and looked at her watch.

"Damn, it's four-thirty," she said to herself. "I'm in my room," she answered back, recognizing her aunt's voice. Her aunt appeared at her door, holding an envelope.

"You have some mail," she stated while handing her the letter.

Pumpkin looked at the handwriting and knew right away it was from her grandmother, who was living in Muddy Waters, Mississippi. She quickly tore open the letter. Her grandmother was telling her how proud she was of her for graduating, especially because of all she'd been through the last couple of months. She told her how she hoped that Pumpkin attended college like her cousin and that she was doing fine, despite her arthritis. The second page of the letter was wrapped around a crisp, hundred-dollar bill. In the corner of the envelope were a thin, gold chain and a locket that said *Best Granddaughter*. Pumpkin put on the chain and read the letter several times before putting it under her mattress.

Pumpkin loved her grandmother so much. This was the only gift anybody had given her, but she couldn't blame the others. Everybody was going through one problem or another.

Pumpkin had a big day planned for tomorrow, so she ate some fried chicken, watched a couple of movies, and went back to sleep.

*   *   *

Several weeks after Mr. Eddie Frost's unusual ordeal, he developed a painful urinary tract infection that caused his balls to balloon to three times their normal size. When his wife finally convinced him to go to the hospital, x-rays revealed that he had a few jagged pieces of eggshells lodged firmly in his urethra. The next day a specialist in urology operated, splitting Mr. Frost's penis down the middle like a Polish sausage and roughly plucking out the shells with a pair of surgical tweezers. Later, after his wounds had healed, Mr. Frost would get a reasonable erection maybe twenty times a year, if he was lucky.

CHAPTER
TWO

Briiiiiiiing.

Pumpkin hit the stop button on her alarm clock. She got up and took a piss and a quick shower. She then dried off and stared at her herself naked in the full-length bathroom mirror. Natasha Monroe, seventeen, better known as Pumpkin, a nickname her grandmother had given her when she was just two. Her grandmother said she had the skin tone of a brownish-orange pumpkin, not to mention her round, prettily-shaped face. The name had stuck with her ever since. Friends, family members, and even the school faculty opted to call her Pumpkin instead of Natasha. She stood five-feet-seven-inches tall with perfectly rounded, perky breasts and a well-sculptured, fat-free body that caused many women, old and young, to be jealous of her. Her hair, which always had a natural luster to it, hung down to her shoulders when let down.

"Pumpkin, when you get through, I need to holler at you for a minute," her aunt shouted from the living room. Pumpkin dressed in a pair of jeans, Nikes, and a light jean

jacket before heading out toward the living room to see
what her aunt wanted.

"What's up, Liz?" Pumpkin asked. Her aunt sat at the
kitchen table, playing cards with her girlfriend's lover,
who preferred to be called 'Storm.' Pumpkin's aunt worked
as a juvenile probation officer while her partner worked
in a meat packing plant. In their spare time, they went to
wife-swapping clubs and smoked danks, which were weed
cigars soaked in embalming fluid.

"Now dat you finished school, you know you can't lay
your ass up in here all day. So what are your plans?" Liz
asked.

"I'm going out right now to see if I can find a job,"
Pumpkin answered. Storm had a smirk on her face, looking Pumpkin up and down, as she always did when they
came in contact with each other.

"You do what you got to do," Liz said as Pumpkin
headed out the door.

Pumpkin hit the mall and outdoor shopping centers,
filling out application after application. It was now four in
the afternoon and she was feeling frustrated from hearing, "We'll give you a call when something opens up," over
and over. Nobody seemed to be hiring. She decided to
give it one last try at the Red Snapper, a bootleg copy of
the Red Lobster restaurant. Mr. Bernstein, the owner, was
a balding, fat, Jewish man. He interviewed Pumpkin and
told her he liked what he saw. Pumpkin took the comment as off the wall since she had no work experience, but
dismissed it as a white people thing. He stated that she could
start tomorrow but she had to provide her own black skirt
and white blouse. She shook Mr. Bernstein's clammy hand
and thanked him for the job.

Afterward Pumpkin went to a department store in downtown Atlanta and purchased what she needed from the
money her grandmother had given her. She then went and

got her hair done, and topped it all off with getting her nails done at Ming Lee's nail salon. She made it home feeling good, but her mood changed when she stepped in the door. Storm was doing pushups in the living room and stood up when Pumpkin entered.

"What's up, Pumpkin pie?" Storm asked while flexing her pumped-up chest and giving Pumpkin the once–over, as always. Storm had been making overt sexual innuendoes and throwing blatant hints at Pumpkin ever since she moved in three weeks ago.

Before coming to live with her aunt, Pumpkin had lived with her mother and older brother in their grandmother's house in a modest neighborhood in Marietta, Georgia. But six months ago, their grandmother informed them that she wanted to move back to her birthplace, Muddy Waters, Mississippi, and had put the house up for sale. A week before her grandmother moved, Pumpkin and her mother got a little run-down apartment in the seedy, drug-ridden side of Atlanta. Her brother moved in with his girlfriend and their young child. It wasn't a big secret that Pumpkin's mother had a steadily growing crack habit, and eventually she got busted on a misdemeanor charge for possessing drug paraphernalia. Pumpkin's mother's sister, Liz, took Pumpkin in because of her underage status.

Pumpkin ignored Storm's comment and thought, *As soon as that old bull dyke bitch cross the line, I'm gonna give her a buck fifty across the face.* Pumpkin then walked to her bedroom, locking the door and turning the radio on full volume. She could make out slight thumping and assumed that Storm was continuing her workout.

CHAPTER THREE

Pumpkin had been working as a waitress at the Red Snapper for close to a month now. She remembered her first day, when Mr. Bernstein complimented her on her outfit. She took it in stride until the remarks became bolder and more sexually oriented in nature. Pumpkin and her coworker, Dallisha, became fast friends and they would often gossip about the owner.

"That nasty-looking motherfucker always finding a reason to brush up against me," Dallisha remarked with a frown.

"Yeah, his fat, greasy ass is always calling me 'baby.' He makes me want to throw up in my mouth," Pumpkin said. Just then Mr. Bernstein walked by and asked both girls if they were all right. As soon as he turned his back and walked a couple of feet, they stuck their middle fingers up and then giggled.

Since working as a waitress and having to wear skirts, male customers almost always gave Pumpkin compliments on her legs, figure, and general appearance. The envious stares of the other waitresses showed that it was a known fact that Pumpkin was a favorite among the regular guys who frequented the restaurant. Dallisha, who Pumpkin considered pretty, gave her advice on how to talk and flirt with the guys, thus getting bigger tips. Pumpkin threw in shaking her ass as she walked away and bending over on occasions when it was a slow day and the weekends, when it was extremely crowded, especially by the bar section. Pumpkin would sometimes bring home one hundred dollars in tips, and phone numbers that she never planned to call.

Pumpkin was now stashing the money she made under her mattress and giving her aunt some money every week. Now that she was coming home wearing short skirts, her aunt's lover was like a dog in heat. Every time they interacted with each other, Storm's eyes were constantly roaming over Pumpkin's body, her look saying, *Yeah, one day, bitch.* Pumpkin would stare back, her own facial expressions clearly saying, *Whenever you're ready, make your move!* The living situation was growing tenser by the day, so Pumpkin decided to work on her off days to stack more money, so she could move out on her own sooner.

CHAPTER
FOUR

"So, Miss Monroe, why do the customers call you Pumpkin? Is it because you're sweet as pumpkin pie?" Mr. Bernstein asked Pumpkin as she stood by the door, waiting for a cab.

"Excuse me?" she asked, only catching part of what he had said.

"I was just saying that I could drive you home, or maybe we could stop by somewhere first and have a couple of drinks?" he asked in a quiet voice, just in case somebody might be listening.

"Why would I have a couple of drinks with you?" Pumpkin asked in a snide manner.

"I know how hard you've been working, and even on your off days. I've been thinking that you deserve a raise, that's all," her boss said as he looked for any signs in the young girl's face that she might be buying his bullshit.

"A raise?" Pumpkin asked in a puzzled tone. Mr. Bernstein continued, thinking that he had this voluptuous, naïve girl hooked.

"I could just give you an advance on your raise right

now. How does fifty bucks sound?" he asked, thinking all he had to do was mention money to change her snooty attitude. But by the time he pulled out a crumpled fifty-dollar bill and tried to hand it to Pumpkin, the unusual conversation finally registered in her mind.

"What! You think I'm some kind of whore? I wouldn't go with you for all da money in da world. What you need to do is take dat money and buy a good bar of soap and some strong deodorant!" Pumpkin spat with fire in her eyes.

"You black bitch. I give you a job and this the way you talk to me? I see the way you shake your ass in front of the homies. What, you think your pussy ain't good enough for a white man?" he asked with a look of pure contempt on his face.

"Who I fuck ain't none of your business. What you need to worry about is your fat-ass wife sucking dick in the storeroom when you're not there," Pumpkin said with a smirk on her face. Mr. Bernstein acted as if he was about to catch a fit.

"Get the fuck out of my place," Mr. Bernstein yelled. "If you come back here again, I'm going to call the cops on you. And don't you worry about your last paycheck. That's for them dishes you broke last week," he yelled. Pumpkin heard the cab beep its horn and she walked out the door, yelling the entire way.

"Fuck you and dis place, and stick dat check up your fat, white ass."

Pumpkin jumped in the cab and gave the driver her address. She sat back, letting out a sigh while thinking about how she would have to start looking for another job. It would make no sense telling her aunt what happened because she would make it seem as if it was all Pumpkin's fault.

I'm not even going to tell her what went down. I'm just going to start searching for something else on the low, she thought.

Pumpkin walked through the door and saw Storm sitting on the couch. She was smoking a dank with her feet propped up on the coffee table.

"Damn, you look as if you just lost your best friend," Storm said when she noticed a this-is-a-fucked-up-world look on her face. For the past four days Storm had been acting friendly and had stopped raping Pumpkin with her eyes. Pumpkin began to think that all those times Storm made those crude remarks, she had just been playing.

"Nah, just my job at the restaurant," she blurted out before realizing it.

"Don't worry. You'll find something else, and no, I won't tell your aunt. I know how uptight she can get when it comes to money."

"Thanks," Pumpkin said humbly.

"Have a seat and relax," Storm offered while moving over on the sofa.

On any other day Pumpkin would have went straight to her room, but on that day she decided to sit down. She then confided in Storm about what had transpired between her and the strange, disrespectful white man. Storm went on a tirade about how men weren't shit and they were only good for reproducing, and even that act was unpleasant.

After listening to Storm rant about men and watching her smoke the dank, Pumpkin decided to ask a question she'd been wanting to ask her aunt or Storm for a while.

"Why do you smoke dem things?" Pumpkin asked. "Dat shit smells like fried roach spray."

"It's not so bad. You have to get used to it," Storm answered. "A lot of people say it gives them a better rush than just plain old weed."

"I'll just stick with my simple weed," Pumpkin decided.

"Just take one pull and I'll leave you alone," Storm said while holding the cigar out to her.

"Fuck it. One pull won't kill me," Pumpkin said as she took the dank and took a puff.

One puff turned to several as she and Storm continued to talk about life. Pumpkin barely noticed that every time Storm made a joke she would put her hand on Pumpkin's knee, pretending to laugh. The knee touch became a thigh touch followed by comments on how well developed Pumpkin's body was. Pumpkin didn't notice Storm's behavior because she began to feel nauseous from the strange mixture of potent drugs. She excused herself and went to lie down on her bed. She was too tired to even take off her sneakers.

Pumpkin soon drifted off to sleep and dreamed of the good-looking guy with the basketball type of athletic build, who always came into the restaurant. Somehow they ended up on an isolated, tropical island with both of them lying on a hammock between two palm trees. His warm fingers massaged Pumpkin's most sensitive parts below her waist as the sun shone on her face.

Suddenly, for some unknown reason, Pumpkin awoke and groggily snapped back to reality.

"What da fuck!" she shouted as she saw Storm kneeling between her open legs like it was the most natural thing in the world. She felt a finger moving around in her vagina and a thick hand tugging at her panties. Without hesitation, Pumpkin kicked Storm dead center in the face with all her strength. Storm flew back into the dresser, knocking over perfume bottles. As Storm started to rise with blood streaming out of her nose, Pumpkin then grabbed the closest thing to her, which was a pair of scissors.

"Bitch, get da fuck out my room before I stab you da fuck up," she shouted, meaning every word. Storm walked out the room, saying that it wasn't over, as she held on to her bleeding nose.

Pumpkin quickly changed out of her waitress outfit, put on her street clothes, and headed out the door.

CHAPTER
FIVE

Pumpkin went to the nearest payphone and called Dall-isha.

"Hello," a female's voice answered.

"Dis is Pumpkin. I need a place to rest for da night," Pumpkin explained.

"All right. What happened?" Dallisha asked in a concerned voice.

"I had a little drama at my aunt's place. I'll explain everything when I get there." Dallisha gave Pumpkin her address, and then the upset girl called a cab.

Half an hour later, Pumpkin paid the cab driver and hopped out in front of a run-down apartment building on Martin Luther King, Jr. Boulevard. She knocked on the door and Dallisha snatched her inside, immediately asking what happened. Pumpkin told her what nasty Mr. Bernstein had the nerve to ask her and half the story about what went down with Storm. She just told Dallisha that she found Storm standing in her room, but left out the molestation part because of embarrassment. Dallisha remarked that she should have kicked boss' little, white dick off and that

she would have went and cut the shit out of her aunt's girlfriend. Then Dallisha fixed up the couch for Pumpkin
and both girls drifted off to sleep.

The next morning Pumpkin waited until Dallisha was
finished with her bathroom duties before she went in. She
washed her face and brushed her teeth with her finger.

"So, what you gonna tell your auntie?" Dallisha asked.

"I ain't gonna tell her shit. I'm outta dat piece today. I
got some dough stashed away to get my own place. I'll get
a room for now, though. At least I won't have to worry
about nobody being all up in my shit."

Both young women took the Marta bus to the Ocean
Creek apartment complex and walked inside Pumpkin's
aunt's apartment. Once they were inside, Liz rushed out
from her bedroom.

"I'm surprised to see you back here after what you
done!" Liz yelled.

"What do you mean, what I did?" Pumpkin asked in a
surprised tone.

"Storm said you came home angry last night after losing your job and then attacked her for no reason. You're
lucky you're my niece because I had to convince her not
to press charges against you."

Pumpkin just stared at her aunt in disbelief. There was
no sense in trying to explain what happened, because in
Liz's eyes, Storm could do no wrong. Pumpkin just signaled her friend to follow her to her room. Pumpkin went
straight to her bed and lifted the mattress. When she didn't
see her money in the spot where she left it, she flipped the
whole mattress, including the box spring, onto the floor.
Liz appeared in the doorway.

"I hope you're not trying to tear my place up," she said.

"Where da fuck is my money I had hidden under the
bed?" Pumpkin asked, getting more vexed by the minute.

"I don't know anything about no money," her aunt

replied. Then Pumpkin noticed that the drawers were open and all her clothes were gone. Pumpkin started shouting hysterically.

"First you steal my money, and then you take everything I have in dis world. Bitch, if you don't tell me where my things are, shit is about to get real up in here." Pumpkin eased her way toward Liz with murderous intent in her eyes. Liz pulled out a cell phone and started dialing 911.

"I'm at—" was all Liz could get out before Pumpkin snatched the phone and threw it against the wall, breaking it. "I'm going to use the phone in the kitchen," Liz yelled, "and then we'll see how tough you and your hoodlum girlfriend are when the police get here." Pumpkin started to run after her aunt, but Dallisha grabbed her arm.

"Let's bounce," Dallisha advised. "You know how quick these Atlanta police be running up on a motherfucker. Plus, I got warrants out in Dekalb County." Both girls rushed out of the apartment, as Liz yelled, "Don't ever bring your young ass back here again!"

When they got back to the bus stop, Dallisha noticed that Pumpkin had tears welling up in her eyes.

"Don't worry. You can stay with us for a while until you get straightened out," Dallisha offered. "I'm just going to let my sister know what time it is, but I told her about you and I know she won't mind."

"Thanks," Pumpkin said sincerely.

"This is some fucked-up morning. Let's stop by my boy's house and pick up some weed," Dallisha said, knowing that mentioning the drug would cheer up Pumpkin.

CHAPTER
SIX

"Y'all niggas are straight up on some wicked shit, but me and my homegirl gotta make tracks," Dallisha stated as she stood up from her chair. She and Pumpkin were smoking weed at White Boy Danny's house with two of his other friends. White Boy Danny was a straight-up Caucasian fitted with pale blue eyes and dark black hair that was always hidden beneath a baseball cap. He seemed to gain the majority of his friends by the endless supply and varieties of weed that he always had on hand. Because he was one of only a few white boys who lived deep in the hood, he had to constantly prove his gangster against disbelievers. Danny was steadily on the lookout for any man or woman who might try to test him.

"OK, doll, but next time you swing by, be sure to bring your cute ass friend on by," Danny stated shyly, looking over and winking at Pumpkin. Pumpkin was now feeling good, forgetting that she was temporarily homeless and broke, not to mention that the only clothes she had were the ones on her back.

"I'll do dat," Dallisha replied. Pumpkin laughed as she

thought about how her peoples would act if she actually brought home a white guy. Pumpkin had nothing against white people, but she had never run across a white boy that ever remotely sparked her interest.

Both girls left the house as the guys prepared to roll up some more blunts while they played the new car-jacking game on their XBox.

"We can walk. I don't live too far from here," Dallisha told Pumpkin. "I can tell he was feeling you," Dallisha continued, looking over at Pumpkin and smiling.

"Who? I hope you not talking about dat nigga with dem busted-ass kicks, who kept asking where I was from."

"Don't try to play dumb. You know I'm talking about Danny."

"Please! What am I'm gonna do with some white guy? I like my men black, with da dick swinging long and low," Pumpkin said, even though she had had sex only a few times.

"I feel you, but word is that he has a little paper, plus his peoples is connected. Hungry, bum bitches around the way always trying to push up, thinking he's an easy motherfucker 'cause he's white," Dallisha stated with sincerity.

"So how you know him?" Pumpkin asked.

"You know how it is in the hood. When a motherfucker got some good-ass smokes, you know niggas and bitches gonna know the route," Dallisha stated, while pretending to puff on an imaginary roach.

"Here we go. This is where me and my sister rest at," Dallisha stated as both girls entered Misty Valley apartment buildings, located in the heart of Martin Luther King Boulevard. There were a couple of young guys loitering around the run-down building, trying to get their hustle off to a good start. Two older men were sitting casually on an old, tattered sofa that someone had obviously tossed out as trash. The men didn't seem to mind that the couch showed signs that the previous owners allowed their pets to use the furniture as their personal bathroom.

"Yo, shorty, you girls look bored, like you all want to get into something. Why don't you two swing dem fat asses by our place, so we could see if we can cure your problems," one of the men sitting on the couch yelled out as Pumpkin and Dallisha walked by.

"First off, you have to get a place before you can invite someone over, you bum motherfuckers. Second, if my pussy was on fire, feening for some dick, I would just have to burn the fuck up, because I wouldn't go near your stink ass," Dallisha spat back as she turned around to face the men.

"Fuck you, you wack-ass bitch. You probably just finished getting dicked down. Dat's why you acting like shit ain't real," the guy shouted back, standing up.

"You probably just finished getting dicked down by your friend. I peeped da way he was sweating your ass when you stood up," Pumpkin said, joining in with the verbal exchange. The men started spitting more profane language, but the girls had sped up their pace and were out of earshot.

Dallisha was putting the key in the door when shouting in the apartment next door caused Pumpkin to automatically turn her head toward the noise.

"Yeah, bitch, don't think I don't know what went down last night," a female voice yelled out from inside the apartment.

"Come on, Shameeka, when you start fucking around with that shit, it always fucks with your mind. Plus, what would I want with him? Please, he's not my type," another woman answered, trying to squash the disagreement.

"So what the fuck you saying? That I deal with crab-ass niggas?" Shameeka asked.

"Oh don't worry about them crazy bitches," Dallisha said casually when she saw Pumpkin listening to the fight.

"They always fighting every weekend about who's fucking whose man."

It's funny how every M.L.K. Boulevard or Street in America is always in the slums, and the most violent parts of town, Pumpkin thought with raised eyebrows.

Both women entered the apartment and Pumpkin's mouth dropped wide open. She didn't expect to see such a tastefully furnished room in this type of environment. When Pumpkin had been over her friend's apartment the night before, she was so stressed out that she didn't take the time to notice her surroundings.

Everything in the living room seemed to be brand new and expensive. There was a widescreen, flat panel, digital TV that gave the room an even more luxurious feel.

"Sit down and relax, while I see if my sister is in," Dallisha said while flicking on the TV with a state-of-the-art remote control. Pumpkin sat down on a butter soft, hand-stitched, cream-colored Italian leather sofa while her friend walked toward the back room and knocked on the door.

"You in there?" Dallisha asked.

"Yeah, I just got in. What's up?" a female asked from inside the room. Dallisha walked in and chatted for about five minutes before she walked back into the living room.

"My sister wanna holler at you for a minute. I told her a little bit about your situation, and she said she'll see how things work out," she told Pumpkin. Pumpkin walked into the bedroom while Dallisha went toward her own room.

"Don't be shy. Come on in and pull up a chair," Dallisha's sister said. Pumpkin did as she was told and took a good look at her friend's sister that she had been hearing so much about.

Sitting cross-legged on a fluffy, king-sized bed, painting her toenails, was a beautiful, light skinned woman who looked to be in her early twenties. She wore a pair of baggy men's boxer shorts with a blood-red bra that matched the hearts on the shorts. She had her long, dyed hair up in a bun, revealing a slender neck.

"I heard you ran into a little drama with your peoples. What da deal with dat?" she asked.

"You know how it is sometimes. Even your own family can flip on you da hardest. My fucking aunt let her dyke friend steal my loot and throw out all my gear, so I had to bounce from da set-up," Pumpkin explained.

"Chill. Don't sweat the small stuff. Anyway, what's your name?" the woman asked as she applied the final coat to her toenails.

"Everybody calls me Pumpkin."

"Only my close friends call me 'Stacey,'" Dallisha's sister said. "Everybody else calls me 'Goldmine.'" When she caught the look Pumpkin gave her, she continued. "Yeah, da very first night I started shaking my ass up on stage, the DJ saw dat I had racked in so much money, he forgot my stage name and said, 'Give it up for uhhh . . . look at all that dough. The pussy must be certified with the government, 'cause she sho'nuff is a goldmine.' When everyone in the spot saw dat I'd become da baddest bitch catching all the duckets, they had no choice but to bow down and call me Goldmine," she stated with confidence.

"Dat's what I'm talking about. I need your type of money to get me back on my feet. First thing I want to do is get me a little place of my own," Pumpkin said.

"Yeah, I feel you, but not everybody got da looks and moves to stack real paper," Goldmine said, looking Pumpkin up and down as if to say that she was way out of her league. "Since my sister said dat you was mad cool, though, I could kick it to the manager and get you a waitress job or something where I work."

"I appreciate that," Pumpkin said as she watched the older girl brush her hair in the mirror.

"We gonna have to get you some new gear. Niggas spending dat paper ain't trying to check out a bitch in some baggy-ass clothes. They want to know what they getting before they start lightening dem pockets. I'm going to get a little rest and we'll see what we gonna do about some outfits for you later on," Goldmine stated as she began preparing herself for some much-needed sleep after being up all night, chasing that dollar.

"OK, I'll check you later," Pumpkin said before she closed the door to the bedroom. She and Dallisha kicked it for a little while before Pumpkin fell asleep on the sofa, watching MTV.

CHAPTER
SEVEN

"You don't want to fuck with them niggas up the block. They have that feedback shit that will leave you with a weak high, plus fucked-up stomach cramps," Jason stated to a potential customer.

"Let me see what yours looks like?" a middle-aged white man who looked like he could be a vacuum salesman asked.

"I'm telling you, I got the ill shit. It will have you feeling like you can take on every black whore on the block," the dealer stated, while smirking slightly as he watched the man blush.

"OK, give me two hundred-dollar bags," the white man stated, darting his gray eyes from left to right as if he were being watched. After the quick transaction, both men continued on with their own personal business.

Jason kept his grind going, fattening his pockets, convincing the fiends he didn't know to buy from him. It was a little after one AM and he had just finished knocking off his bundle of coke and crack. The customers were steadily slithering by and he hated telling them that they had to wait. He knew damn well that a person who was feening wouldn't wait for anybody or anything. All they cared about was copping their dope and then scheming on how they could acquire their next hit. The only thing he could do was call his peoples, and let them know he was out and the block was still pumping.

"Yo, dis is Jason. I'm over at da west end spot. You know what time it is," he said into his Nextel when he recognized the voice that picked up.

"Hold tight. I'll be there in a minute. Peace." Jason ended his call, knowing that a minute could be anywhere between fifteen minutes to an hour. He decided to call his girl, hoping she was close by so she could keep him company until more product arrived.

"Hello, who's this?" a polite female voice asked.

"Hi, is this Camay?" Jason asked.

"Yes, it is. Who's this?" she asked again.

"I met you at Greenbriar Mall last week. You were rocking a tight-ass jean skirt, so you know I had to push up with da quickness with all dem other cornball niggas hawking," Jason said, trying to disguise his voice.

"Nah, you got me all mixed up with some other female. I don't give out my number to guys who patrol the mall. Anyway, I got a man," she stated loudly so the male caller could hear her.

"So do you think we could meet sometime, and maybe become friends?"

"What are you, deaf? I said, I got a man. Why don't I give you his number and then you can ask him yourself if we can be friends!" she shouted into the phone.

"Chill, shorty, it's me, Jason. I was just fucking around," he stated.

"You know I don't play that shit," she said, smiling.

They kicked it for a couple more minutes before she told him that she would hop in a cab and come check out her boo. Jason bought a forty-ounce of Old English and guzzled his brew, watching money slip from his hands as the fiends strolled by him toward the other drug dealers doing their thing down the block. He was always telling his so-called boss that he needed more work because he often ran out and soon the customers would consider him undependable.

"Hey, small fry, don't fucking tell me how to run my business," his boss would say. "The only reason I put you on is because your brother was a street warrior who got down for his." Jason didn't like the way the boss talked to him or how he conducted his flow. He had been planning to save up so he could cop his own brick and flip it on the other side of town.

"Fuck that nigga. He's gonna see how a real nigga blow up, once I get rolling," Jason said to himself just as a cab pulled up alongside the street.

A stunning, honey mustard-complexioned young woman with unassuming eyes hopped out and walked toward Jason, smiling. She had on a tight Spelman College sweatshirt that fit as if it were masterfully painted on her body. She ran over and gave her man a hug, causing him to spill beer on his new Timbs.

"What's up? Damn, girl, I can almost see the outline of your pussy. Who you wearing that tight shit for?" he asked jokingly, taking a look at her outfit.

"You so nasty," Camay replied, punching him in the shoulder. She sat on his lap as they talked about what she did in school while he sipped his beer, feeling good just to be hanging out with his girl.

Beep, beep. A car horn caused the couple to look up. A gold Eddie Bauer Expedition that looked as if it had just come back from getting a hot wax, was pulling up slowly. Jason knew who it was immediately, so he got up, finished the last of his brew, and approached the vehicle.

"What's up? Is Doc with you," Jason asked the driver. The driver slightly twisted his neck as if to say that he was inside and for Jason to climb in.

"I'll be a minute," he told his girl as he jumped in the back seat, flopping down on the hand-stitched, leather seats.

"So what's the big motherfucking hurry?" Doc asked, turning around to face his worker.

This motherfucker knows damn well what I called him for. I hate niggas who always got to play the hot shot role, Jason thought as he stared at the man who really wanted to be the man.

"I was saying that shit is hot right now, and I ran out of work again" Jason responded, putting strong emphasis on "again" as he handed Doc a large roll of money.

"I told you before, when you young niggas get blessed with a little weight, you wanna get a little rabbit in your blood and take off. I usually don't fuck with too many young bucks because I know sooner or later, I'll have to put them to sleep. You understand me, boy?" he asked with a sharp Southern twang.

"I feel you, but I'm just trying to get mine, like the next nigga," Jason answered.

"Hit him off double," Doc stated to his driver and bodyguard. The driver reached in his jacket and threw Jason two pre-packed bundles of crack and coke, which Jason quickly placed in the lining of his coat. "Oh, I see you got your little shorty out there rocking with you," Doc said as he lifted his shades to get a better look at the college girl.

"Nah, she just dropped by to give me a shout out. I'm about to put her in a cab, so I can finish handling mines."

"We can't have a pretty young thing like that traveling at night by herself. I'll drop her off and make sure she gets home safe," Doc replied, unconsciously licking his lips as he lustfully watched Camay putting on a fresh coat of lip gloss.

"She's all right. I called the cab already," Jason lied, thinking how foul Doc was to openly disrespect him like that.

"OK, I'll see you in a day or so," Doc said, letting Jason know that it was time for him to get out of his ride. Jason got out without saying a word, still a little heated from his boss' comments.

"Everything cool?" Camay asked as she noticed the look on his face.

"I'm straight. I just wanna stack this paper so we can one day get out the hood," he said, while giving a customer the signal that he had product again.

CHAPTER EIGHT

"What's up, girl? You ready to roll or what?" Gold-mine asked while standing over Pumpkin, who was sprawled out on the couch.

"Yeah, I'm ready to bounce."

As they were heading out the door Pumpkin really took a good look at Goldmine, who was dressed casually in a pair of tight blue jeans, high-heeled leather boots, and a form-fitting sweater that revealed all of her melon-sized breasts except the nipples. The women both jumped in a clean Mitsubishi Galant and peeled off.

"Dis is a fly whip. How long you had it?" Pumpkin asked.

"Dis piece of shit? Dis is only a rental. I cop a different one every week. I can't be like dem other bitches, catching cabs all da time or asking some stalker for a ride home. Bitches really gonna be hating when I pull up in my own shit real soon," Goldmine said, looking over and smiling at her impressed passenger.

About twenty minutes later the girls arrived at the Body Shop, a fashion boutique that mainly catered to women in the adult entertainment business. Every once in a while a die-hard female from the block, slinging that ass, would stroll in, but the prices were usually out of their range. Goldmine parked the car in the rear of the shop and the girls got out.

They walked around the front, where Goldmine gave the bifocal-wearing security guard a hug and little peck on the cheek. They quietly talked for a minute, with Pumpkin trying to make out what they were saying. Their body language suggested that the nerdy white flashlight cop was asking Goldmine where she'd been at and she was responding that she'd been busy trying to keep her head above water. She whispered something secretive in his ear as he tried to palm her ass. Goldmine slightly pushed his hand to the side and blew him an insincere air kiss as she told Pumpkin to come on in.

Pumpkin's eyes lit up when she saw all the exotic-looking outfits hanging on the wall, and swinging from the red ceiling with a touch of blue swirls.

"Fuck dat cheap shit. You wash dem outfits a couple times and you have string coming out your ass," Goldmine stated as she grabbed the younger girl and led her to a different part of the store. Both women spent close to two hours in the boutique, trying on various seductive clothes, footwear, and sleeping apparel. They both finally made it to the sales counter, each carrying an armful of expensive clothes. Before the woman working at the cash register could ring up any of the purchases, Goldmine spoke.

"Oh my God, I left my Mastercard in my other bag."

"I'm glad you told me real quick before I rang up everything. That would have been a headache," the middle-aged but well-kept woman said.

"Oh, yeah, it's definitely not here. I got to go back home and get it," Goldmine stated while still pretending to search around in her limited edition Frenchie bag. Goldmine then grabbed an armful of clothes, signaling Pumpkin to snatch up the rest of the enticing garments. "I'll just put these to da side. Sorry for the inconvenience."

"No problem," the saleslady said as she started ringing up another customer's purchase.

The women then headed for the exit. Goldmine winked at the guard as they headed back to the car. Pumpkin knew that Goldmine and the security guard were running some kind of scam, so she knew better than to ask what was going down.

Both girls sat in the car listening to music as they talked about the sick gear they had just picked out.

Ten minutes later the back door swung open and the same security guard looked around, with his Coke bottle glasses gleaming in the afternoon sunlight. He finally emerged from the doorway carrying two large bags with the store's insignia on them. The scheming woman beeped the horn twice as he nervously trotted over. Goldmine quickly got out of the whip and snatched the bags from the man.

"Thank you. You're a real sweetheart," she squealed, giving the now smiling man another light peck on the cheek. He moved in closer for the kill, trying to pin her up against the side of the car.

"I keep risking my job for you, so when can I see you again? I get off at seven," he said.

"Slow down. Someone might see us. I definitely want to get with you. You know I have been waiting for dat white snake for a while," Goldmine told him in her most seductive voice as she roughly squeezed a handful of his crotch. He took that as a hint, so he pressed her toward the car and tried to kiss her directly on the mouth.

"Norman, chill out. I just got my hair done. Give me your number again, so I can make sure I have it on me when I call you tonight," she stated. After maneuvering away from the stale odor of Old Spice and sweat, Goldmine practically dove into the car as Norman wrote down his number, praying she wouldn't lose it again. She had the window already rolled up, but left it cracked a little so that the salivating man could slip her the piece of paper.

"Please call me," he shouted over the music as spittle splashed onto the driver's side window. Goldmine just waved as she screeched out of the parking lot.

When she drove a good half a block away, she tossed the number out the window and turned to Pumpkin.

"Dat's how us bitches do it up in ATL."

"You got his ass strung out. I know you had to fuck him at least once?" Pumpkin asked.

"Hell motherfuckingno! Dat blind redneck gonna have to come up with some serious cheddar if he hopes to get into these panties anytime soon," she replied while laughing up a storm. A couple minutes went by and Goldmine told her that she had to make a couple of moves before she went to work that night.

"I'ma let you out right here. Go get your hair and nails tightened up. Later on, I'll swing by to pick you up so I can introduce you to the night manager at my spot." She handed Pumpkin some money, which Pumpkin acknowledged with a quiet thank you.

"Don't think dis is a handout," Goldmine said. "Da money and gear is a one-time loan, just because I got a good heart," Goldmine stated before pulling off, leaving Pumpkin on the sidewalk.

Pumpkin wasn't used to people talking to her like that, but she knew she wasn't in any position to complain. She then walked off with her bag of clothes, hoping one day she wouldn't have to depend on anyone for anything.

CHAPTER NINE

"Yeah, who is it?" White Boy Danny asked after hearing a soft knock on his front door.

"You probably don't remember me, but I came here with a couple of my friends a week ago. Anyway, my name is Tiffany," the girl answered, hoping he would let her in, even though it was so early in the morning. Danny lifted the heavy wooden bar from across the door and opened it. There was a brown-skinned girl of about fourteen standing on the stoop, carrying a bright orange book bag on her back.

"Oh, I remember you. Come on in out the cold," he told her, opening the door wider so she could squeeze by.

"Thanks," she said.

"Sit back and chill. Let me throw some cold water on my face to wake up fully," Danny stated as he walked back toward the bathroom. The young girl did as she was told, watching Danny walk away like he had more soul than the average black guy from the hood. He had on a pair of Fila slippers, a pair of matching Fila basketball shorts, and a doo-rag tied neatly on his head, even though it was impossible for the texture of his hair to acquire waves.

"So, what's up, shorty?" Danny asked as he walked back into the living room. "You look a little stressed the fuck out."

"My homeroom teacher started bitching about bullshit, so I broke out. My peoples told me about a ditch party today, but I forgot where it was at," Tiffany said.

"Fuck school! Them teachers don't know a goddamn thing. The only thing that matters is that dollar," Danny responded as he turned on the CD player, flooding the room with Young Dro's "Shoulder Lean."

"You're right. Mr. Green is always talking about education is the key to success, but why his ass be on the city bus like the rest of us?" she threw in and started laughing, revealing a mouthful of shiny braces. "You got a little weed?" she asked. "I don't have money right now, but my brother promised me something tomorrow. I'll pay you back then," she said, hoping he'd give her credit.

"Don't sweat the small stuff," White Boy Danny said as he went into another room and came back with a small plastic bag.

"I heard you got some bomb-ass shit," Tiffany said, looking at the drug as he laid it out on the coffee table.

"I got that Sour Diesel to help you get your mind off that school shit," Danny stated as he prepared to roll an extra fat blunt.

Danny knew right away that the girl wasn't a true smoker by the way she inhaled the fumes, and how she held on to the Philly. The more Tiffany puffed on the Diesel, the more she relaxed, talking non-stop about everything that came to mind.

"I feel a little sick," she said after a while. "I think it was that fish I ate last night. Do you mind if I use your bathroom?" she asked, getting up slowly and feeling the effects of the drug.

"Go right ahead," Danny said, knowing it wasn't the fish that made her feel sick, but something he had slipped in the blunt to make it three times stronger.

White Boy Danny sat back on the couch after Tiffany made her way to the bathroom, and he started thinking about his family.

It seemed that Danny's world started to unravel when his dad, who at the time was a two-year rookie cop, got wounded in a shootout. The confrontation left Danny's father with a missing piece of his intestine, thus forcing him to wear a colostomy bag (shit bag) on his right side. Danny's mother stood by her husband, answering his every beck and call, plus maintaining the household. The strenuous recuperation took its toll on both parents, so they decided to hire a nurse/housekeeper to ease the burden. Danny, being only twelve at the time, didn't fully comprehend what was happening when he started hearing the arguments between his parents.

"You haven't let me get close to you for months. What? You find me vile and disgusting because of this bag attached to my side?" his father would scream.

"What do you expect? Do you think I feel sexy after dumping your shit and piss away all day?" his mother would shout back.

Sometimes the house would be deadly silent, and at other times it would get so loud that the sound of Niagara Falls would be just a little drip in comparison to their shouting.

Danny's mother often shared her marital problems with the black housekeeper. One day Danny arrived home from school with an extreme headache. The house was in one of those quiet times, so Danny knew that both of his parents were in different parts of the house doing their own thing. He quietly crept up the carpeted stairway, hoping to go straight to his room and go to sleep. He passed his parents' bedroom, but something, which he couldn't explain even to this day, caused him to stop dead in his tracks. His sweaty hands turned the doorknob as he peeked into the master bedroom. What Danny saw next would remain in his memory forever.

Danny's sweet mother was lying on the bed, naked from the waist down, with her milky, white legs wrapped around the black housekeeper's nappy head. The black woman had her face buried deep in his innocent mother's privates, taking advantage of her moment of weakness. He closed the door quickly, wishing the black lady would get hit by a bus and die on her way home. For a long time Danny couldn't get the sounds of his mother's moans of passion out of his head.

Danny suspected that his father knew something peculiar was going on, but he never openly let on. Soon he went back to work, maybe too soon, just so they wouldn't need Helen, the housekeeper, anymore. Once his father returned to work he began coming home saying things like, "Those porch monkeys are like roaches, living on top of each other. All they do is fuck and breed. Filthy jigga-boos, causing the city to go to hell. Them nigger bitches are the worst. They all are on welfare, while their men get rich selling dope to our children."

Danny had to agree with his father's rants because all he ever saw on the news were daily accounts of what his pop constantly spoke about. Little by little, Danny subconsciously adopted his father's belief system and worldly outlook until he grew into a man much like his father.

"That's some wicked shit," Tiffany said, startling Danny out of his thoughts as she came back out of the bathroom after throwing up a couple of times.

"Why don't you lie down on the soft bed for a few minutes?" Danny suggested as he hugged her by her tiny waist and half-carried the girl to his bedroom.

As soon as the young girl hit the bed, she was snoring as

if she hadn't a care in the world. Danny lifted up her T-shirt and stared at her tiny breasts before biting one so hard, it left teeth imprints. Tiffany moaned a little, but was still out. After biting the girl a couple more times, bruising her soft, tender flesh, he unbuttoned her jeans. Her white cotton panties had a few black pubic hairs peeping out near the waistband. Danny smiled as he got up and went into the bathroom, returning with a wooden toilet plunger. Just as he licked the tip of the handle he heard a couple of hard knocks on the door. He threw the plunger down, closed the door, and went to see who was interrupting his fun.

"What's up?" he asked.

"Danny, what's up? I got a couple of my peoples with me. My homegirl Tiffany said she was heading over here," the guy said in a good-natured tone.

"Yeah, she's here," Danny answered as he opened the door. A group of guys and one girl walked in saying hi, and giving him five. Danny then casually walked back in his bedroom and quickly fixed the girl's rumpled-up clothes.

"Shorty had just finished smoking some weed and said she was mad tired from before," Danny told the group as he opened the door so they could look inside. Tiffany was sleeping like a newborn baby.

"Yeah, that's how Tiffany do. Wants to smoke up a nigga shit and then get all comfortable," the female said while giving another guy some dap.

The group of guys and the girl bought some Northern Light weed and smoked up as Tiffany slept in the next room. When they were ready to go, they woke up their friend and left, telling Danny that he was cool peoples. But once the group was gone, Danny showed his true self as he threw a table lamp against the wall, shattering it and cursing because his private party had been stopped short.

"There's always more where she came from," he said to himself as he prepared to make a couple of phone calls.

CHAPTER
TEN

Pumpkin was still trying on her brand new clothes, trying to figure out which combination went best with
what, when Goldmine walked into the apartment. Goldmine took a long, hard look at the young girl standing in
her bra and panties and had to admit that she possessed
star quality attributes almost equal to her own, if not even
greater.

"Nah, throw on dat black prism skirt with those thigh
high boots," she told Pumpkin. Pumpkin looked up, startled, and tried cover herself with a midriff cut belly shirt.
Goldmine laughed. "You gotta get dat shy shit outta you if
you wanna roll with da big dawgs." She then walked toward her bedroom to freshen up and prepare for the
night at the club.

The owner of the strip club had a habit of fining the
dancers fifty dollars if their hygiene wasn't up to par. He
also fined the dancers if their outfits weren't to his liking.
Sometimes the women would be rushing to work and
carelessly grab mismatched outfits. If he caught them, the
fine would be ten dollars. The girls talked amongst them-

selves about how the owner seemed to make up the rules as he went along.

An hour later both women headed out the door, with Pumpkin wearing the outfit that Goldmine had suggested. Goldmine was dressed in street clothes, carrying a leather Gucci bag containing her stage gear along with various cosmetics. The girls drove silently, listening to music while Goldmine puffed on a small weed joint rolled up in White Owl. Soon Goldmine was pulling in the parking lot of Adina's Jewels, a popular strip club. It was still early in the evening, so the place wasn't as thumping as it would be.

"Chill right here and I'll go holla at da manager about you," Goldmine said as she smiled to a couple of regulars, while walking to the booth where the DJ did his thing. A few minutes later she came back with a tall, dark guy who sported a dried-out perm.

"Dis is my little cousin I was telling you about. See what you can do," Goldmine told the manager, who was already introducing himself to Pumpkin. Goldmine sexily walked off in the direction of the dressing room to get ready for work or, as she put it, "separating those fools from their money."

"I'm Rich," the manager told Pumpkin, poring over Pumpkin's body with his lazy eye.

"My name is Natasha, but everybody calls me Pumpkin," she replied.

"I like it. It has a nice ring to it. Anyway, how old are you?" he asked, looking at her fresh face for the first time.

"I've been eighteen for about three months now," Pumpkin lied, trying to sound more mature.

"OK, but I need to see some ID the next time you come up in here. A girl just quit on me yesterday, talking about she's going to L.A. to make it as an actress. Yeah, right! I'll be seeing her broke ass on the box of a skin flick. Well, anyway, you ever had a job working as a waitress?" Rich asked, getting back to the informal interview.

"Yeah, I worked as one for about six months," Pumpkin responded, lying again.

"Cool. I'm gonna let you work with one of my girls for half the night, and then we will take it from there," he said, waving over a waitress. "The dress code for the ladies is a black skirt, which you already have on, and a matching bikini top. I'll let you work today with what you rocking, but have the right attire tomorrow night," he stated. As the woman walked over, he introduced her to Pumpkin and told her if she needed anything else, just ask.

The lady who was training Pumpkin nearly ruptured her eardrums, kicking dirt on the other dancers' names and how she should stay away from all of them.

"Them hoes do anything for a buck—fuck, suck, and lick a dog's dick if there was enough dough in it for them."

Pumpkin noticed that the waitress had a long, thin razor scar on her face, which Pumpkin later found out was bestowed on her from a stripper about whom she was spreading rumors.

Some bitches just don't learn their lesson, Pumpkin thought.

Throughout the night Pumpkin learned the names of crazy drinks that the customers ordered. She also learned how to lead guys on without hurting their feelings, so she could still get the big tips. Goldmine mostly stayed in the VIP section with the high-paying patrons, who knew their money could buy practically any and everything they desired.

Toward the end of the night Pumpkin heard an unusually loud roar and swung her head toward the stage. A dancer was in the middle of the stage, strutting her wares. She licked and massaged her thick titties, causing her nipples to be fully erect. After warming up the crowd, she grabbed some sort of tube and squeezed out what looked like green toothpaste onto both of her nipples. She then lit the mysterious cream on fire, causing flames to create even more of an illusion for the crowd. The dancer then turned around, dropped to the floor and thrilled the men with her humongous ass. One butt cheek had 100% tattooed on it in big letters, and the other one had Beef tattooed in bold letters. The thick girl then had another dancer carefully place two shot glasses filled with Hennessy on each meaty cheek, and she skillfully moved them up and down without spilling a single drop of alcohol. After her act she threw her hair over her shoulder, downed both the cognac shots, and strolled off the stage after grabbing her pile of dollar bills.

"Dat bitch sure got down for hers," Pumpkin said to herself as a customer started waving her over for more drinks before the bartender called last call. A few times throughout the night, guys asked Pumpkin to join them for drinks, but she politely told them that it was against the rules. She told them that they could buy her drinks, which they did. The bartender only gave the waitresses colored water and they split the money with the waitresses. On the down low, Pumpkin sneaked a couple glasses of Alizé to help her relax.

A short while later, she and Goldmine were in the Galant, talking and laughing about the different events at the club that night.

"Yeah, I made almost eight hundred duckets up in dat piece tonight," Goldmine bragged. She failed to mention that three hundred dollars came from one tricked-out customer who was trying to blow his load by receiving consecutive lap dances in the VIP room. Goldmine expertly studied his facial expressions and when she suspected that he was about to climax, she eased off a bit to cool him down just enough to have him try to get back where he almost was. That was one of her favorite money-making tricks that the horny customers always fell for.

"I clocked about a two and change, plus some numbers," Pumpkin said while smoking a Newport.

"Da money is all right for your first day, but throw away dem numbers. Wasn't no real players out tonight. Wait for da weekend and you'll see how niggas try to ball," Goldmine advised as she pulled up to the housing projects.

Pumpkin and Goldmine made it inside. Goldmine went straight to her room, and Pumpkin looked in on her friend Dallisha to see if she was still up. She was out cold with the TV still playing. Pumpkin quietly crept in, cut the set off, and got some fresh linen to make her bed on the sofa.

CHAPTER
ELEVEN

Doc, his driver, and Jason were cruising in the Expedition after they picked up Jason from the block.

"So you really think you can handle a little more work?" Doc asked, puffing on the sickly sweet smell of his dank. Jason had to roll down the window from the back seat because the aroma of the cigar was making him a little nauseous.

"I'm telling you, it ain't nothing. I got this," Jason answered with confidence.

It was just getting dark when the trio pulled up in front of Blazen Cuts, a popular barbershop that Doc owned. When there was a big boxing fight scheduled on pay-per-view, he often threw big parties with food, liquor, and strippers, which drew the majority of the crowd. Depending on the event, he would charge between five and twenty dollars at the door and sell shots of a variety of drinks. The dancers put on a show equal to the main event, racking up money in lap dances and private fucks, if you were willing to spend two hundred dollars. Doc had someone carefully watching the girls, not for safety reasons, but to make sure they didn't pocket anything extra because he split the money with them at the end of the event.

As soon as they walked into the spacious shop, Doc stopped to talk briefly with some of his skilled barbers. Some customers waiting their turn were either watching television or gossiping about which neighborhood girl did what freaky thing to someone the night before.

"What's up, Doc? I've been cleaning up real good," the obviously slow young man said, looking at his employer for approval.

"Yeah, you're doing a good job. Make sure you feed the fish before you go home," Doc replied and patted the floor sweeper on the head like an obedient puppy as he slipped him a five-spot. The floor sweeper's sister used to work for Doc, and when she received a twenty-year bid for transporting drugs across state lines, Doc promised her that he would look out for her younger brother by putting him on. What he didn't tell her was that he would be cleaning up and running errands for the barbers, getting them their lunch and so forth.

"Come on, player," Doc said to Jason, leading the way into the locked back room, which held a screen that revealed what the cameras placed around the shop recorded. The driver then opened a door that was located in the floor and led to a damp basement.

Oh, this is where this nigga keeps his stash, Jason thought, but then he realized that Doc wouldn't slip up and let him know where he kept his weight. Doc hadn't stayed in business for so long by being careless.

Jason had to accustom his eyes to the dark basement that only had a tiny, low-watt light bulb hanging by a string at the far end of the room. The group reached the other side of the basement, with Doc's white smile gleaming like he had a secret that only he knew about.

"What the hell!" Jason suddenly shouted. He was momentarily startled when he saw a man hanging upside down from one of the rusty water pipes. The man's hands were tied firmly behind his back, with strong evidence that he had been viciously beaten. Standing next to the hostage was a well-muscled, fair-skinned man whose face was peppered with light brown freckles. Doc walked up to the battered man, stood inches away from his face, and spoke.

"So you wanted to be that nigggga and have one of my spots hit up, huh!" Doc then turned to Jason. "It wasn't enough that I let the nigga eat," he said. "I let him live, and good at that. Can you believe he was buying a brand new coupe every four months, but he wanted more," Doc stated, now getting angry, but working to maintain his composure. Jason looked at the light-skinned man, who had his arms crossed, staring blankly as if he wanted another workout at the terrified guy's expense.

"You see, this is what happens when a nigga thinks he has a little paper and a couple of guns. Now the mother-fucker's crying and begging for another chance when just a couple days ago, he was telling his peoples how I'm washed up in the game and now it's his turn to shine." Doc then ripped the duct tape off the man's mouth and continued in a serious tone. "The only thing that's gonna be shining is the handles on your casket."

"Doc, I swear to God I didn't know it was your spot. Please, I could get the money back in a couple of days," the captive begged through half-shut, swollen eyes.

"Nigga, you don't even have a couple of minutes," Doc replied as he placed the tape back over the man's mouth while the man continued to try to talk his way out of his permanent position. Doc turned to face Jason, who was wondering why he was being shown all of this.

"My pops told me an old trick the Ku Klux Klan used to practice on black folks in the old South, who they deemed too uppity," Doc said. "See, they would have victims like player right here upside down, then they would have a couple of real strong, bruiser-type crackers pound the man's stomach until his intestines slowly unraveled, eventually strangling the unlucky person to death. They called this the Devil's Fingers, and I guess you can understand why. The process took approximately four hours of steady pounding. Now that's why I got my man, Life. He used to box in the heavyweight division, so I know he won't disappoint me."

Doc then looked at Life, who quickly threw some punching combinations at the struggling man's mid-section. The man's eyes grew wide with fear as he knew his last days spent on earth would be in agonizing, unbearable pain.

Soon the three men were back in the SUV, leaving Life to finish his high-paying assignment, which he would have done for free.

"Now, Jason, I like the way you handle your business, so that's why I'm gonna up your packages from now on. But remember, if you ever think about trying to play me, just think about ol' boy back in da basement," Doc said intensely while looking over and handing Jason ten times the product that he usually gave him. Jason took the wrapped-up coke that was in a knapsack and started thinking how he wanted to make enough money so he could break cleanly away from this man who enjoyed his dirty work a little too much. They dropped Jason off at his house that he shared with his grandmother and younger sister, so that he could prepare himself for that night's rush of fiends.

CHAPTER TWELVE

"Yeah, that nasty Mr. Bernstein still trying to push up on all the young girls," Dallisha told Pumpkin one day as they sat in Dallisha's bedroom.

"Word?" Pumpkin said.

"You know how his fat ass gets down. This new girl started working there the other day as a hostess and he was all over her, kicking some different shit. After her shift, she started talking 'bout she ain't the one and that she had cousins in da Folks gang who will be waiting for his white ass when he comes out," Dallisha stated, smiling while imagining the owner getting the shit kicked out of him.

"I'm glad I broke out, 'cause I definitely would have caught a charge," Pumpkin threw in.

Both girls talked for a while, with Pumpkin describing all the wild things the girls up in the strip club were willing to do for a dollar. Time passed so quickly that soon Dallisha said she had to get ready for work. Pumpkin decided to get some rest because she had to be on her feet all night.

Pumpkin woke up later and realized that Dallisha had

gone to work and Goldmine had left also, to do whatever she did when she was not at work. Pumpkin kept herself busy by getting her work clothes ready for the night, straightening up the living room, and watching a little cable.

Goldmine walked in smiling, in a good mood because it was Friday, a night when all the guys came out to unwind and spend their hard-earned money.

"So, I see you up and about," Goldmine said, sitting down next to Pumpkin.

"Yeah, I guess so. I just wish I had clocked your paper," Pumpkin answered.

"Like I told you before, every female can't trap dat dollar like me. When I get a chance, I might put you on to a couple of my trade secrets. So, where's my sis?" she asked.

"Oh, she bounced to work a couple hours ago."

"Well, anyway, I'm about to get ready. I left a little something for you in da bathroom," Goldmine said as she walked toward her room.

Pumpkin went into the bathroom and saw a gold wire basket filled to the brim with all kinds of expensive-looking beauty and feminine products. She picked up a strawberry-flavored douche and had to laugh to herself. *Yeah, she definitely got style,* Pumpkin thought. She soaked in a hot bath with Chinese herbal bath beads and used a couple of the products Goldmine had left her, including the douche bag.

An hour and half later, both girls were speeding off to the club while they shared a Philly blunt. Pumpkin noticed that Adina's was starting to fill up more quickly than normal. Less than twenty minutes after Pumpkin started work, a commotion erupted in the direction of the dancers' dressing rooms. Staff and customers alike rushed toward the noise, with the guys hoping to get a glimpse of a cat-fight that they knew often went on in a place like Adina's.

"Bitch, I know it was you! I saw you creeping by my

locker just before I looked in," a short woman shouted as a bouncer tried to restrain the struggling girl.

"You don't have nothing I want, sweetie. What the fuck I need to steal from a dope fiend ho, who sucks a man's dick just to keep her habit straight," the second girl, who was taller and slimmer but had deep scratch marks on the side of her neck, responded.

The crowd busted out laughing at the remark, causing the first girl to struggle even more and spit out even more obscenities, mainly because she knew that what the second girl said about her was the cold truth.

"You talking that good shit right now, 'cause a bunch of motherfuckers standing around giving you heart, but when I catch your skinny ass outside, you'll be singing a different song," she spat. The second female just smiled.

"Whatcha gonna do, stab me with your needle?" With that comment, a high heel came flying through the air, missing the second girl's head by inches, but hitting a by-stander in the shoulder. Before the enraged dancer could get off the other shoe, the bouncer pinned her arms tightly against her sides while she continued to scream.

"Get your faggot hands off me, 'fore I shut this place down for real!"

Just then, Rich, the manager, finally showed up and or-dered some of the other strippers to take the second woman over to the bar, so he could calm things down. But the first woman broke free from the bouncer's grasp, grabbed her bag, and headed out the door, yelling that shit wasn't over. Soon after, the second girl jetted home, telling Rich that she wouldn't be working for a couple of days because she was marked up from the scratches she received.

"What was all da drama about?" Pumpkin asked the waitress who was training her.

"That wild bitch was talking about Topaz stole some platinum heart chain that some regular gave her. What

Rich needs to do is get rid of both of them ghetto bitches."
Before she could rattle on about how everybody was foul,
Pumpkin said she had to go. Pumpkin did catch the waitress rolling her eyes and muttering something under her
breath as she went to attend to some customers.

Moments later, everything went back to normal and the
club started to steadily fill up. The DJ started rocking "Pop
That Pussy" when Goldmine strolled out on the stage,
wearing a skimpy *Arabian Nights* outfit with a thin veil and
cloth shapes cut out like horses to cover her shapely nipples. Goldmine was graceful taking off her clothes, teasing
the audience, and nimbly sliding down the pole. She turned
around, doing the stripper ghetto shake, and Pumpkin saw
that she had an artistic tribal tattoo on the small of her back.
She then put both her legs behind her head, giving the
lusting guys a long frontal view of her completely shaved
vagina, making each one think that the pussy could be his if
the price was right. Just before her act was over, she gave
Pumpkin a wink and walked back toward the dressing room.

"Pumpkin, let me holla at you for a second," Rich said
as Pumpkin walked behind him into his office. "I know I
hired you as a waitress, but how would you like to work as
an exotic dancer just for tonight?" he asked.

"Me? But why?" she asked, not really believing her ears.

"A couple of girls got into it earlier tonight, as you probably heard, and two more broke out because they said
they was sick. I'm not stupid, though. I know some trick
offered them a little paper for their time. Anyway, I've
seen the way you carry yourself. You're a natural. Plus you
got the fresh, young, new face. That's just what this place
needs right now. Do you have an outfit to perform in
tonight?" he asked, imagining the young woman giving
him a private show in the office.

"I got a little something," she answered, still deciding if
she should really go through with it.

"Cool. Head home and I'll schedule you in for a show," he said, opening the door and leading her out.

Pumpkin's head was spinning as she thought about how everything was moving so quickly. She made up her mind to go through with it when she thought back to how much money Goldmine made in one night.

I could at least make half of what she made, Pumpkin reasoned. She quickly located Goldmine sitting on some fat guy's lap and giggling in his ear as he rubbed her back, hoping to turn her on. She told Goldmine what Rich had asked her and explained that she would be back with an outfit.

"Hurry on back. Da way da spot is pumping, it's like the money just jumping in your pockets."

As Pumpkin excitedly walked away, Goldmine chuckled under her breath. The guy she was entertaining wondered what that was all about, but when Goldmine slightly brushed her long fingernail against his crotch, his thoughts centered back on trying to bust a nut without spending all of his rent money.

The cab, which one of the bouncers had called, pulled up, and Pumpkin jumped in. Goldmine stayed close to the exit, hoping to catch Pumpkin before she went to the dressing room. An hour later Pumpkin was back, strolling through Adina's wearing a long, borrowed leather coat.

"Don't worry. We black women are in tune with nature's energy, so we know how to shake yhat azz," Goldmine told Pumpkin when she caught up to her in the club. "Let me get you a shot of Hennessy Reserve to help smooth out your first dance. I'm just looking out for you like a big sis." Unknown to Pumpkin, Goldmine had slipped a whole tablet of the drug Ecstasy into Pumpkin's drink.

"Thanks, I needed dis," Pumpkin said while taking the drink.

"Drink up before you spill it on yourself," the more experienced woman said.

Just then Rich popped up, wishing Pumpkin luck. He asked her if there was any particular song she wanted the DJ to play.

"Just some hard core, up-to-date rap," Pumpkin responded.

Goldmine then led Pumpkin back to the dressing room where she introduced her to a couple of other dancers, who studied Pumpkin for any flaws so that they could joke about her later. When one of the women couldn't find any obvious physical defects she asked, "Do your mother know you up in here?" When she was ignored, the jealous woman got the hint and busied herself, trying to brush the kinks out of her old weave.

Goldmine noticed that Pumpkin had taken only a sip out the tainted drink, but she didn't want to take the chance of mentioning the liquor again because it might raise suspicion. She knew Pumpkin was young, but not dumb.

A little while later Rich let Pumpkin know that she would be on in a few minutes. Goldmine showed a look of disappointment on her face when she noticed that Pumpkin had put her drink down to the side and was busy looking at her hair in a cracked mirror. She wanted the drug to take effect so that Pumpkin would make a fool out of herself during her first time out on stage. But Goldmine knew it was too late when one of Ludacris's hottest singles came on. It was time for Pumpkin's debut.

"This charismatic new girl is sure to get you out your seats and have you on a natural high. Give it up for Pumpkin's High," the DJ shouted out over the music.

Pumpkin slowly strolled out, forgetting to take off her leather coat. When she realized her mistake, she seductively slid it off, revealing a Catholic schoolgirl outfit. Pumpkin danced to the hip-hop song, getting into it and eventually getting most of the guys to cough up their dough. When she showed the crowd her fully erect nipples and firm breasts, along with her jet-black pubic hair, more dollars began to be separated from their owners. She slipped one time in her high heels, so she threw them off and got busy, getting more hype by the second. Pumpkin finally walked off the stage, feeling a sense of power from so many men going crazy over her for simply shaking her ass.

Pumpkin did one more stage performance for the night, and the rest of the time she couldn't even go to the bathroom without a customer grabbing her arm and requesting a lap dance. When she felt the men's jeans bulging, she knew she was doing it right. To her surprise, she expertly turned down guys in a polite way so as not to offend the paying customers.

Pumpkin received requests ranging from, "What will it take for you to come home with me tonight?" to "Fuck a lap dance. Just sit on my face!"

Four o'clock finally rolled around and Pumpkin took another cab home because somebody told her that Goldmine had stepped off with someone. She finally made it back to the apartment, took a quick, steaming hot shower, and fell out without even counting her money. Pumpkin drifted off to sleep, thinking about how she was soon going to have her own place and a phat whip to push around, with everyone hating on her.

CHAPTER
THIRTEEN

White Boy Danny cruised through the streets in his perfect condition, '66 Chevy Impala SS with the expensive flip-flop custom paint job. He rode on eighteen-inch Lowen Hart black edition rims with matching tires. Danny rode most of the time in silence except when he had company, and this time was no exception. He was soon on I-285, doing the speed limit so he wouldn't attract the attention of the state troopers as he puffed on his fatly-rolled blunt. The night seemed to grow even darker as he pulled up in a quiet park that was exclusively used by the local Elk hunters. A dark sedan was already parked and waiting on his arrival when he threw his car into park.

Danny got out of his Impala, wearing a red Ecko Unlimited sweat suit with his trademark baseball hat pulled low to cover his eyes. He walked over to the other vehicle and got in on the passenger side.

"Everything running smooth? How they liking the stuff?" the driver asked as he tapped his pinky diamond ring on his pudgy belly.

"They can't get enough of the stuff. It's like I got fried chicken or something," Danny replied.

"I know what you mean, but we need to step the game up a notch or two," the man said.

"What you have in mind?" Danny asked.

"I came across a good amount of PCP. I'm giving you an even pound to give away. Make sure everybody you come in contact with tries a little, even if they don't know it. You got me?" the man asked while raising his voice.

Danny nodded as the man gave him the mind-destroying drug, plus a hefty supply of cannabis. Just before Danny was about to get out, the man continued.

"Let your gangbanging buddies know that next week, you should have that artillery they been asking about."

"OK," Danny said as he got out and jumped back into his own vehicle. Danny was just making it back to Atlanta when his cell phone began ringing.

"Yo, who's this?" he asked.

"What's up, nigga? Dis is Chase. Act like you know," the voice answered, playing around.

"Yeah, whatever. So what's the deal, player?" Danny asked.

"You got something for me or what?" Chase asked, using a more serious tone of voice.

"You know I got you. I was just about to head to your side of town."

"You know where I beez at. I'll catch you then. Peace," Chase said, clicking off.

A little while later Danny was driving through Little Vietnam, a small but brutal Atlanta neighborhood that earned its infamous nickname due to the violence that erupted on a daily basis. The remaining families still living there took the shooting, stabbing, and constant police harassment as a normal part of everyday life, just like getting bills in the mail. Politicians had long ago given up on this once quiet, respectable neighborhood, saying off the record that it was too much of a burden on the taxpayers' pockets. Just before the Atlanta Olympic games, some liberals even suggested that Little Vietnam simply be bulldozed for the good of Atlanta and its honored visitors.

Danny pulled up to a decrepit–looking, two-story house, but before he could finish parking, a young boy in his early teens ran up to the passenger's side window.

"Whatcha need?" he asked.

"I'm cool. I'm looking for Chase," Danny responded.

"You best to get on. I don't know no Chase," the boy stated, eyeing Danny suspiciously while looking around in his car.

"Just tell him White Boy Danny's out here," he said as he pulled out a Bic lighter to light up another blunt.

The young guy went over to a group of guys drinking forty ounces of malt liquor on the stoop and whispered a few words to them. Danny then saw everyone looking over at him as another guy walked inside the house. Moments later, a tall figure emerged from the house, accompanied by two other men. All the men were wearing gray bandannas tied in the Tupac style.

"Oh, dat's just my nigga," Chase said to his boys, who were sporting screwed-up faces since they were wary of all strangers, especially the pale ones. Chase leaned in Danny's window, revealing a tattoo on his neck of Jesus crying red blood while looking over a drawing of the city of Atlanta. He gave Danny five as his henchmen went to take care of a carload of dope fiends who had just pulled up.

"So you got dat or what? You know it's hot around here," Chase said, knowing that if police were to see him talking to a white guy, they would definitely want to fuck with him.

Chase was the head of the Folks gang-turned-drug-pushing-crew, because it was more profitable to sling rocks than to run guys who crossed the gang borders out of their neighborhoods. He and his boys sold everything from weed, dope, and stolen car systems to exotic women's lingerie. Anything in which Chase could make money, he was involved, but he concentrated mostly on the steadily-growing drug game.

"I got that Indica from Holland you asked about. I have two pounds of that, and I also got three pounds of that purple haze. So you already know what I want for everything," Danny said, talking fast.

"What, you trying to retire on me or something?" Chase asked jokingly.

"You know with my shit, motherfuckers always gonna come back to hit you up."

"You're right about dat, and the bitches just seem to get freaky after a couple of pulls. Fuck it, I'll take it all," Chase said as he gestured for one of his partners to come over. He then told the guy how much money he wanted him to bring back out.

"I'm going to throw in a little something extra for you," Danny said, grinning.

"Whatcha got?" Chase asked.

"I got some leaf farrilla that's sure to have niggas bugging."

"You hitting me off for free?" Chase asked, raising his eyebrows a little.

"You know I got you," Danny said.

The guy came back out the house and handed Chase a plastic pack. Chase hopped in the car as Danny drove around the back of the house and into a dark alley. After Danny finished counting the money and Chase carefully checked out his weed, they gave each other some dap.

"Oh, yeah, I should have some ill heat for you early next week," Danny said.

"For sho'. I need some new high-power shit. We got some bitch-ass niggas from New York trying to move on in.

We sent one of dem New York cats to ICU at Grady Hospital. I know if his ass makes it, he's gonna take a one-way trip back home," Chase said, chuckling as he thought about the incident.

"Yeah, you can't let them come in here like they own shit, when you been here your whole life," Danny replied, knowing that drug beefs were good for business.

After the transaction, Danny peeled off just as a cop car was pulling to a stop, to question a young boy on a bike.

CHAPTER
FOURTEEN

"**D**amn, girl, you really did it up," Dallisha stated with enthusiasm. She and Pumpkin were in her bedroom, counting the money that Pumpkin had made the night before. She had stacks of crumpled-up dollar bills along with fives, tens, twenties, and two hundred-dollar bills.

"Yeah, I put it down Dirty South style, but you wouldn't believe what niggas were whispering in my ear all night," Pumpkin said, smiling at the money on the bed.

"I can imagine. My sister used to tell me some wild shit. This one guy wanted to buy my sister's used maxi pad for a hundred bucks," Dallisha said, frowning.

"What da hell he wanted dat for?" Pumpkin asked.

"She said he just wanted to use it as a tea bag, talking about it contained all kinds of vitamins and nutrients."

"Dat's bullshit. He was just a freak! So what she do, anyway?"

"I don't know. She never told me," Dallisha answered, but she suspected that her sister did what she had to do to get that money.

"Anyway, you should get down with me at Adina's so dat way, we could clock dat serious paper together," Pumpkin said, smiling as she thought about the idea.

"Nah, I couldn't. I wouldn't want everybody staring at my body."

"Not to sound like a dyke or something, but you got a little something dat niggas might want to see," Pumpkin stated sincerely.

"I don't think niggas gonna want to check for this," Dallisha responded, lifting up her shirt. There, on Dallisha's tender, soft skin, was an ugly burn mark that resembled something that looked like it belonged on a piece of Freddy Krueger. The hideous scar was on her left side, which is why the girl never wore a belly shirt, no matter how hot it was outside.

"Oh shit, what happened?" Pumpkin asked in a soft voice.

"Mom Dukes was hitting the gin and juice real hard, and when she mixes it up with the crack rocks, she gets in one of her flip modes. When Stacey, I mean Goldmine, got older, she let me bounce with her," Dallisha said.

"Dat's some wicked shit," Pumpkin said. "My mom is in jail right now. She got caught up in some bullshit, chasing dat dope. I don't really remember my father. She told me he got stabbed up in a dice game when I was like around five," Pumpkin added, throwing in her own ghetto story.

Just then both girls turned toward the doorway after hearing the front door open. A few seconds later Goldmine appeared in the doorway, looking like she had a rough night. Her eyes were bloodshot and she walked as if she could sleep for a good two days straight.

"I see you got dem niggas open last night. How much you hit 'em up for?" Goldmine asked after spotting the money lying on the bed.

"Six twenty-five," Pumpkin responded. Goldmine's jaw dropped a little before she fixed it.

"Dat's good. We girls call it da first night lucky break. Niggas see you for da first time and they try to impress a bitch. My first night I clocked in over a gee," Goldmine lied.

"That's an ill chain. Is it platinum?" Dallisha asked, staring at the long chain with the diamond-encrusted heart pendant that swung down between Goldmine's breasts.

"Oh dis? I copped it last week at dis new jewelry shop down in Buckhead," she responded. Pumpkin started to think how those two girls got into it at the club over a chain just like the one Goldmine was rocking. Since she really didn't know Dallisha's sister very well, she made a mental note to stay on point and to find a safe place for her loot. She didn't want to take a chance on what happened at her aunt's apartment to jump off again.

"Anyways, I'm tired da fuck out. Catch you all a little later," Goldmine stated as she headed toward her room.

Since it was Dallisha's day off, both girls decided to hang out for a minute and kick it. They took a cab to the mall, where Pumpkin bought outfits for her and Dallisha. They hit Music Factory, picking up the latest R&B and rap CDs, and then headed to the food court, where they ate with some guys they had just met. They were about to catch a movie at Magic Johnson Theater, but Pumpkin started feeling a little tired. She admitted that she wasn't used to this kind of late night work. Dallisha just laughed, saying she was going to check out one of her homeboys to get her smoke on. So Pumpkin gave her a hug and jumped in a cab.

It was Thursday evening and Pumpkin was preparing for a night at Adina's Jewels. She had Wednesday off, so she had relaxed at the apartment, going out only briefly to buy two new dance outfits. Goldmine reluctantly helped her rent a maroon Altima through one of her connects. Goldmine was now pushing a brand new, cranberry-colored

Mustang that she insisted she paid for with straight up cash, but Pumpkin soon discovered that Goldmine had a habit of claiming she possessed more than what she actually owned or had.

Pumpkin was finally out the door and on her way to the club. *I definitely need to get my pockets up,* she thought to herself while lighting a Newport. She spent almost $2,500 on a variety of things, from paying Goldmine back for getting her those expensive clothes, to the rental car and a new cell phone, not to mention day-to-day living expenses. She only had enough money left to fill up the gas tank and buy a pack of cigarettes.

While walking through the strip club, she ran into her friend Marisza, who went by the stage name Chi-Chi. She was a good-natured, full of energy, beautiful Dominican woman who recently relocated from Miami to Atlanta with her three children. Chi-Chi always had the customers sweating her to get lap and wall dances.

I just don't see why she don't get her teeth fixed, Pumpkin thought while staring at Chi-Chi's buckteeth.

"How you doing? You ready for another night?" Chi-Chi asked.

"You know me, I'm always ready for some more dough," Pumpkin said.

"I know that's right," Chi-Chi agreed as both girls gave each other high fives and started laughing.

When they got to the stage, Pumpkin noticed that it had been transformed into a small boxing ring complete with ropes.

"What da fuck is dis shit?" Pumpkin asked, wondering how someone was supposed to dance with the stage hooked up like this.

"Oh, you didn't know? The owner thought it would bring in more money if he started setting up different theme nights at least twice a month," she answered.

"What da fuck bitches supposed to do? Beat da shit out of each other and den be all up in a nigga's face?" Pumpkin asked.

"The girls are supposed to have on boxing gloves, and you can fight only if you signed up a couple of weeks ago, plus the winner gets two hundred fifty dollars."

"Word? I wish I could have been around to sign up. I would love to pound on dat ape bitch dat's always looking me up and down, and get paid for it too! Hell, yeah!" Pumpkin said, laughing at the idea.

Soon the spot was packed with guys and a few sprinkles of women wanting to see the spectacle. Later, when Pumpkin left the VIP room after giving some white college student a couple of lap dances, she heard a bell and two strippers began to circle each other in the made-up ring. Both women were almost equal in stature. The deep brown girl threw the first punch, snapping the other woman's head back. The blow looked as if it was hard, but in reality, the clownish, oversized boxing gloves absorbed all the impact. Both women threw wild, swinging punches at each other, eventually ending up wrestling. Some guy, who was dressed in a referee-type of shirt, broke up the struggling women as the bell rang. The huge crowd cheered and booed at the same time, wanting to see more of the bikini clad women tussling around.

The bell rang again, signaling the start of round two in the three-round event. Both women came back to the center of the ring to the sound of a cheering crowd. Some patrons even had side bets going on for who would be the victor. Halfway through the round, one of the dancer's tops came off as the embarrassed girl tried to cover up. Her opponent kept swinging at her, with the half-nude girl finally deciding that it was better to have her titties show than to get her ass whooped.

For the start of round three, the embarrassed girl came

out like a person possessed, really trying to knock her opponent out. The second girl took her actions as personal and started throwing blows with more force than ever. Before anyone knew what was going on, both women tossed their gloves to the side and started going at it for real. The crowd went crazy, shouting for more as the ref announced that the match was over. He declared the girl that lost her top the winner, awarding her the cash prize. The customers thought that both women put up such a good fight that they started throwing fives, tens, and twenties into the ring. Later, both contestants were seen drinking and laughing together about the match.

Toward the end of the night Chi-Chi told Pumpkin that a customer wanted a dance in the VIP room.

"Can't you take it? I'm beat," Pumpkin said.

"He specifically asked for you, plus he's already there," Chi-Chi responded, ready to head home herself.

A little more money won't hurt, Pumpkin thought as she stepped inside the VIP section. The room had a soft blue light glowing with a hip-hop mixed CD blaring.

"I see you want to get high off of Pumpkin," she stated, smiling and walking over to the man. Pumpkin wore her new see-through dress, with only a dental floss thong underneath. The guy was relaxing on the leather sofa in his extra baggy Dickies khakis, drinking straight out of a Moët champagne bottle. "You know it's thirty dollars a song up in here," Pumpkin said while trying to catch a glimpse of the guy who had his baseball cap pulled down real low, covering half of his face. Without answering, he pulled out six twenty-dollar bills and laid them on the table next to the steel ice bucket. Pumpkin started doing her thing, shaking her ass as she slowly stripped for the guy who had started to breathe heavily.

There's something crazy familiar about dis dude, Pumpkin thought as she threw her soft breasts up in his face while trying to take off his hat, acting like it was getting in the way. He gently took her small hands and placed them on each one of his knees.

Pumpkin felt a strong, funny vibe that she couldn't shake. She was on her third lap dance song and here she was giving her all, and he still hadn't even said a single word to her, much less taken off that stupid cap. Curiosity just got the best of her as she quickly snatched off the baseball cap. She couldn't believe what she saw as she stood there speechless, staring directly at Storm, her aunt's girlfriend who had molested her a couple of weeks ago.

"Don't act like you ain't with it now. Go ahead and finish swinging that tasty ass. I paid good money for mine," Storm said slickly as she stared at Pumpkin's nude body. Without hesitation, Pumpkin grabbed her dress from the floor, covering herself. Still too shocked to speak, she tried to leave the room.

"Hell no. Where the fuck you think you breaking out to? Nah, bitch, you gonna stay right here and give me mine," Storm said forcefully as she blocked the smaller woman's path.

"I suggest you get da fuck outta my way," Pumpkin yelled as she tried to go around the persistent, thuggish woman.

"Oh, I see you want to play me. I've peeped the way you been throwing that sweet ass pussy around for a couple of days. Now that I want my fair share, you want to act brand new," Storm replied, spraying Pumpkin with her musky breath.

"Fuck you, you crazy bulldog man bitch!" Pumpkin yelled as she threw a punch that was way off its mark. Storm ducked the blow, rushing the girl as they both fell onto the couch. Storm quickly had Pumpkin's arms pinned beneath her own body as the bigger woman sat on the struggling girl with a hand around her throat. With

her free hand, Storm viciously slapped Pumpkin, dazing
her a bit.

"Now talk that good shit now, huh? I don't hear you,"
Storm said as she maneuvered Pumpkin's legs open with
her knee.

"Get off me, get off me," was all Pumpkin could say over
the loud music. Storm was just beginning to slobber over
the struggling girl's breasts when a waitress walked in to
ask if they wanted more champagne. She stopped her sentence in mid-speech when she saw the unusual scene. She
ran back out to the floor and started yelling.

"Rape! Rape! A girl's getting raped in the VIP room."

The bouncers, along with the remaining people in the
club, joined in the mad dash to the room. Storm was so
into her lustful attack that she didn't notice the room
being filled up. The next thing she knew, two sets of powerful hands snatched her off the terrified girl and flung
her to the floor. The men began punching and stomping
Storm unmercifully until someone in the crowd yelled,
"Holy shit, it's a woman." The bouncers let up and snatched
Storm to her feet as they took a good look at the bloody
person.

"This shit is better then the boxing match they had earlier," one person said as a couple of people broke out into
laughter.

"I don't care if it's a bitch or not, they can't get away
with drama like that up in here," a stripper said with dead
seriousness. By now a couple of dancers were consoling
Pumpkin and asking her if she was all right. Without warning, Pumpkin grabbed a half-empty bottle of Moët and
rushed toward the bouncers, who were taking Storm outside. She cracked the hard bottle onto the already-beaten
woman's head, causing her to slump into the bouncer's
arms.

"Chill, Pumpkin, before you kill her," a voice called out

as the deadly weapon was taken away from her. Pumpkin looked up and noticed that it was her long-time friend, Junior. "Let me take you home," he said as he pushed his way through the crowd.

"Hold up, hold up! Who the fuck are you? Where you think you're taking Pumpkin?" a dancer known as Bright Eyes asked. Before Junior could respond, she continued. "Pumpkin, you know this guy?" The crowd turned their attention toward the new altercation, hoping more action jumped off so they could have still more things to talk about.

"It's all right. He's my cousin," Pumpkin lied, just wanting Bright Eyes to drop it.

"That's cool. I was just looking out for you. You know how niggas in the Dirty South get down. They see a bitch in distress, and they want to come running, pretending to be our savior, but all they really want is some thank-you pussy," she said as Junior led Pumpkin away.

Ten minutes later Pumpkin had her street clothes on as Junior walked her to her car. Junior took the wheel, and Pumpkin lit a cigarette. After the music relaxed Pumpkin a bit, she spoke.

"Why didn't you say something to me earlier at the club?"

"I saw you, but every time I went to approach you, you went off to do something else. Anyway, how long you been dancing, and what was that all about?" he asked as he pulled off and parked. Pumpkin told him everything, about how her aunt's girlfriend tried to wild on her before and how she got put on to dancing by her friend's sister. One minute Pumpkin was pouring her heart out to him, and the next thing she knew they were passionately tongue kissing.

"You sure you're all right? You remember what Shorty

spat out about knights-in-shining-armor bullshit?" Junior asked.

"Shut up and just kiss me," she replied as she placed one of Junior's hands on her titty. The moist feeling in her panties let Pumpkin know right away that she wanted Junior to fuck her right here and now, even though they were good friends. She opened her legs slightly and moaned a little, signaling to the guy that it was all right for him to go further. A second later they had both climbed into the more spacious backseat. Junior had her soaked panties pulled to the side as he gently stroked her to orgasm after orgasm. He started to tremble and speed up his pace when Pumpkin said, "Please don't cum in me. I don't want to get pregnant."

When the time came, he splashed Pumpkin's thigh with hot semen. Pumpkin wished they could stay in that moment forever. Junior helped her clean up, laughing and joking about funny things that had happened in school all year. Junior finally began driving himself home, taking his time. Pumpkin gave him her new cell phone number and told him where she was staying temporarily. They both promised to keep in contact as Pumpkin took the wheel, slowly pulling off and still looking in the rearview mirror at the guy who she had always considered a good friend. She felt on top of the world, even though only hours before she was attacked by what she considered a very deranged woman or man, depending on how you viewed the situation.

CHAPTER FIFTEEN

Jason had just finished counting all the money he made from the weight Doc had given him. He smiled, admitting to himself that he had gotten everything off in a very short time. He didn't do it all quite by himself, though. He had enlisted one of his boys, who was always complaining that paying child support for his three kids was killing his pockets. So when Jason asked him if he wanted to get down, he eagerly jumped at the chance. From the money he made in the last week, plus the dough he already had stashed away, Jason was ready to cop a whip to be a little more mobile. Getting around every day by cab was starting to be costly, but the main reason why he wanted to buy a vehicle was to impress Camay and let her know that he was finally starting to come up.

"You finished getting dressed, dear?" his grandmother asked in a raspy, shaky voice through his locked door. Jason opened the door after stuffing the money in his jeans.

"Yeah, Grandma. How you feeling today?"

"I'm still getting these back pains, but where is Lamont? I set up a breakfast plate for him and I couldn't find him anywhere in the house," she said, wondering why Lamont never ate at the table anymore.

"Grandma, I told you that Lamont is away in the army. He should be back real soon," Jason replied, giving the bent over old woman a hug.

Lamont, Jason's older brother, was awaiting trial for attempted murder and a whole host of drug-related charges. His brother was a certified street hustler, who set his own rules when it came to the game. Many people were envious of his rapid success, including those in his inner circle. Jason remembered that at the trial, a lot of his so-called "ride for life" friends came out the woodwork to testify for the prosecution, saying that Lamont, a.k.a. Free, had an ongoing dispute with the victim, who was also a major player in the underworld of Atlanta's drug trade. What had Jason's mind doing back flips was when his brother's baby's mama took the stand, swearing under oath that Free told her about his plan to murder the intended victim, which would have made the crime premeditated. Jason knew for a fact that the only reason she took the stand and lied was because his brother had cut off her drug supply. Free had discovered that she'd gone from sucking the crack pipe to sucking his competitor's dick, for scraps of table crumbs.

The first trial was declared a mistrial when the judge died of a brain aneurysm and when certain members of the jury openly expressed opinions about Free's guilt before all the evidence had been presented.

"Where's little sis? Did she leave for summer school yet?" Jason asked, knowing that his grandmother, who was in the beginning stages of Alzheimer's disease, might not know.

"Who you talking about now?" she asked.

"Forget about it," he responded. After a cold breakfast of fatbacks and grits, Jason headed out the door. He arrived at the car lot and after some quick paperwork, he drove away in a late-model Honda Civic.

It's all right for now, he thought as he flew around the corner to scoop up his girl.

"How you like it?" Jason asked as Camay climbed inside.

"It's phat. I know you gonna let me push it," she replied as she turned up the music full blast.

"You know I gotta open it up first," he replied as he threw her a bag of weed and a Philly blunt for her to roll. After she amateurishly rolled up the cess, they smoked and enjoyed the comfort of their new ride.

"Damn, Jason, that blunt got me with the munchies. Let's go get something to eat," Camay said.

"I know what you mean. You wanna try that new rib spot over by the college?" Jason asked.

I'm with that. My girlfriends tell me they got some banging-ass catfish dipped in a secret Louisiana Cajun batter," she said excitedly.

Halfway to the rib shack, Jason saw an unmarked police car in his rearview mirror with its lights flashing.

"What the fuck they want now?" Camay asked as she turned around to get a better look.

"Chill, I got this," Jason whispered as the undercover cop approached his car. "Why you pulling me over, officer? Did I do something wrong?" Jason asked as the officer looked quickly around the inside of the car.

"First off, I'll ask the questions. I stopped you because the temporary tags on your vehicle weren't properly displayed. How long have you had this vehicle?" the obese, red-faced detective asked.

"I just bought it a couple of hours ago."

"Let me see your license and registration. You too, miss," he ordered.

After finding that they didn't have any outstanding warrants, the detective came back to the car, determined to find something on the boy who he thought had to have something illegal on his person. Smelling the familiar scent of weed, he ordered the couple out of the car.

"I got all my paperwork in order," Jason stated, raising his voice a little.

"Get out the car or I will drag your black ass out, along with your girlfriend here," the cop said, hoping for a confrontation with the young man.

"Jason, let's just do as he says so we can be on our way," Camay whispered. The cop then had them sit on the sidewalk as he searched the car, knowing this angry black guy must be concealing some kind of weapon.

"Look what we have here," the officer said, holding up a tiny piece of blunt that Camay had put out in the ashtray. The couple looked at each other as the sloppily-dressed detective walked over and demanded that Jason stand up. He started patting Jason down and then carefully went through his pockets, throwing the contents onto the sidewalk. When he couldn't find any more incriminating evidence, he started searching the now fully angry man's waistband. He had Jason drop his jeans as he ran his chubby, fish-white finger around his boxer shorts.

"OK, you clean. Is this what you call a man? This ain't a man!" the cop said, directing his comments to Camay, who was now staring at Jason in shock as if she couldn't believe what had just happened. Jason snatched his jeans up and started gathering his belongings, not looking his girlfriend of two years in the eyes.

"That motherfucker's lucky I didn't have my steel on me," Jason said as they were pulling off. "I would have had his cop friends giving him a twenty-one gun salute." When Camay didn't respond, he looked over and thought for a second that she was now looking at him through different eyes.

CHAPTER
SIXTEEN

"You should have at least pressed charges against dat dyke bitch who tried to push up on you," Goldmine stated while she splashed on some silver and turquoise body glitter.

"Nah, I don't think she be stepping up here anytime soon. Plus you know how da police gonna be asking all kinds of questions. I wasn't ready for da bullshit," Pumpkin said. Both women were in the dressing room, getting ready for their shift at Adina's: It was in the middle of the week, so the dancers who were scheduled to work weren't hyped up because they knew it would be a slow money night.

"Yeah, I know how po-po can get. If you want, I can holler at some of my peeps on the east side to straighten shit out."

"I'm cool. I just want to forget about it," Pumpkin replied as she adjusted her skimpy, Hawaiian print dress.

"Fuck that shit! I would have cut that bitch from elbow to asshole. How someone gonna try to raise up in my spot? I'm not having none of that bullshit from anybody," another dancer said, raising her voice so the rest of the women in the room could hear.

"Who do you think you're trying to front for? You up in here spitting all dat gangster drama like you 'bout it 'bout it," Goldmine said. "I've seen many times when you done dragged yourself in here after your man done walked up and down your ass," Goldmine spat out as she turned around to face the girl, and the room erupted into giggles.

"Whatcha talking about?" the woman asked, darting her eyes around, now sorry that she had butted into their conversation.

"You know what I'm talking about, and so does every bitch up in here. When he doesn't think you shook your stank ass enough to get dat paper, he goes upside your fucking head," Goldmine responded. Pumpkin just stood there, enjoying the show, wishing she had some dirt on the girl to throw in.

"Why you trying to flip on me like that? I was just trying to help Pumpkin out. Ain't that right, Pumpkin? You know how we get down," she said, looking over at the smiling girl, hoping she would put an end to the verbal onslaught.

"Don't be trying to have Pumpkin cosign for you. Next time, you should try to keep your cum-stained lips from flapping and we won't have to go there again," Goldmine stated coldly, then turned her back on the now-humiliated girl, letting her know that she was done with her.

The club was extremely slow that night. Even Goldmine and a few other strippers who were go-getters, and usually could convince the cheap customers to get lap dances, were seen occasionally sitting down chit-chatting with each other, with not much else to do. The bar was giving away complimentary thick slices of watermelon that had Grey Goose vodka frozen inside. Folks in Georgia termed the fruity intoxicant "Hunch Punch." Pumpkin had been at the club only an hour and she had already consumed five slices. She just wasn't in the mood for loud music, petty arguments, and customers with foul body odors, trying to be suave with only a handful of dollar bills.

Soon a guy wearing a one-piece car mechanic type of garment approached Pumpkin.

"I know how you chicks get crunk up in here. What can I get for a dove on the low?" he asked as he grabbed her arm with caked-up, dirty fingernails.

"Nigga, what you need to do is get your hands off me. Number one, I don't trick, and if by a slim chance I was to get turned out and in desperate need for a rock, I still wouldn't consider fucking you," she spat out, waiting for the guy to say something else so she could throw a drink in his face. The guy knew he was in no position to flip with the bouncer, who was standing close and looking bored. After the customer turned his attention back toward the stage, Pumpkin knew she had enough for the night. She let the manager know she was leaving and downed a shot of Rémy Red before she left. She lit up and smoked the remaining half of her joint as she sat in the rental car, listening to a little music.

Pumpkin finally arrived home and decided to take a hot bubble bath. She couldn't find Dallisha's bubble bath beads, so she did it up ghetto style and used a good amount of lemon Joy dishwashing liquid. After the relaxing, therapeutic soak, Pumpkin flopped down on the couch and flicked on the TV, wishing she had another blunt. She wondered why Junior hadn't called her since the last time they ran into each other. Feeling bored, she decided to call one of the many phone numbers the guys tossed her way at the club.

"Hello, is dis Tareek?" Pumpkin asked, not knowing who the guy was or what he looked like.

"Yeah, who this?" came the response.

"Dis is Pumpkin from Adina's."

"Oh shit, I thought you would never call. I went by the club hoping to see—"

Before the excited guy could finish his sentence, Pumpkin hung up on him. *Nah, dis nigga sounds way too desperate. He gots to be lame or a stalker,* she thought. Pumpkin crumpled up the piece of paper, tossing it to the side as she grabbed another number.

"Is Knowledge around?" she asked.

"You're hitting me up on da cell, so what do you think?" the male voice asked.

Dis nigga ain't no Georgia boy, Pumpkin thought after hearing a slight accent in his voice.

"I'm da girl you met at da strip club," Pumpkin replied, testing him a little.

"Bitch, I don't have time to be playing little girl games," he shot back. The harsh remark threw Pumpkin off balance and she quickly tried to recover.

"I'm just playing. I'm Pumpkin from Adina's."

"What you look like? I was probably bent dat night, so if you ain't correct you might as well save yourself da trouble and hang up now," Knowledge said.

Pumpkin described herself truthfully, thinking how different he was from the other guys who were always sweating her. They talked for maybe a full minute before he stopped her.

"Yo, Shorty, you caught me at da wrong time. Give me a shout out another time," he said. Before Pumpkin could respond, he said peace and hung up.

Just then, the house phone rang and Pumpkin decided to answer it after about ten rings. It was Dallisha, yelling excitedly into the receiver. Pumpkin told her to slow down and explain what the fuck was going on. Dallisha told her that she had got caught in the mix of things with the police, and now she was in Atlanta's pre-trial detention center.

"Fuck da details. How much is your bail?" Pumpkin asked.

"They found out I had a warrant in Dekalb County, so they holding me until they talk to someone over there," Dallisha said.

"Don't worry about it. I'll be up to see you tomorrow," Pumpkin said as she heard a rough female voice say that time was up. Pumpkin got off the phone, smoked her last Newport, and knocked off to sleep.

CHAPTER
SEVENTEEN

Doc was pushing a clean, silver-nickel Bentley Continental GT down Memorial Drive while listening to a little jazz. He rarely took his Bentley out, especially in the hood, because it attracted unwanted attention, mostly from the thirty-thousand-dollar-a-year jealous cops. Today was different, though, because he was meeting some important men from Augusta. He had just recently finished getting his precious hair permed and fluffed, and now he was heading to Buckhead to see his private tailor, who had fitted him two weeks ago. Doc pulled into a plaza when he spotted a music store, thinking about how he needed some new CDs.

"Yo, kid, you wanna make a quick twenty dollars?" Doc asked a young kid who had just come out of a wing spot.

"What I gotta do?" the guy asked, looking up and down at the man, knowing exactly what he did for a living.

"I'm gonna run in the music store for a second. I want you to watch my whip and make sure nobody comes within ten feet of it."

"I could do that," the guy responded, holding out his hand.

"You'll get paid when I get back," Doc said as he hit the car's alarm and headed toward the store. He walked over to the rap section and started going through the latest southern crunk, and threw it in the store CD player. The cover had a picture of a couple of pretty, ghetto fabulous girls wearing hooker shorts and showing ass cleavage to the max. They were at some sort of car show that was prevalent in cities like Atlanta. Doc liked what he heard so he headed toward the counter, grabbing a few more CDs on the way.

When he arrived at the counter, there was only one other person in front of him. The girl in front of him had a thick, Coke-bottle figure with long, flowing hair. Her jeans seemed to coincide perfectly with her body structure. Doc stared at her, thinking, *I'd pay to lick the crack of her ass*. He was already feeling a little horny after looking at the women on the CD cover.

"Excuse me," the girl said as she tried to walk past Doc, who was lost in his temporary fantasy.

"What's up, Shorty? Whatcha doing in this part of town?" he asked after recognizing her. The girl looked at him for a few seconds and then she spoke.

"Oh, hi," she said as she started to walk away. Doc quickly paid for his CDs, telling the well-nourished, flirting woman at the cash register to keep the change. He made it outside the door just as the girl was headed toward the Marta bus stop. Doc jogged up to her in his expensive, dyed gator shoes.

"I thought your man was out here. Why he got you riding the bus like that?" Doc asked, trying to sound like he was concerned about her well being.

"He had to take care of something. I'm all right anyway," she responded.

"Well I'm not all right with you riding a hot bus. Come on. I'll give you a lift," he said, taking her bag. She cautiously walked behind the man she had only seen a few times, wondering what his real motives were.

"Everything's cool?" Doc asked the young guy who had just finished eating his hot wings meal. After the boy nodded, Doc pulled out his money knot, slowly searching for a twenty-dollar bill for the benefit of the girl. When he was certain she peeped his drug roll, he gave the youth his easily earned money and turned off his alarm.

"Come on and relax those pretty feet," Doc told the girl as he unlocked the doors with another push of a button. The girl walked to the passenger side with her eyes as big as eggs, thinking she had only seen cars like these in rap magazines.

They were now cruising through the streets, listening to a new CD. The girl leaned back comfortably, feeling like she was floating on air. Doc saw the effect his most prized possession was having on the young woman, so he smiled and pressed a button on the armrest to seal the deal. A hidden console slid open quietly, revealing a small bottle of champagne with two crystal glasses.

"Your drinks, sir," a computerized woman's voice said.

"Have a drink," Doc said, smiling and showing his diamond-studded, gold teeth. She did as she was told while remaining in a trance-like state, never believing that cars like this one existed, much less that a black man from the hood could own one. Doc soon hit another button on the console, causing the passenger seat to vibrate, giving the wide-eyed girl a full body massage.

"So your man got a whip, huh? You should never be walking," Doc said.

"He got a little something, but nothing like this," she replied, wanting to take her Nikes off to feel the plush floor carpet.

"Well he could get it if he really wanted to," Doc threw in for good measure.

He asked her where she was going and she told him where her girlfriend was supposed to be meeting her. Doc felt her vibe that she just wanted to ride around with him in this ultra-luxurious rolling machine. Although he badly wanted to peel this beautiful Georgia peach, business came first. Just before Doc dropped her off, he gave her his number, which she stuffed in her sneakers. Doc saw the overly impressed young woman staring at him as he pulled off, and he chuckled to himself.

It was now late in the evening and this time, Doc was parlaying in the passenger seat of the Bentley while his driver drove. They were on their way to meet some guys who were heavy hitters in Augusta, dealing primarily in Nigerian heroin. Doc had been trying to negotiate a deal with the Africans for a while, after finding out they were planning on expanding their territories in Atlanta and the surrounding area. From what he heard, these guys didn't play, making examples of their enemies in the most gruesome ways imaginable. His sources told him that they once butchered an entire family, including a newborn baby, by stuffing the child in the family's refrigerator and freezing it alive while the parents watched helplessly in horror.

Doc sniffed up some of his top-notch cocaine, which he rarely did, to loosen up a bit. He was always quick to tell his workers, "Don't fuck with the product. Let them other fools have the habits."

An hour later Doc met up with the Africans and their gleaming black 600 SL Mercedes Benz followed the Bentley. Doc checked the men into the presidential suite that he had previously reserved at the newly erected Mandalay Bay Hotel, that was located in the business district in Buckhead. As the Africans were climbing into the back of his car Doc thought, *Damn, that's a tall, slinky motherfucker.* One of the Africans was six-foot-six with a wiry frame. His partner was of normal height, but had cruel eyes that never seemed to blink, which could cause the average person to turn away.

"I'm sorry Mooka couldn't make it. I was looking forward to meeting him in person," Doc said, not directing his comment to any of the men in particular.

"I'm sure he told you he had urgent matters to attend to. We are willing to listen to your proposal and relay the message back to Mooka," the tall African stated without changing his facial expression. Doc, being in the ruthless, unpredictable drug trade, knew that most men on top of the game would never meet another guy in the same business, especially if he didn't know the person. Doc knew that Mooka had sent a couple of his lieutenants just in case something went wrong. They were expendable and easily replaced.

The four men soon reached Adina's Jewels and headed straight to the VIP room that had previously been reserved for them. Doc let the manager know that he didn't want to be disturbed or pestered by the dancers, who saw nothing but dollar signs. Doc had the waitress bring in a couple of bottles of Hardy Perfection cognac, which for a single shot starts at $600. Doc fixed his guests their drinks with slices of miniature, Hungarian-aged lime as his bodyguard/driver stood watch outside the room. Twenty minutes later the waitress brought back a sterling silver platter filled with roasted Maine frog legs sprinkled with sesame seeds. All three men talked business, ate, and drank while discussing their future plans.

"Now, gentlemen, let's relax and have a little fun," Doc said after their meeting was concluded. He then walked out the room, bumping into Goldmine.

"Goldmine, what's up? Let me holler at you for a minute," Doc said.

"Doc, I'm kind of busy right now. Can we talk a little later on?"

Goldmine knew exactly what she was doing. All the other girls fell over themselves, hoping to snatch up a piece of whatever Doc happened to be throwing their way, whenever the drug dealer came in the spot. But the experienced Goldmine always acted like he was just a regular customer, making her more desirable in his eyes. She knew very well that he ran the streets, and if she played her cards right, she hoped she could retire on a nice, sizable chunk from the proceeds of the dope game.

"Fuck all them other bird-ass niggas for right now. I want you to bring back four of the baddest bitches in the joint and have them come into the VIP room," Doc said with an air of unchallenged authority.

"What's in it for me?" she asked.

"Let's just wait and see what kind of chicks you bring back. And don't be bringing no project bitches with bullet wounds, scars, and all that other silly shit," he responded, letting his driver know what time it was.

Goldmine arrived a short time later with four other stunning strippers, who were all smiles when they realized it was Doc who had sent for them. Goldmine thought for a second about putting Pumpkin on to the easy money party, but she quickly dismissed the idea, fearing that Doc might just choose the young girl over her. Goldmine had already found out through the club's grapevine that her regular money-spending customers were asking for Pumpkin now.

The four women stood in the middle of the room, trying to look their best as if they were on a slave auction block. To Doc's surprise, the tallest African chose a pretty, dark-skinned dancer with smooth, thick lips. In his vast experience dealing with men, especially the darker ones, they almost always went for the light-complexioned girls, but not this African.

The tall African's partner pointed to a short, mulatto girl who went by the name of Lethal. She sported a bright red, hanging-tongue tattoo on her belly with the word LICKABLE written underneath.

Doc then waved his diamond hand, dismissing the remaining two women. Once the other two dancers were sitting comfortably with their men, hugging on them and smiling, Goldmine looked at Doc, ready to get down to business. He took the hint as he led the woman outside the room. Doc pulled out a roll of hundreds and gave the eager Goldmine $1,200.

"That's four hundred for each of you," he stated, knowing that all parties involved knew what was expected of them. Forty-five minutes later, after the couples became well acquainted with each other, Doc's bodyguard let him know that the other car was there. Just before the intoxicated group left the club, Goldmine gave each woman two hundred dollars and pocketed the rest.

Both cars arrived at the hotel and the men and women went up to the suites, with Doc telling the now relaxed Africans to enjoy themselves. He and Goldmine had the other high-priced suite. Goldmine went straight to the huge bathroom, which had heated floors.

"It's all yours now," she said as she stepped out of the bathroom after taking a steaming hot shower. She wore a wide, white, fluffy towel and a pair of crystal clear pumps that had multi-colored bubbles in the heels.

"I'm good," he said, taking a long, hard look at Goldmine's tight form which hugged the towel. He lay sprawled out on a bed that sat on a raised, oval platform.

Oh shit, please don't tell me he's one of dem niggas who don't like taking more than one shower a day if he don't have to, she thought, putting on a fake smile. *At least he goes out in style,* she thought as she stared down at the beautifully decorated, custom-made aquarium that had exotic Japanese fish swimming peacefully.

"How about some sounds?" Doc asked, pulling out a

platinum-colored remote control and hitting a button. Some R&B flooded the room as Doc pushed another button, causing a fully stocked mini-bar to slide out from behind a glossy mahogany wall. Goldmine brought back an already-chilled bottle of fifty-year-old champagne, along with a pair of crystal wine glasses. Doc was lying on his back in his boxer shorts, with his hands behind his head.

"Doc, let me give you a massage. You look as if you had a rough day," Goldmine said as they both drank two glasses of the champagne. He willingly turned over as she poured a little hotel lotion on his back and expertly began giving the man a deep tissue massage with her delicate fingers. Her long fingernails went up and down his spine every now and then, slipping down the bottom of his ass crack to tease his nerve endings. She finally slipped off his purple silk boxers and began slowly rubbing his butt, occasionally tickling his balls.

Dis nigga gonna give up da dough freely after I finish with him, Goldmine thought as she let her towel fall to the three-inch plush carpet. She began passionately kissing his lower back and then his ass. Without warning, she slid her wet tongue in between his butt cheeks, finding the intended, ultra-sensitive target. She stroked his waiting anus with her slippery tongue a couple of times before she almost gagged. Goldmine had caught an ass booger and spit it out. It took all of her will power to keep from throwing up as she told herself that what she was doing was all worth it if it meant getting closer to the big drug dealer.

"Everything all right?" Doc asked like he was doing her a favor. Goldmine tapped him on the leg for him to turn over as she reached for his still limp penis. She milked his organ into hardness and then using her mouth, she slipped a glow-in-the-dark condom on his dick.

Dis motherfucker got some wack equipment, Goldmine thought as she took a look at his now stone-hard member. It was pencil thin and not long at that. She climbed on top of him and rode Doc like she was riding into the sunset in an old western movie. When his hand began digging deeper into her tender breasts and his moans became shallower, she knew he was about to blast. Doc finally let off with a grunt and afterward took a long swallow of champagne.

Goldmine didn't even give the man a chance to have his sweat dry before she sucked him into a fresh erection. After Goldmine placed another condom on him, she got on all fours and tooted her ass in the air like a seasoned Dallas cheerleader. Doc happily obliged her as he took the waiting, swollen pussy like a wolf would take an innocent, unsuspecting sheep. Goldmine had been practicing contracting her vaginal muscles at will for a while to make it seem as if she had a smaller hole. When she was sure her muscles were firmly around his shaft and squeezing, she yelled out, "Oh God, it's too big. Da dick is too big. Please hurry up and cum."

"Nah, girl, this is what you came here for. You fuckin' with a real nigga now. You in for a real ride," he replied as he grabbed her ass cheeks even tighter and began pounding harder and quicker, like a jackhammer on overdrive.

"Oh shit, I'm cumming again. Cum with me, daddy," Goldmine screamed out, lying. That did the trick as Doc started shaking and then collapsed on the girl's sweaty, red back.

Goldmine was gonna wait ten minutes before she put it on him again, but Doc fell out before the minutes were up.

Yeah, I got dis weak dick trick nigga in my hands now, or should I say da pussy, Goldmine thought to herself as she went to take another shower and use all the bottles of the hotel's mouthwash.

CHAPTER
EIGHTEEN

Danny pulled up to the local twenty-four hour Waffle House for his usual steak, eggs, and double order of smothered and covered hash browns. Before he could exit his car, a young girl ran up to the driver's side window.

"What happened that day I was at your house?" she asked. Standing inches away from his face was Tiffany, the young girl he had at his mercy in his room before he was rudely interrupted.

Danny was caught completely off guard by her question, and all he could say was, "What? What you talking about?"

"A couple days ago after I went home from kicking it with you at your spot, I found some bite marks on my chest. What was that all about?" the girl asked, looking as if she was getting more pissed by the moment. Danny knew he had to de-escalate the situation before it drew unwanted attention his way.

"Chill, Shorty, let me explain. When you started feeling sick, I let you rest up on the bed, remember?" he asked, talking in a tone that a concerned father might use.

"So what the fuck happened?" Tiffany asked, wanting him to continue quickly.

"Well, being that you're peoples and everything, I ran out to the pharmacy to see if I could get you something to settle your stomach. I came back and saw this dude I barely knew on top of you like he was trying to rape you or something," Danny said.

"Who was he?" the girl asked. By now Danny knew she was believing the unbelievable story. "It's some buster I used to hit weed off to for making little runs for me. I cut him off because he started getting real shady around my peoples. Anyway, I tossed his ass around a bit and the motherfucker started crying and begging, saying he was sorry. He tried to tell me that he thought you was some wild jump-off bitch from the hood. That shit just got me even more amped up. When I went to get the gat to double-tap his headpiece, he ran off like a bitch," Danny explained while watching Tiffany as she stood there with her mouth open.

"Word! You should have blasted his ass. Why didn't you tell me?" she asked, already caught in the trap of his lies that only a naïve, fourteen-year-old girl would believe.

"I felt fucked up for leaving you there by yourself, and even more fucked up for forgetting to lock the door," Danny answered, looking as if he was about to shed a tear.

"When you see him again, let me know, so I can have my folks get into that ass," Tiffany stated.

"I'll definitely look out for you. Anyway, I was just on my way to pick up a load of some good strawberry hydro. I feel bad about what happened the other day. Let me hit you off with an ounce," Danny said, changing the subject.

"I'm kicking it with some friends inside. Can they come too?" she asked.

"It's only around the corner. Plus I don't want everybody knowing my business," he answered.

"I feel you. Niggas are always up in somebody else's biz," the eager girl replied as she climbed into the passenger seat. Danny drove out of the parking lot, forgetting that he was even hungry. He drove his Impala in no particular direction.

"I thought you said the weed was just around the corner," Tiffany commented, wanting to get her hydro and get back to her friends.

"Oh shit! I must be smoking too much of my own product. I forgot I had picked it up already," he replied as he pulled out a filled up Ziploc bag. Tiffany's mouth transformed into a wide smile as she thought about how she just knew she was going to be the center of attention when her friends saw how much weed she brought back.

"I told you I always come correct with my folks, but let's smoke a quick joint before we head back," Danny suggested with a toothy smile.

"Fo' sho'," the young teenager said as her tiny hands grabbed at the bag.

White Boy Danny parked behind an isolated, shut-down Amoco gas station and quickly rolled up two Philly blunts. Unknown to Tiffany, he handed her the blunt that was spiked with PCP, and he took the normal one.

This is one cool motherfucker. Let it be a nigga with this much weed. He wouldn't be trying to give up shit, Tiffany thought as she took a strong pull.

"Why we way back here anyway? I can't see shit," she said, thinking an axe murderer was going to jump out the woods at any minute.

"You know how it is. We don't want anyone rolling up on us," he answered, watching the drug starting to take its toll on the young girl's lungs and mind.

"You have some pretty eyes. I wish I had blue eyes. I can just imagine all those bitches hating on me and the niggas wanting to buy me anything I wanted." Tiffany was rambling on, often repeating herself as her body became more relaxed and unaware of her surroundings. "Damn, I feel so good. I wish I had a bed to lie down on," she stated as she started putting on makeup with an imaginary lipstick.

"You can chill out in the backseat where there's more room," Danny said as he guided the girl toward the back.

"I never smoked no hydro like this before. My mouth tastes and feels like sandpaper." Tiffany then started to lick the back of the car seat while laughing. Danny knew that having a cottonmouth was one of the side effects of smoking the hallucinogenic drug, not to mention doing off-the-wall things.

"You seem hot," he said. "Let me take these stuffy pants off so you can cool off a bit," Danny offered as he unlaced her sneakers and then slid her Guess jeans completely off.

"I'm still hot," the half-conscious girl said as she proceeded to take off her shirt. Once she had taken it off, her fried brain cells told her that the shirt was still on, causing her to take it off a couple more times. By now Danny had retrieved a small bottle of Jack Daniels from under his seat and practically poured it down the girl's throat. Tiffany was now having a conversation with her dead father.

The older man knew that the young girl was now in never-never land as he snatched her panties down around her ankles. Danny just stared at his defeated prey, drooling at what he considered the ultimate specimen. He took a long drag of his blunt and then drove his tongue into Tiffany's untouched vagina. The girl moaned lightly and tried to turn on her side. He roughly pushed her onto her back as he continued his assault while unbuttoning his own jeans.

Everything Danny was told about blacks, mainly black women, made him loathe them; and at the same time he was drawn to their unmistakable sexuality. He knew that black women, especially the ones who patrolled the ghettos, were up for grabs with men of all races. The years of rhetoric preached by his father taught Danny to believe that African American girls had to be taught their roles, by force if necessary, because most of the time their absent mates did a poor job of controlling them.

Danny jerked his small, stubby, pinkish penis in his hand, thinking about the time when he had caught his deeply religious mother with her eyes half closed, being eaten out by their housekeeper. Many nights in bed Danny tried to make sense in his young, still-developing mind about what magical power that black witch had over his mother, to cause her to lay with the animals who their ancestors taught to walk and talk.

Danny looked down at the now-twitching, helpless girl as he unsuccessfully tried to become aroused. Lust turned to uncontrollable rage as he lit his lighter under one of the girl's dark nipples, trying to get some kind of reaction. The unconscious girl just started shaking even more violently as her torturer lit the fire under her other still developing, exposed breast. Danny then climbed on top of her with his still flaccid penis, hoping he could capture the magic that overwhelmed his mother years before.

In the darkness Danny never noticed Tiffany foaming at the mouth as dark urine flowed down her legs and created a puddle on the backseat. Danny's thoughts were flipping back and forth from his mother to the girl on the backseat, who was now lying very still.

He then put his face back down toward her pubic area and began biting the girl's thighs as if he were eating a tough piece of meat. After quite a few sadistic bites, when the girl didn't respond, Danny started slapping her face to bring her back to consciousness. He had no way of knowing that young Tiffany had been born with a rare genetic heart condition that required her to take medication three times a day. The mixture of alcohol, PCP, and her heart medication aggravated her ailment, causing her to join with her father sooner than she expected.

"Damn, this black bitch done went and died on me," Danny said out loud, rushing to put his clothes back on as he nervously looked around in the darkness. Once Danny was dressed, he went to his trunk and brought back a heavy, gray blanket, which he used to cover the girl's body. He then threw her in the trunk next to his spare tire, gulped down the rest of his drink, and cautiously drove to Little Vietnam.

"What's one more body in this fucking hell hole?" he asked himself as he drove his car into the middle of a weeded lot that was covered with debris. He found the perfect hiding place, which was an old, burned-out car that had been stripped before it was lit on fire. He took a quick look around before taking the corpse out and stuffing it under the wreck. For extra safety, he placed a couple of trash bags around the car before heading off. As Danny slowly drove away, curious eyes watched his every move.

CHAPTER NINETEEN

Jason had just finished dropping his shorty off at the mall, so she could cop some new outfits for a party one of her girlfriends was throwing. Jason couldn't pinpoint the reason for Camay's distant attitude toward him recently. When he questioned her, she just dismissed him, saying it was all in his head and giving him a wet kiss with her soft, full lips. The only thing that really bothered him was that after the traffic stop involving the racist detective, Camay asked him what he would have done if the police had tried to make her strip also.

"Come on, you know the jakes know niggas in the hood be stashing all kinds of shit in their pants. They wouldn't fuck with a chick on the level," he responded.

Right now Jason wanted to put that particular moment on hold. He was now headed into downtown Atlanta to see his older brother, who had been on lockdown for almost a year. It seemed that the redneck DA kept pulling unsolved cases out of her ass, trying to pin them on his brother. For every new charge, it just so happened that the state had a so-called reliable and confidential informant who saw or heard something relevant to the case. Jason knew that they were just trying to make sure Free never touched the gritty streets again. The courts deemed his brother a security risk for the upstanding citizens of Atlanta, so they placed an injunction on him, only allowing visits from his lawyer and immediate family members.

When Jason arrived at the prison, he dropped $500 on his brother's books for commissary and then talked with him for the allowable half hour. Free told Jason in so many hidden words to check out a source his lawyer told him about, that was possibly turning state's evidence against him. Jason promised to come check him again sometime next week and bring more money to help pay for his defense.

After that short visit, Jason sped his Honda Civic toward the Red Roof Inn, where his boy L.B. was holed up.

"What's up? Who's there?" a voice yelled from behind the seedy hotel room door.

"Yeah, nigga, you better recognize," Jason said as he removed his thumb from the peephole. The door swung open and the two men gave each other five. "Damn, nigga, why don't you clean up every once in a while?" Jason asked, as he looked around the room that was littered with old food wrappings and empty forty-ounce bottles.

"You know me, I ain't with that cleaning-up shit. I'm only worried about making this paper," he said, while digging in his jeans and pulling out two huge knots of money wrapped in rubber bands.

"That's what the fuck I'm talking about," Jason replied, while taking the money and flipping through it. "Who's that?" Jason asked when he heard a sound that originated from the bathroom.

"That's just a shorty I met from the first floor. Yo, she got some banging-ass friends," L.B. said, hoping Jason would go along with his party.

"Fuck all that other shit. Tell that bitch to get the fuck outta there," Jason shouted loud enough so that whoever was in the bathroom could hear.

"Yo, Shorty, my man wants to meet you," L.B. said, trying to save face.

The door cracked open and a female in her early twenties wearing only her panties and a white bra that was beginning to turn gray around the straps, walked out, not bothering to cover up. She had heard everything through the door and peeped L.B. handing Jason the drug money. Being from the streets, she knew that the guy she had just fucked and licked was just a worker. She knew that the guy who had just arrived was the head honcho. Even though both men wore no jewelry, she considered Jason a better catch than his friend.

Jason watched the woman, who had a slight kangaroo pouch for a stomach, walk sexily over to L.B. and put her arms around his waist.

"Hi, I'm—" Before the girl could finish introducing herself, Jason cut in.

"I'm not trying to break up your little whatever, but me and my boy got some business to handle, so you gots to spread out." L.B. then whispered that he'd check her later, and she began gathering up her clothes. She took an extra long time bending over and pretending to look for her dress for Jason's benefit, but he just ignored her and lit up a Newport.

"What the fuck you doing?" Jason asked once the girl was out of the room.

"Whatcha talking about?" L.B. asked like he had no idea what the man was saying.

"Didn't I tell you don't be having no hood rat bitches up in the spot? You don't know who the fuck she is, or who she could be working with."

"Nah, she ain't like that. Her peoples buy from me on the regular," he stated, trying to plead his case.

"How the fuck you know how she gets down? And her peoples are smokers, which is all the reason for her to set your dumb ass up," Jason said, knowing that it only took one stupid mistake like this to throw a monkey wrench in his plans before they even got off the ground.

After Jason hit L.B. with another package of coke, plus a nice amount of pre-packaged crack rocks, he headed off to his other spot to get his own hustle on.

CHAPTER TWENTY

Pumpkin was sitting on Dallisha's bed, painting her toe-nails and puffing on a fat spliff. The other day she tried to see Dallisha at the jail, but the officials made it clear that Pumpkin had to be over eighteen to visit some-one unless she was accompanied by an adult. So Pumpkin just put thirty dollars in Dallisha's account and bounced.

"Dis is some good ass weed," Pumpkin said to herself as she reached over to turn the music up even louder. A week ago she had gone to White Boy Danny's house and bought a dime bag. The next day, she went back and copped a straight up ounce of purple haze. Since she started dancing at the club, she didn't really have time for anything else except sleeping, eating, and an occasional shopping spree to keep her wears up.

* * *

Pumpkin awoke from her sleep after hearing Gold-mine walk in talking noisily on her cell phone.

"I'm telling you, I swear to God dat motherfucker has some foul ass breath. Yeah, I know. I still don't give a fuck

if he is pushing a Lex, dat nigga's mouth smells like somebody took a shit on his tongue," Goldmine replied, then
burst out in a laugh. "OK, girl, I'll see you later," she said
before clicking off her phone.

"Your sister called yesterday and asked when you were
going to check her," Pumpkin said as she walked into the
living room.

"And I'm not going to. I told her to stop running around
with dem tack-head bitches and bum-ass niggas who wanna
be ballers. She wouldn't be locked da fuck up if she had
listened to me," Goldmine replied, her facial expression
changing drastically.

"Dat's between you two. I'm just giving you the message.
Well anyway, that rental your peoples hit me off with, it
overheated on me twice," Pumpkin stated.

"Oh, I've been meaning to tell you da broad I've been
getting da whips from got caught, so now you gonna have
to bring back the whip tomorrow," Goldmine said, spitting out an outright lie off the top of her head. She figured Pumpkin had begun acting like she was a prima donna,
trying to steal Goldmine's customers and shit, especially
after Goldmine put her broke and homeless ass on. *Let da
bitch try walking again*, Goldmine thought to herself. Pumpkin knew for a fact that Goldmine had just made up that
story seconds ago, but she was in no position to try to chal-
lenge the older woman while still living in her apartment.

"I'll bring back the car in the morning," Pumpkin stated
as she made a frown that Goldmine caught. "Anyway, you
going to work tonight? Bright Eyes told me dat some high
rollers are supposed to be throwing some kind of party,"
Pumpkin said, trying to change the subject.

"Bright Eyes! I wouldn't believe shit she has to say. Dat
bitch is high most of the time and plus, she wouldn't know
a go-getter if she was partying in the middle of the all-star

weekend," Goldmine responded as she took off her high heels and carried them in her hands toward her bedroom.

Since Pumpkin had decided to get rid of the rental car so Goldmine wouldn't have anything else to beef about, she now sat in the back of a cab, smoking a cigarette and thinking that she definitely needed some kind of transportation. She had to admit that she had gotten comfortable pushing her own temporary vehicle, coming and going as she pleased.

"What da hell going on?" Pumpkin asked, not expecting an answer as the cab driver pulled up in front of the strip club.

There was a whole squad of uniformed police officers milling around with a few detectives thrown in the mix. The police were busy trying to keep the gawking neighborhood residents back as they tried to get a good look at the carnage that wasn't new to them. Pumpkin paid her fare and jumped out, joining the curious spectators. She looked past the yellow police tape and saw a body sprawled out on the sidewalk with a small, circular, red bloodstain in the middle of her chest. She took a closer look and realized that it was one of the dancers from the club. Her first thought was that some psycho stalker who couldn't take no for an answer had just flipped the fuck out. Except for the blood on the woman's shirt, she looked as if she could have been sleeping after a long night of shaking her ass.

Pumpkin then spotted the waitress who had trained her, blabbing to a couple of guys who seemed to be deep into her story. Pumpkin pushed her way over, knowing that she would know the full history of what went down.

"Cathy, what happened?" Pumpkin asked after she tapped the still-gossiping woman on the shoulder.

"Oh, you didn't hear? Remember them two wild bitches that got into it about that chain last week?" Pumpkin nodded her head, now clearly remembering the face of the girl lying on the cold sidewalk. "Well the shorty she had drama with was waiting for her tonight. When she tried to show up for work, the shorty stabbed her in the heart with a big ass butcher knife. I told Rich he should have fired those project hoes a long time ago." Before Cathy could go on with her constant tirade, Pumpkin needed to know about her income situation.

"So what about da club? Is a bitch gonna make some money or what?" Pumpkin asked.

"The police said a little while ago that shit is gonna be closed for a minute until they do a complete investigation. I don't give a fuck. I'm going back to school, so I—"

Pumpkin once again cut her off, saying that she had to go. *What da fuck they got to investigate? A bitch got done in over a bullshit chain,* she thought to herself as she got on her cell phone to call another cab. She didn't feel like going home and being by herself. For some reason she wanted to hear loud music and get a little twisted.

While waiting for the cab, she noticed strippers coming and going, hopping back in their rides, knowing that their pockets would be lighter because of the unexpected drama.

Pumpkin arrived at a small bar called Moments, which was located not too far from the famous Atlanta's Underground. The place wasn't packed, but it would do as the underage girl sat at the bar and ordered a Kamikaze. The DJ in the booth had a talent for mixing old school R&B with the latest rap hits. Pumpkin ordered another drink, wishing she had brought some of her weed with her so that she could have fired up in the bathroom.

As Pumpkin happened to look over at the front entrance, she saw some guys coming inside. The first guy had a short haircut and wore a light brown, two piece Carhartt jeans suit with matching beef and broccoli Timberland boots. He didn't wear any jewelry except an Ice-Tec watch that was encrusted with flawless diamonds. Pumpkin knew he looked familiar but couldn't quite place the face. The group came straight to the bar and ordered their drinks.

"Don't I know you from somewhere?" Pumpkin asked, her curiosity getting the best of her. The guy turned around, expecting some fat chick trying to run that played-out game on him.

"What's da deal, shorty? You forgot dat you hit me up on da cell a couple of days ago?" the guy asked as the bartender brought him and his boys their drinks.

"I got to lay off da ganja for real. Knowledge, right?" she asked.

"You know it," he stated as he took a step back to get a better look at the girl sitting at the bar. She had on a short, red, strapless dress that let the world know that she was braless and had erect nipples pressed firmly against the thin fabric.

"So you rolled up in here with some of your friends? We can have our own little private get-together, if they up to par," Knowledge said as his boys went toward the back, where the pool table was located.

"Nah, I'm solo. I came up here on a humble. I was supposed to be at work, but da fucking police shut shit down just because a bitch caught a bad decision," she stated, stirring the tiny straw in her drink.

"Things happen," Knowledge responded nonchalantly.

Knowledge and Pumpkin decided to join his friends in playing pool. He snatched up a big bottle of Rémy Martin before heading out toward the back. Pumpkin had never played pool before, but she enjoyed herself, making bets with the guys.

"Nigga, I bet you two hundred you can't make that shot."

"I got twenty on that one," the guys would yell back and

forth as they downed their drinks. The place started getting packed later on, but the men practically took over the pool tables, only letting females get in a game or two with them.

Time flew by and before Pumpkin knew it, it was four AM and the DJ had called last call. People started to move slowly toward the exit, trying to see with whom they could hook up, so they wouldn't have to go home to their lonely apartments. Knowledge told his boys to go pull the whip around front while he went to take a piss, so Pumpkin decided to sit at an empty table and wait for him.

"Yo, what's up! Can me and my boy get a private dance?" a male asked. Pumpkin looked up and saw a smiling guy holding a mixed roll of tens and twenties.

"Excuse me?" she asked.

"Don't you strip at Adina's? Or are you trying to act brand new?" he asked as his partner started laughing.

"Yeah, I dance, but I'm not dancing right now. Don't try to play me, offering me money like I'm a ho or something," Pumpkin shouted as she stood up.

"Come on, now. Don't be like that. I've seen the way you spread them ass cheeks, like you was begging for a nigga to run up in you. I'm just saying, you could make some quick dough," he stated with a huge grin.

"Fuck you and your weak-ass roll, fronting with your rent money. You corny-ass motherfucker," Pumpkin said.

"I bet you if I was in the VIP with a bottle of Moët, you would be quick to slob the knob," the man spat out as he told his friend to roll out. Just then, Knowledge came out the bathroom and told Pumpkin to come on. They were walking a couple of feet behind the two guys when one of them turned around and started laughing, while giving his friend some dap.

"Who da fuck they laughing at?" Knowledge asked Pumpkin.

"Dem niggas ain't nobody. They tried to push up on me and I had to shoot dem down. They just salty, dat's all."

"Word?" was all Knowledge said, but he took their behavior as a total lack of respect.

Soon the sidewalk was filled with patrons exchanging phone numbers and chit-chatting. Knowledge made eye contact with the guy who had propositioned Pumpkin.

"You got a problem?" he asked. The guy turned around, made eye contact with Knowledge, and spoke.

"You talking to me?"

Knowledge walked quickly up to the guy, with Pumpkin following behind him.

"Yeah, nigga, I'm talking to you. I seen you laughing earlier and now I see you watching me. So what's up?" Just as the two guys started to screw their faces up for drama, a Suburban Jeep with tinted windows slowly pulled up.

"Knowledge, what's up? You all right? You know these clowns?" his boy asked, pulling out his gat and cocking a round into the chamber.

"I'm cool. I'm just trying to find out why dis nigga was staring at me, like I was a bitch or something," Knowledge responded, opening up his jacket and showing a shiny, nickel-plated nine tucked in his jeans.

"Man, I don't have nothing against you. This is about that bitch, isn't it?" he asked in a shaky voice.

"Who you calling a bitch?" Pumpkin asked, stepping closer to the much taller man.

"I didn't mean it. It just slipped out."

"Did it just slip out when you said you wanted to fuck me for some chump change?" she asked loud enough so that everyone could hear.

"So dat's how you niggas get down when a person in da bathroom?" Knowledge asked.

"I didn't say shit. He said everything. I was telling him to leave her alone 'cause I thought I peeped her with somebody," his partner said, wanting no part of what was about to jump off. Knowledge's boys just looked at him with their guns at their sides, letting him know that he was stuck just like his boy.

"So you want to pay for some pussy? Let's see how much you working with. Turn dem motherfucking pockets out," Knowledge demanded. The frightened guy took out his money as Knowledge told him to hand it to Pumpkin, who eagerly took it. His partner also got the same treatment.

"I apologize. Can I go now?" the guy practically begged.

"Pumpkin, show dis trick a little respect," he said. Pumpkin looked at him, her eyes asking what she should do.

"Bitch-smack him a couple times," Knowledge ordered. Knowledge knew there was nothing worse than to be pimp-smacked by a female in front of a crowd of people, when you couldn't do anything about it. Pumpkin reached up and slapped the guy in the face as hard as she could, causing the watching crowd to break into a loud laughter.

"Why it got to be like this?" the guy asked while holding his eye. Pumpkin then balled up her small fists and started rapidly punching the guy in the face, relieving all of her pent-up stress from asshole guys like this one, who thought they could treat her any way just because she danced.

"Damn, shorty cold," Pumpkin heard someone in the crowd say.

"Fuck dat! Niggas shouldn't be running off with da mouth if they can't hold their own," a female in the crowd responded.

"OK, let's bounce," Knowledge finally said. "Dis bitch-ass nigga crying like he want his mama. You country boys lucky I'm in a good mood tonight," Knowledge said as he took Pumpkin's arm, leading her to the jeep. One of Knowledge's boys tapped both of the humiliated men on the head with his gun.

"Now bounce 'fore I let loose," he said. The two guys stumbled down the block, praying that a bullet wouldn't catch them in the back.

Knowledge took the wheel and Pumpkin sat in the passenger seat, while his crew sat in the back and started joking about the whole episode. Pumpkin kept looking at the driver, feeling his don't-give-a-fuck attitude. She gave him her cell phone number just before he dropped her off at the apartment.

I definitely want to get with this nigga again, Pumpkin thought as she watched the Suburban speed off.

CHAPTER
TWENTY-ONE

Danny finally hustled the remaining weed smokers out of his house and threw the heavy wooden bar across the door, after deadlocking it.

"What's up, Chase? I got them things we been talking about," Danny said into his house phone.

"Word? Bring 'em over right now, so I can peep what you working with," Chase said.

"I'm already caught up in something right now. I'm gonna hit you up in about five hours, when I'm on my way," Danny stated.

"I can work with dat," Chase responded before hanging up.

Danny proceeded into his bedroom, locking the door behind him. He then retrieved two large, dark blue duffel bags from underneath his bed and opened them. The bags contained old machine guns, along with ammunition and a couple of slightly used handguns. His special connect came through last night with the artillery he was waiting for. Danny began the tedious task of cleaning and trying his best to shine each weapon thoroughly. He checked each component and spring, making sure they were in satisfactory working order. After what seemed like an eternity to him, he finally finished, flopping down on the mattress to take a breather. He then rolled up his own personal super-sized blunt. Danny grabbed his jeans, going through the pockets, searching for his lighter. His hand touched on a pair of panties and he slowly took them out. Danny had momentarily forgotten that he had stuffed little Tiffany's underwear in his pocket after tossing her lifeless body away like last week's trash. He barely remembered seeing the pink material dangling from one of her feet as he carried the body. For some unknown reason at that particular moment, he wanted those pink panties more than anything in this world.

Danny got up and walked toward his lamp, carrying the dead girl's underwear loosely in his hands. He brought the lamp back to his bed as he lit his Philly blunt. He lay back on his bed in his oversized boxer shorts and took the shade off the lamp. He then held the panties up to the bare, bright light bulb as he carefully examined them inside out, like a CSI professional investigator. Danny then began rubbing the underwear against his face as he inhaled the pungent odor. He took a final strong pull of his weed and he laid it on the ashtray. Closing his eyes, he wondered how Tiffany's private parts would be smelling right at that moment. He hoped her vagina was giving off as mind-enhancing of a smell as her panties. Danny had unconsciously slipped out his already stone-hard dick, wrapping the undergarment tightly around his organ. A few seconds later he climaxed, a long stream of semen rushing toward the ceiling. Danny gradually slid back to reality as he placed the panties under his pillow for future use.

A while later Danny was climbing into his ride, with the guns tucked safely in the trunk. On his way to Atlanta's

Little Vietnam, he called Chase to let him know that he was on his way.

"Everything's cool?" Chase asked Danny as he led him, carrying his weapons of war, into the rundown house. Chase was followed closely by his first lieutenant, Head, who sported two well-groomed Afro puffs that were held in place by rubber bands. Danny laid the machine guns on a long table that doubled as a card table when the crew decided to gamble at the card game, Georgia Skins.

"So what you got dat a nigga could get busy with?" Chase asked as he picked up a freshly cleaned Russian AK-47 machine gun.

"I got these two Israeli Cobra M-11s the army uses over there to cut motherfuckers in half," Danny replied.

"What up with dis one?" Chase asked, picking up another weapon.

"Niggas ain't gonna want to fuck with you when they find out you have this shit. That's the British L1A1 battle rifle with a mounted suppressor," Danny answered, flashing a smile.

"You got any American shit?" Chase asked jokingly, picking up two nine-millimeter pistols and holding them in both hands like he was fighting in Desert Storm.

There was a loud knock on the front door, causing all three men to freeze in mid conversation.

"Go check it out!" Chase said to Head, who quickly walked off. Head moved the window curtain to the side, recognizing the young kid standing at the door. Head looked around one more time before opening the door and stepping outside.

"Whatcha want? We in the middle of something right now," Head stated to the young boy who ran errands every now and then for the men.

"I got something important to holler at Chase about," the kid replied.

"He's busy right now. You can tell me whatever you got to say," Head barked, wanting to get back to the table so he could look over the guns some more.

"That white boy you're chilling with, I've seen him doing some foul, sneaky shit," he said.

"What you talking about? He's working with the jakes or something?" Head asked, his curiosity building.

"Nah. I peeped him dump a body a couple days ago over at that lot by 62nd Avenue."

"How do you know it was a body, and how do you know it was him?" Head asked, still not fully believing the boy.

"I saw an arm hanging from a carpet or something, and you always tell me if I see any white faces hanging around to follow them, to see what they up to," the young boy answered.

"But how do you know it was him?" Head asked.

"When I saw his car pull up with them fly-ass rims and crazy paint job, I knew it was him from the other day."

"Where exactly did you see him put the body?" Head asked, now believing the youth's story.

"He put it under an old, burned up car way in the back," the young boy answered quickly.

"Check it out. I don't want you to tell no one, I mean no fucking body, what you just told me. If I hear you running your mouth, you gonna be under the car too," Head said, reaching into his pocket and handing the kid a small roll of fives and tens. "Remember, keep your mouth shut!" Head reminded the young teen as he got on his bike and pedaled away.

Head walked back into the house just as Chase and Danny were wrapping up their transaction.

"Who was dat?" Chase asked.

"Just a fiend trying to sell some broken-down laptop computer," Head lied.

"Well we got something for these bitch-ass New York niggas now," Chase said, giving Danny some dap. After White Boy Danny left, Head was still deep in thought, wondering how to use his newly-acquired information to his advantage.

CHAPTER
TWENTY-TWO

Doc sat in his five-bedroom, early Italian design house, located on the ritzy side of Alpharetta, Georgia, smoking a Cuban cigar. He really didn't like the taste of the cigar, but he thought it gave him the aura of a professional businessman, even though most of his white neighbors considered him nothing more than a drug pusher.

His wife and ten-year-old daughter were in Miami, Florida, searching for another house and vacationing at the same time. Doc put the cigar out after smoking less than half of it and decided to hit the Jacuzzi and soak for a minute, while drinking a shot of Hennessy Paradise Extra.

As the strong water jets massaged his whole body, Doc sat back, thinking about how his plans were finally starting to materialize.

That crazy African Mooka finally decided to hit me off with some of his heroin that the friends are always buzzing about, he thought while starting on his second glass of Hennessy. He still hadn't even met the man or had any idea what he looked like.

The nigga could be a ghost, for all I care. As long as he deliver, Doc thought as he set the temperature a couple of degrees higher. He had a second meeting with the African at his house, mainly to talk about what they already had discussed. Doc knew that the head honcho wanted to know where he laid his head at, just in case things didn't go as smoothly as everyone had planned. A couple of days after the so-called meeting, he had a strange feeling that someone was staking out his house, probably to make sure he really lived there. That was another reason why Doc decided to push the idea about getting another residence in Miami.

He was hoping Mooka blessed him with fifty kilos, but he was sticking to giving him around thirty for now, to see how he handled himself. Doc had distributed a large portion of his remaining coke and cooked-up rocks to his workers, giving Jason a nice, sizable amount of the product. Doc knew that Jason was destined to blow up on the scene like his older brother, Free. Every night Jason outhustled other workers on his level, bringing in stacks after stacks of money.

Rinnnngggg!! Doc answered his cell phone that was lying on a clean, folded towel. He talked for about five minutes and then hung up, smiling to himself like a cat who had just swallowed the canary. Shorty had called him, saying that she just wanted somebody to talk to. Doc had been around long enough to know exactly what that meant. It was the first time since he was a teenager that he had a wet dream, fantasizing about the sexy, young female who was willing to go all out.

Doc got out of the hot, swirling water and quickly got dressed, forgetting his plans that seemed unimportant at the moment.

"Was you waiting long?" Doc asked the girl as she climbed into the Beemer coupe.

"Not really. I had time to buy a slice of pizza," she answered as Doc sped off.

"So what you wanted to talk about?" he asked, playing along with her game.

"Huh, what?" she asked.

"Well, it's not important right now," he responded, hitting three on CD changer and causing some Beyonce Knowles to come on. Doc was seriously thinking about bringing this beautiful Georgia peach to his home, just to see her naked body floating in his Jacuzzi. When he looked over and saw her short, Baby Phat skirt riding high and showing off those perfectly golden, sculptured thighs, Doc screeched to a halt at the first hotel he saw. He usually didn't patronize this type of rundown spot, but under these circumstances, all he needed was four walls, a bed, and a strong pipe game to lay on a willing ghetto bird.

"Why you brought me here?" the girl asked on their way to the room, acting like she had no idea what was going down.

"I was up all morning driving here and there, and I just wanted a place to relax for a minute," he answered, opening the door to the cheap room. "I gotta go take a piss," Doc said, flicking on the TV. Once in the bathroom he plopped a one-hundred-milligram tablet of Viagra in his mouth. He then flushed the toilet, acting like he had used it before heading back out.

"You don't mind if I spark up?" Doc asked, trying to sound like a gentleman as he pulled out a swollen dime bag of smokes.

"Whatever," the girl responded as she sat on the edge of the bed, flipping from channel to channel. After a while, each of them was pulling on the L. Doc noticed the girl relaxing more and taking off her shoes. His dick became more rigid by the second.

A little while later, the young woman said that the room

was hot and sticky so she decided to take a cold shower. Doc heard a click behind her, knowing that she had locked the bathroom door. She was not really sure if she should go through with the escapade or not. Once he heard the shower running, Doc took off all his clothes and used a credit card to open the bathroom door.

"Whatcha doing in here?" she asked, trying unsuccessfully to cover up. Her eyes were glued to Doc's penis that stood straight out, like a sword ready for attack.

"Everything's all right. I was feeling a little hot myself," he responded while looking at her soapy pubic mound. She stood shyly in the corner as Doc climbed into the shower and began gently massaging her back.

This shit's taking way too long, he thought as he fell to his knees and started eating her pussy like a man possessed. The cold water pounded her body as Doc's tongue pounded her sensitive clit.

The loud moans and the fingers grabbing his ears revealed that it was her first time having someone go down south on her.

"Your man don't do this, does he?" Doc asked, already knowing the answer.

"No, no. God, no!" was all that she could say between gasps. After the second shudder, Doc took her to the bed and laid her down on the worn bedspread, not caring at this point. Just before Doc was about to enter her, she momentarily regained her senses.

"Please put on a condom," she requested. Doc reached in his slacks, producing a rubber, which he put on his throbbing shaft. Once she saw that he had the condom on, she moaned out, "Come on, put it in." At the same time Doc was guiding his dick toward the waiting pussy, he slipped off the condom.

I want to feel all this pussy, Doc thought to himself while pumping with all his might, trying to slay the pussy. The girl couldn't hold back any longer as she screamed, spasmed, and came, saturating the older man's organ.

"Can your man fuck you like this? Can he?" Doc asked in a loud voice as he turned the girl over on her flat belly and began his sexual assault doggie style. Her screams seemed to have the weak walls vibrating, echoing throughout the whole structure. Doc just knew somebody was going to call the police, thinking someone was being murdered. The girl fell down in an exhausted, sweaty heap after releasing so many orgasms. Doc knew he had to finish this episode, so he exploded like a water hose, flooding the young girl's deepest depths.

"When can I see you again?" she asked once they were back in his ride.

"Call me in a couple of days," he answered, still tasting her musky juices in his mouth. Doc wished he had more time to spend with the ferocious, sexually insatiable young college girl, but he had more pressing issues to tend to.

CHAPTER
TWENTY-THREE

"Do you mind if I kick it with you for a minute?" a male voice asked.

"I'm kind of busy right now. Probably some other time," Pumpkin responded in a kind but firm voice. The guy walked off, mumbling something she couldn't make out.

Pumpkin was sitting at the food court in the mall, writing her grandmother a letter. It had been a while since her Nana had written her. Pumpkin wrote how she loved the gold chain that her grandmother had sent her, and that she would never take it off. She didn't want to mention anything negative that had transpired between her and Aunt Liz, or that she had been recently stripping at a club. Pumpkin just said that she was still working at the Red Snapper restaurant and had filled out a couple of college applications. She also lied and said that she had moved into her own apartment but was looking for something else in a better neighborhood. She then licked the envelope and closed it, wishing that she didn't have to put Goldmine's address down as a return address. She wanted to write Dallisha, who was still on lockdown, but two letters back to back was too much for her right now.

Even though Pumpkin was short of money since the closing of Adina's, she purchased a couple of CDs, which always made her feel better.

Pumpkin rode the bus back to Martin Luther King Jr. Drive, thinking of trooping it to the Warehouse Strip Club, hoping to get hired. She had run into her friend Marisza a week ago, who told her that she had been dancing there for a couple of days.

"It's not the best club in town, but I got kids and they gots to eat," Marisza told her while giving her the club's business card. Even though Pumpkin didn't have any children, her pockets were hurting since the detectives had padlocked the club. To make matters worse, Goldmine was stressing her for more money, saying that since Dallisha was gone, she would have to cough up half the rent and utilities. Pumpkin had planned on saving, but the dough came fast and went just as easy, leaving her with nothing to show for all those hours she put in swinging from the pole.

Later on that night Pumpkin jumped in a cab, carrying a nondescript bag with her dance clothes, hoping to start work that night. She arrived at the Warehouse, which was located in the heart of the infamous Red Light District. It was her first time in that particular area, but Pumpkin had heard stories on how the district was a breeding ground for washed-up strippers, hookers, and sometimes ordinary girls whose men had turned them out with the aid of that powerful rock.

Pumpkin strolled inside the club after the bouncer waved her in and was hit full force with the unmistakable smell of woolie smoke (crack mixed with weed). Already from jump street, she knew the owners didn't give a fuck what took place in their establishment.

"Yeah, come on in," a voice growled from behind the door after Pumpkin had knocked. "What can I do for you?" the guy asked, his voice softening up a little after getting a good look at Pumpkin.

"My friend told me dat you might need some new girls," she said.

"You ever dance before?" he asked, noticing how young Pumpkin looked in the face, but with a body that said otherwise.

"Yeah, I used to do my thing over at Adina's Jewels," Pumpkin answered, thinking how ugly he looked with his bumpy pug nose.

"Oh, I heard about what happened over there. So now you wanna come over here?" His facial expression said, *I want you to do what you gotta do for this gig.*

"I just came for a job. I didn't come here for you to try to get on me just because I used to work somewhere else," Pumpkin replied, ready to say fuck it and keep it moving.

"Relax, relax. It ain't that type of party. Go in the dressing room and get changed up so I can see what you working with, and we'll take it from there," he said while standing up and showing the young girl where the women changed.

Them bitches are all the same, the owner thought as he watched Pumpkin walk away. *Pretty, young things with a little fire in them. But once they start hitting the pipe, they be begging just to suck my dick.*

Pumpkin walked through a narrow hallway that had the women's bathroom on one side and the men's on the other side. She walked down a short flight of stairs to the dressing room, and the whole room became instantly quiet as everyone stared at the new girl. Seconds later, everything returned to normal with Pumpkin luckily finding an empty, rusted locker way in the back. Just then, Pumpkin's nostrils were blasted with the strong mixture of ass and unwashed feet.

Damn, I see I'm gonna have to bring a can of Lysol with me on a regular, Pumpkin thought as she scrunched up her nose.

"Can you see the string?" a stripper asked as she stood nude with one foot on a metal chair, trying to push her tampon deeper into her vagina.

"Bitch, ain't nobody trying to be all up in your coochie," another woman yelled in a joking manner.

"So is this your first night up in here? Where you from?" a woman asked Pumpkin.

"I'm from around," she said coldly, letting the woman know that she wasn't in the mood to be making any friends.

Soon Pumpkin was back upstairs and standing in the middle of the owner's shabby looking office. Pumpkin had on a silver, sheer, mid-thigh length skirt with a long split up the side. In the right lighting, you could make out Pumpkin's thong and matching push-up bra. Her open-toed Marc Jacob pumps set the outfit off just right. The owner said she could start that night, if that was OK with her. Normally he would have had the girl dance for him slowly, stripping for him until she was completely nude like a newborn baby. On most occasions he would have gotten head and then told the girl that she was hired. But the way Pumpkin acted when he first met her, he decided to wait a little while before putting his game plan into action.

"Whatever you do outside the club is your business; just don't come to work high or drunk. All girls have to pay a fee if they want to attend private parties." Even though Pumpkin had been in the game only a short while, she knew what private parties meant to him—straight-up fuck parties—where the quick money always came with a heavy price, and the owner also got his cut. The owner finished his speech, saying that she would pick up the rest of the rules as she went along.

Later that night Pumpkin danced on stage, which wasn't really a stage at all—just a square wooden platform that looked as if the local handyman had put it together. The so-called stage didn't even have a pole, and could only hold two dancers at a time.

Pumpkin had changed back into her street clothes at the end of the night, vexed that she had only made eighty dollars. She was even more upset that every guy kept try-ing to shove his fingers into whichever hole was closest to him at the moment. Just as Pumpkin finished calling the cab service, she heard a high-pitched female's voice yell out.

"Yeah, daddy, show him what time it is." Pumpkin turned toward the sound of scuffling and spotted a small gathering. Being the curious person that she was, Pump-kin walked up the block to see what the commotion was about. Lying on the ground, balled up in a fetal position was a plump, middle-aged white man, getting the shit kicked out of him. Doing the beating was a pimp who ob-viously didn't mind getting blood on his new lizard skin, multi-colored shoes.

"Yeah, daddy, dat trick tried to say your pussy wasn't worth seventy-five dollars," a prostitute shouted.

"Show this redneck how we do it up on the District," an older guy, who had nothing to do with what was going on, threw in. The pimp then began kicking the man in the ass, trying to tear into his nuts with the tip of his pointy shoes.

"Please, just let me go. I wouldn't disrespect your woman like that," the man begged, trying to get up, but he was sent flying backward with a sharp kick to the face.

"Should I give him the pimp's salute?" the pimp asked his women, who obviously wanted more action.

"Yeah, da pimp salute, da pimp salute," all the observers sang at the same time. The outraged pimp then proceeded to take out his penis and empty his full bladder all over the man, as everybody cheered him on.

"Now get the fuck off my street 'fore I really get gorilla on you," the pimp spat, pulling out a small silver pistol. A hooker then approached the pimp and placed a whiskey-colored mink on his shoulders as another hooker held out a fresh pair of gators.

The white man slowly got up on wobbly legs, looking around as if the next thing the man was going to do was shit on him.

"Oh shit!" Pumpkin yelled. It was her old boss from the Red Snapper, Mr. Bernstein. Their eyes met for a split second as Pumpkin broke out into a loud, ear-shattering laugh. She hopped into her cab, still laughing, thinking about the wild spectacle and forgetting that she was ever angry about her night at the club.

CHAPTER
TWENTY-FOUR

"You sure you ready to get down right now?" Head asked cautiously.

"Hell, yeah! I'm tired of niggas trying to come to my town, making noise. Them New York cats are some funny-style motherfuckers, rocking Timberland boots no matter how hot it is outside," Chase responded as he puffed on his blunt.

A group of four men were in an average-looking living room, preparing for what would seem to the casual observer to be an all-out war on American soil. All the men were busy loading bullets into their weapons of destruction, and every now and then they pulled on their weed or drank some Beefeater gin.

"I feel you, but once we spray Knowledge and his soft-ass crew, One-Time (the police) gonna know from jump that we had something to do with it," Head stated, knowing that participating in mass murder was bad for business.

"You know da motherfucking police don't give a fuck what goes on down here. If a nigga gets his shit pushed back, da most they might do is sit on a corner for a day or two. Da only time they might bring out da big dawgs is if a cracker was to get robbed or something. Ain't dat right, boys?" Chase asked. The other guys nodded in agreement with Chase as Head admitted that their leader was right.

The police didn't give a fuck what happened in Little Vietnam. They already knew the details about the ongoing beef that had been brewing in the hood, but they never took any preventive measures to squash the predictable, disastrous outcome. In most inner cities, especially Atlanta, the police swooped down only to clean up the carnage with their insincere questions and yellow police caution tape.

"Come on, y'all, let's take care of dis. I wanna get something to eat afterward," Chase shouted, slinging his gun over his shoulder.

The murderous foursome rode around in an old, stolen Cutlass, looking intensely for their intended victims.

"Where the fuck they at?" a guy about nineteen asked from the back seat. All the men rode in silence, anxious to end this little drug turf war. An hour later they spotted a group of men gathered around in the shadows, behind a known crack house.

"What the fuck they up to?" the second guy asked Chase.

"Shhhhh, be quiet. Kill da lights and back up," Chase ordered, his finger sweating anxiously on the trigger. Head did as he was told, sliding his ten-millimeter gun into his free hand. He then slowly backed up the heavy car so that it was sitting at the entrance to the alleyway.

There were about seven guys huddled around three glass dice, playing the New York favorite, cee-lo. There were various amounts of money in front of each of the player's feet. A slim, doo-rag-wearing guy blew on the dice and shook them in his fist.

"I got fifty that says he falls," one guy shouted.

"I'll take that bet," someone answered.

"What's up, cuzzo? Anybody seen Knowledge?" Chase asked, leaning out the window on the passenger's side. The men froze, looking down the dark alley at the sound of the strange man's voice, not even realizing that the dice had already been rolled.

"Nah, he ain't here. Who are you?" a husky guy wearing a crisp white tee asked, while squinting his eyes and trying to make out who he was talking to.

"I'm a friend of his. Give him dis message for me," Chase said, then swung his British battle rifle out the window and let loose. The rifle barked as the men who were already on point scattered, trying to find cover. Chase jumped out of the car, running up the alley. The rest of the guys followed suit.

One dice player, who felt that the money on the ground was worth more than the slight danger, tried to scoop up the twenties and fifties. He ran maybe a couple of feet before a high-powered bullet pierced his spine and tore through his lung. He fell to the ground, still clutching the money in his hand, as liquid started to fill his lungs. Before he could drown in his own blood, a series of bullets created a hole in his chest.

Head emptied his clip into a fast-moving figure, not sure if he had found his mark.

"Come on out, you scary motherfuckers. I wanna talk with you," Chase called out, still holding the gun close to his body. By now all of Chase's hit squad was gathered together, with one of guys kicking the obviously dead man to see if he was still alive.

Brinnnng, brinnnng. A cell phone went off, causing all the men to turn toward the sound. Chase slowly crept up to a row of Rubbermaid garbage cans and kicked them to the side.

"Don't move, motherfucker!" Chase growled, pointing his machine gun dead center on the young guy's forehead. All the guys now surrounded the frightened teen, who couldn't keep from shaking as if he were caught in a blizzard without a coat.

"Please, I don't know what's going on. I was just watching the game," he pleaded, holding up his hands.

"Dat's too bad. Maybe in your next life you'll understand da meaning of guilty by association," Chase said with a cold-hearted grin as he let the barrel touch the boy's head.

"Come on, man. He can't be no more than fifteen. This little nigga can't do nothing to us. Let him ride so he can tell his peoples what time it is," Head said, knowing very well what Chase was about to do.

"Fuck dat shit. I've seen twelve-year-olds murder grown-ass men. If dis nigga had a burner, he wouldn't think twice about blasting my ass," Chase answered without a trace of sympathy in his voice. The young teenager sat there speechless as the men discussed his fate like he was a lamb about to be slaughtered. Before another word could be uttered, Chase pulled the trigger, causing the night air to echo once more. The kid fell backward with his wide eyes still focused on Head, praying that this man would save his life. The young kid's last thought was that he would never disobey or disrespect his mother about staying out all night again.

A week after his funeral, this young boy's mother would move his two younger brothers to a different state, hoping they wouldn't end up like their older sibling. But what the heartbroken mother failed to realize was that there were countless ghettos across America, just waiting to swallow up more black youths.

"We out!" Chase said, walking quickly back to the car. Moments later the group was blocks away from the crime scene, laughing with Chase, who was boasting the loudest.

"You seen da way those cowards spread out? Man, I wish I had a camera."

Head took a swig of the liquor, thinking that his boss was going to bring everybody down with him. He then passed the bottle, knowing what he had to do.

CHAPTER TWENTY-FIVE

"Grandma, have you seen sis today?" Jason asked just as he finished stashing away three kilos of high quality cocaine that Doc had thrown his way. Doc had told him the reason he was giving him this much product on consignment was because Jason had finally proven himself a bonafide street hustler. But Jason suspected from the jump that the older man wanted to be a drug kingpin, and he had ulterior motives for the unsuspected move. Jason planned to cook up the majority of the coke to transform it to the most sought-after crack cakes. The young man knew that he would almost quadruple his profit if he slanged them "can't get enough" rocks.

"I think she said she was staying over at one of her cousin's houses. Baby, you want to sit with me and watch the *Addams Family* marathon?" Jason's grandma asked, with a slight glimmer of hope that she might have some company today beside her cats.

"Can you remember which cousin, Grandma?" he asked.

"No. You know how fast you young people talk nowadays. You sure you don't want to watch TV with me? I'll make some tunafish sandwiches if you like," she said, already heading toward the kitchen.

"Nah, I got to go. Probably some other time," Jason called out as he snatched his car keys from the table and jetted out the door. As Jason backed his hoopty out of the driveway, he made a mental note to make some phone calls to find out exactly where his little sister was.

Twenty minutes later, Jason was pulling up to a decrepit-looking house just off of Bankhead. He grabbed a bag of brand new baby clothes from the backseat and walked up to the front door. He tapped lightly on the old wooden door before he noticed that it was cracked open.

"Hello, anybody home?" Jason shouted.

"Who is it? What you want?" a female voice asked, sounding as if someone had disturbed her sleep.

"It's me, Jason," he said as he stepped into the hot, musty house.

"What's up, Jason? You should have told me you was dropping by. I would have straightened up," the woman said, getting up from the sofa and trying to dust the lint from her clothes.

Jason looked around the house, thinking that every time he came over to this place, he knew it was on the verge of becoming a full-fledged crack den, and this was home to his two-year-old nephew. The living room was littered with old newspapers and discarded food wrappings. Piss-stained bedsheets, hung by large nails, covered the dusty windows.

"Where's little man at? Jason asked, walking a couple of feet and accidentally kicking a forty-ounce bottle under the sofa.

"He's in the back room, sleeping," the mother of Jason's brother's son answered as she busied herself throwing garbage into an oversized plastic bag that was already filled to the top. Jason walked into the bedroom that had a pile of dirty clothes in a corner, and saw his little nephew sleeping on a bare mattress. His nephew seemed to be resting comfortably in a deep sleep, sucking on his thumb.

"Vicky, get your ass in here!" Jason yelled out when he spotted little man wearing a sagging, smelly diaper.

"What's wrong?" Vicky asked, rushing into the room.

"You can't see or smell what he's wearing? What the fuck you been doing all day? Laying on your lazy ass?" he asked.

"I was waiting for a friend to bring over some money she owed me. I was going to change him as soon as I came back from the corner store," Vicky replied as she walked over to the bed and quickly took off the dirty diaper. She then threw the soiled material on top of the pillow as she proceeded to wrap a T-shirt on the sleeping child's bottom.

Jason took a long look at the woman who used to be considered top choice among the drug dealers from the hood. Free, at the time, was an established player in the game, running a successful twenty-four-hour dope house. As the money and fame began to cling to him, so did the women who wanted to be known as "Free's girl."

"Don't fuck with her," was the standard comment about the women who belonged to someone of Free's status and power. Vicky was soon driving Free's cars and posing as she cruised through the ghetto, rocking expensive jewelry along with the latest hip-hop fashions. Not only was Jason's brother fattening his pockets from his illegal racketeering enterprise, but he had bagged some of the illest shorties from the hood, causing the other guys to hate on him even more. It seemed like a hundred years ago that Vicky had a well-proportioned body with long, slender legs. Now she was just a shell of her former self, staring at Jason with sunken cheekbones and desperate eyes.

"This here is for little man," Jason stated, handing a bag

of designer baby clothes to the girl who still had a small trace of beauty from her better days.

"Thanks. Tell Free I'm going to come see him some-time next week," she said while rifling through the bag, thinking what she could sell first.

"What you talking about? He's been on lock for more than a year and you haven't set foot nowhere near the jail!" he yelled.

"It's been hard trying to raise this brat, I mean his son, by myself. I've been putting in job applications every-where, but you know how it is with white folks. They don't want to do nothing for a nigga bitch unless we kiss they ass," Vicky answered, hoping he believed her lie. Jason just looked at her with disgust.

Yeah, them white folks didn't put the pipe to your fucking lips. You fucked up your own life and now you're looking for someone or something to blame for your downfall, Jason thought as he twisted his face into a scowl.

"Anyway, I gotta spread out," Jason responded, turning around ready to head out the door.

"Wait a minute. You can't leave a little something for your nephew?" she asked.

"What! You talking about money?" he asked, knowing the answer already.

"They talking about cutting off the gas. We can't be freezing up in here. The baby was sick for a whole week when they shut off the heat last time, plus I need a little food money. Somebody must have stolen my check. It should have been here already," the woman begged. Jason just couldn't take any more.

"OK, take this, and you better buy some grub and dia-pers. I'll be back in a couple of days. Have the gas bill ready. I'll pay it myself," he told her while handing the woman some money.

"Thank you, thank you, and don't forget to tell your

brother that I'll be up real soon," Vicky said as Jason jumped into his Honda Civic.

The whole scene of his innocent nephew trapped in a fucked-up, unwholesome environment brought Jason down a bit. He stopped by the liquor store and picked up a medium-sized bottle of Hennessy. Just after he finished his first cup, his cell phone rang.

"Jason, what's up? This is L.B. I'm almost done. Why didn't you bless me when you was up here yesterday?" he asked.

"Up where?" Jason asked.

"The Red Roof Inn. I saw your shorty Camay leaving, but I didn't see your whip. I figured you had a rental or something."

"Word! You saw my shorty at the mo? Are you sure it was her?" Jason asked, hoping his worker was wrong.

"Yeah, kid, I'm positive. I was about to ask her about you, but a couple of fiends rushed me," L.B. said, just then putting two and two together, and realizing that Camay probably had just finished getting her guts blown out by some other guy.

"She probably was just out looking for me. Anyway, I'll see you later tonight," Jason said, ending his call and immediately calling Camay. After about twenty minutes of calling her house and cell phone and not having anyone pick up, he decided to jet to her house. He raced to her place while drinking his liquor, dying to question her about the information that had to be a mistake.

"Jason, I'm kind of busy right now," Camay said through the closed door after Jason had furiously pounded on it.

"Why you got the door locked?"

"I'm not dressed," she replied.

"Why didn't you pick up your phone? You know it was me trying to holla at you," he shouted.

"I told you I can't talk right now. I'll call you later," she said, still looking through the peephole.

"My peoples told me they saw you at the Red Roof. What the hell was you doing over there? Don't lie, because L.B. looked you dead in your grill," Jason shouted while thinking of kicking in the door.

"I was playing cards with some of my girlfriends," Camay said.

"Who do you think you talking to? Don't no group of bitches go to the telle to play fucking cards, unless they had niggas with them. Open the door so we can talk," he demanded, growing more impatient and curious by the second.

"No! You acting wild, bugging the fuck out. I'm not gonna talk to you with you calling me a liar," she yelled.

After continuing their heated verbal exchange for about ten minutes, Camay finally told Jason the truth.

"OK, you really wanna know? Don't step to me. Go ask your man Doc what the deal is."

Jason stood silent for a while, staring off into space as if he was in a deep trance, before he slowly walked back to his vehicle.

CHAPTER TWENTY-SIX

"Why do you folks keep harassing me? I told you, you will get your money when I get it," Goldmine shouted into the receiver. There was a slight pause before she continued. "What! What do you expect, me to pull it out of my black ass?" She then slammed the phone down and lit up a long Newport cigarette.

Since the temporary closing down of Adina's, Goldmine's funds had been stretched to the limit. The owner of EZ Ride Auto had been stressing her for the car payments on the Mustang. She cursed herself for dealing with a buy here, pay here car lot who was quick to repossess your ride if you were a couple of weeks late. She definitely needed some flashy shit to show the jealous bitches this was how it was done. The bank wouldn't even fuck with her because she never held what they considered a steady job in her life, so she had to resort to EZ Ride. When Goldmine was sure that she wouldn't have the cash for her payment, she went straight down to the office in her best come-fuck-me outfit.

"Come on, Mr. Riszote, you know me and what I do.

Business has been slow. Niggas must be going through a recession or some shit," Goldmine stated, not willing to tell him that she was now out of work.

"Well I'm very sympathetic to your plight, but you have to understand that I have bills also," he replied, not at all moved by her hard-luck story.

"What I do is hard work! People think dancers just walk around shaking their asses, raking in dough, and everything else is peaches and cream. Just da other night, some crazy guy tried to manhandle me, thinking I wasn't paying him enough attention. See what he did?" Goldmine stated as she stood up and placed her leg up on the chair, causing her short skirt to rise up even farther into her crotch area. "You see, Mr. Riszoto, he must have bruised me somehow," she said as she gently rubbed her upper thigh, giving the man a full view of her baby blue, silk panties. Goldmine made sure she wore this particular pair of underwear because she somehow thought it made her vagina look more puffy and irresistible to the weaker sex.

"I'm sorry to hear that you were attacked, but like I said before, my children have to eat also. They'd starve if everyone's problems became my problems. I'm sure you can understand that," Mr. Riszoto said, barely looking up as he busied himself with papers that cluttered his oak desk.

"You'll have your fucking money!" Goldmine shouted, thinking that the Italian fuck had to be a faggot, or some weird closet freak, for not even missing a beat after what she threw at him.

"Is everything all right?" the nosey, bored receptionist asked, hoping to hear a good story.

"Mind your goddamn business," Goldmine responded as she stormed out the door and sped off in her new car.

"So what you got for me today?" Goldmine asked Pumpkin as she walked into Dallisha's old room, still upset from the phone call she had received a little while ago.

"I know I don't have much, but I would like a little privacy every once in a while," the younger woman replied while putting on a light denim jacket that matched her form-fitting Apple Bottom jeans. Goldmine just stood in the doorway, staring at Pumpkin.

What da fuck is going on dis morning? Do I have a sign tattooed on my forehead dat says, play me? Goldmine wondered.

She couldn't believe Pumpkin had the audacity to speak to her like she was one of these ghetto-out bum bitches walking around. Here she was, kind enough to take in a stray cat and give it warm milk and now when its belly was good and full, it wanted to take a snap at its savior.

"First off, dis is my motherfucking house. I can go anywhere I damn well please," the slightly older woman yelled, her eyes tearing through Pumpkin.

"I know it's your place, but I could have been changing or something," Pumpkin responded, not backing down from her first statement.

"I just hope you realize dat. You know I left you a note saying dat I needed two fifty for rent a couple of days ago," Goldmine lied.

"I didn't see no note, but all I have is a buck fifty right now," Pumpkin responded, digging in her Etro bag and giving Goldmine some money. She then walked out of the bedroom, not waiting for Goldmine to start counting the money.

I'm definitely not in da mood for her bullshit, Pumpkin thought as she went outside to wait for her ride.

Pumpkin's Nextel went off and she quickly answered it. The voice on the other end told her that he was just a couple of blocks away and would be there in a minute. True to his word, the dark blue, big-bodied Suburban swirled into the front of the building on M.L.K. The SUV stopped directly in front of Pumpkin, and a tinted window rolled down.

"Come on, shorty. Let's roll," Knowledge said, unlocking the power doors. Pumpkin climbed in as the driver peeled off.

"I'm glad you came right away. My fucking roommate is really starting to lose it," she said, throwing a different CD in. Some old Notorious B.I.G. flooded the luxurious interior.

"What, she on her period or something?" Knowledge asked with a smile on his face.

"I don't know what's wrong with her. She's probably on dat yak. I really don't care. I'm fed up with da setup already," Pumpkin said as she sat back in a more comfortable position. "Enough about me. So what's up with you lately?" she asked, changing the stressful subject.

"I was up in da hospital early dis morning to see what da deal was with my boy," Knowledge said.

"Is he all right?"

"If by all right you mean is he alive, yeah, he's dat, but da doctors had to take a rib out and make him a new jaw."

"Was he in an accident?" Pumpkin asked.

"We had a little drama, but it's nothing we can't handle."

A short while later, the couple pulled up to a restaurant and took a booth facing the door. Knowledge always had a habit of sitting in a position so that he could see whoever came into the restaurant. Their meal came and they continued to have casual conversation. Every now and then, Knowledge's phone would go off and he would tell whoever had called that he was in the middle of something, and that he would touch base with them later. Pumpkin liked a man who had enough respect not to talk on the phone during lunch, instead of trying to act like a wannabe player.

Just as the waitress was taking away the dishes, his phone went off again. Pumpkin peeped the change in Knowledge's face as he spoke into the phone.

"Hold down da fort," he said. "I'll be right there."

"Shorty, some real serious shit jumped off. I'm gonna have to get with you another time," he said, throwing a fifty on the table as he got up.

"You can drop me off right here," Pumpkin said as Knowledge pulled up a couple of feet away from White Boy Danny's house.

"I'll hit you up once I straighten shit out," Knowledge said before peeling off.

Pumpkin walked toward the house, hoping Danny had some good smokes. She had planned on hanging out with Knowledge because it was her day off. She really didn't have any other plans, so she decided to at least get lifted and asked if she could dance tonight. She definitely needed the cash after giving Goldmine almost all of her money just to shut her up.

CHAPTER TWENTY-SEVEN

Knowledge raced to meet his peoples, blowing through stop signs and almost mowing down an elderly lady. By the time the old woman regained her senses and gathered up the strength for a weak middle finger, the driver was already blocks away. When Knowledge finally reached his boys, he jumped out of the jeep, scuffing his fresh, six-inch Tims in the process.

"So what da fuck jumped off?" Knowledge asked, leaving his SUV in the middle of the street with the door swung wide open. Knowledge's right hand man, Daquan, signaled for someone to move the Suburban to the side so it wouldn't draw any unwanted attention.

"Yo, niggas was just maintaining, throwing them bones around when a car pulled up, asked for you, and just started licking shots," Daquan explained.

"Who was there?" Knowledge asked. Reese, a short kid about eighteen with a half tied doo-rag hanging from his head, spoke.

"Like Daquan said, niggas just asked for you and began letting off."

"So who got touched?" Knowledge asked, knowing that it was the Folks gang who was behind the shootings.

When Knowledge and his crew first set up shop in Little Vietnam, it wasn't no big deal. When they started getting major paper, selling more product for less, that's when the local heads started to take notice of the new boys from out of town. They soon sent word by different messengers that New York niggas weren't welcome in the ATL. Knowledge just laughed and smacked around one guy a couple times, telling him to tell whoever sent him to step to him like a real man. They knew they were being watched, but they made the first mistake of being overconfident.

"Fuck dem country motherfuckers. They can't touch us!" Knowledge would say. A month later, one member of the crew was caught late one night by himself, slinging crack rocks. A group of guys rushed him, beating him to the pavement with golf clubs. They robbed him of his work and money, leaving him unconscious and naked. Luckily, one of the few remaining residents of the drug-infested area made a much needed but anonymous phone call to 911, saving the young man from becoming a permanent cripple.

"They hit up that new kid who's been trying to get down with us, and they wet Little Ty. By the time we found out, the police had the place on lock," Daquan said, glad that he had decided to hit some new skins instead of playing cee-lo with the unlucky guys.

"You sure they caught Little Ty?" Knowledge asked.

"Yeah. When we came back, we peeped both guys covered up with them white cloths, the ones they use if they know you went back to the essence already. Plus, the coroner van was just pulling up," Reese replied, telling the cold, hard truth.

"Dem faggot niggas! I promised Ty's people dat I'd look out for him. Fuck dat shit! We gonna show motherfuckers how our gats bark," Knowledge shouted, ready for an all-out war.

"That's what I'm talking about. I know a couple of their spots. I say we say 'fuck it' and murder everything moving," Reese said, eager to prove that he had an ill trigger finger.

Much later that night, around two AM, Knowledge, Reese, and two other guys were rolling in the Suburban while Daquan rode with another guy in his death grey Astro van. The group rode around, spotting nobody but an occasional cop car riding by for decoration.

"Yeah, dem bitch ass niggas know what time it is. They want to blast their heat and go run and hide behind closed doors like motherfuckering old women," Knowledge said to the guys in the Jeep, while slowly turning a corner that was usually populated by their rival drug dealers.

"I'm telling you, they out here somewhere. Them niggas not gonna close up shop because of a few bodies," Reese said while tightly gripping a blue steel .45, desperately wanting to murder anyone tonight, mostly because he would have a carload of witnesses to see firsthand on how sick he got down.

"Be on point. I see somebody," Knowledge said, slowing the vehicle. It was a forty-something black man hunched over and staring at the ground, hoping to find a cocaine rock that maybe somebody might have dropped.

"That's nobody, just a fiend," Reese said.

"Yo, come here and let me holler at you for a minute," Knowledge yelled out to the man as Daquan pulled up behind them. The man trotted over to the driver's side window.

"What's up, man?" the guy asked. His eyes, which held a sickly yellow color, became as big as dinner plates.

"I heard some bodies got dropped last night over by

South Hill. I think it might have been my little brother. You know anything about it?" Knowledge asked as he lit up a cigarette.

"I saw all the police sirens and ambulances. I heard people from the neighborhood talking about it last night. I think it had something to do with drugs or gangs," the dope fiend replied as he picked his nose.

"This crack head don't know nothing," Reese shouted as he hopped out of the SUV and walked around toward the man, who towered a good four inches over him.

"Get the fuck outta here. We got shit to do," Reese said while grabbing the man by his shabby collar.

"Why you gonna treat me like that? I didn't do nothing to nobody," the man said, looking over at Knowledge for sympathy.

"Cool out! I got dis," Knowledge ordered. "I just want you to find out exactly what jumped off last night," he told the fiend. "Keep your ears to da streets and I'll hit you off with a little something," Knowledge finished as he handed the fiend a business card with his cell phone number on it.

"I'll call you as soon as I hear anything. You have a little something right now?" the man asked meekly.

"Give him a bag," Knowledge said to Reese, since he was already out of the car. Reese did as he was told. The man took his medicine, which caused a huge smile that revealed brown, decaying teeth.

"If you don't call, next time I see you I'll put you out your fucking misery," Reese growled, letting the fiend know that he was packing a rachet.

The man quickly walked off, thinking to himself that a good ten years ago he would have had the young kid begging for his life if he had ever dreamed of talking to him like that.

CHAPTER TWENTY-EIGHT

Jason was up and out the door, still feeling the effects from drinking all night. After what his so-called girl had told him, he decided to call Doc to see what the real deal was. When's Doc's phone went straight to voicemail, he decided to hit up a strip club to relieve his stress, but subconsciously he wanted to feel that he could pull any woman he wanted, never mind the fact that strippers flirted for a living as long as that money kept flowing. Jason headed over to Adina's Jewels, but when he found out they were closed down, he shot over to the Warehouse. The women there were a little more thuggish, but it beat kicking it with nobody at all. He didn't quite remember everything he did that night except that he drank more than he was used to and almost set the record for getting the most lap dances and wall dances in a night.

Jason had momentarily forgotten his little fucked-up conversation with Camay, but it all came back to him the next morning, even fresher than before.

I definitely need to straighten shit out with Doc, Jason thought as he pulled up his Honda Civic to the corner of

Blazen Cuts. He spotted Doc standing by his truck, laughing and talking to a very attractive, red-boned chick. As he walked closer, he recognized the slow guy who usually swept the floors of the shop. The guy was hand-waxing the Expedition and smiling like it was an honor to keep Doc's possessions sparkling.

"What's up, Doc? Can I holler at you for a minute?" Jason asked, trying his best to conceal the anger in his voice.

"What you doing, running up on me like that? I told you to call me if you ever want to meet up with me," Doc stated, turning around to face the much younger man. He was smoking an illegal Cuban cigar, holding it away from his body so that the ashes wouldn't blow back on his custom-made, all-white, imported Egyptian cotton suit. The woman looked at Jason like he had interrupted an important corporate meeting or something.

"One of my boys told me he spotted my shorty at the Red Roof Inn with a nigga, and when I asked her about it, she said I should holler at you," Jason stated, unable to hide his emotions any longer. Doc just looked at his best worker for a split second and then broke out in a long, deep, hardy laugh. When Doc finally regained his composure, he answered the boy.

"Ain't this some shit. You're ready to die for some pussy that wasn't even yours to begin with." Doc puffed on his cigar and looked past Jason. Jason felt a presence behind him and glanced his eyes down toward the ground, where he saw a huge shadow. At once he knew it was Doc's bodyguard, who was always strapped. Jason didn't bother to look behind himself, but he suspected that if he made any type of threatening move toward his boss, there would be a strong possibility that in an hour he could be floating in one of the many nondescript creeks that populated Georgia.

"Yeah, I fucked your bitch, but that's all it was, just a fuck. Shorty threw the pussy at me and like a player I caught it, bagged it, and sent it on its way," Doc stated without any feeling attached to his words. Meanwhile, Jason fought the overpowering impulse to go for his own gat and get busy right in the middle of the afternoon on a busy sidewalk. Doc, being on the streets for a long time, recognized the look of hatred and contempt in the young man's eyes and continued.

"Listen, your girl tooted her ass in the air for me. If it wasn't me, it would have been somebody else. When a female does her thang, don't try to explain it or understand it. Fuck her! Keep it moving. Get your paper like a true baller ought to," Doc said.

Jason knew that Doc was 100 percent right. What could he say? Nothing. He knew that he would make himself look like a bigger fool if he tried to defend the girl who played him like a bitch. Jason started to walk back toward his car when Doc called out to him.

"Hey, Jason, remember: don't let a bitch come between you and your dough. And if you ever step to me like one of your punk friends again, I'll personally make sure that a freaky bitch would be the last thing on your mind!"

Jason got into his car, still hearing Doc's deep laugh. He couldn't decide who he wanted to kill more—Doc or Camay. At least Doc was right about the money issue. He still had to get paid, no matter what happened. Jason had already made up his mind that once he got off Doc's kilos, he would have more than enough money to start his own hustle. He would stop fucking with Doc altogether and maybe one day, he would have Doc working for him. He had seen how the script got flipped too many times for overconfident, cocky Big Willies. Early on, he had begun talking to some of his peoples about moving some weight and going into business together.

As Jason walked though the door of his house, he still had in the back of his mind that he would let Doc know who the real man was, when the time was right. He knew he was in no position, financially or manpower–wise, to go toe to toe with Doc. Jason went straight to his room to retrieve the drugs. He had planned to cook up the coke over at his man's house.

"What the fuck!" Jason said out loud when he first realized the coke wasn't where he had left it. His first thought was that someone from the hood had found out where he had his stash. Then he came to the conclusion that they would have trashed his room looking for more coke or money. "Maybe I put it somewhere else," he said as he began searching and turning over everything in his room, working up a sweat.

"Dear, are you all right in there?" his grandmother asked, walking into his now messy room.

"Yes, Grandma. I'm just looking for something very important," he said, still trying to figure out where he could have hidden it.

"I wish I could help you, but I came to ask you if you had any more dirty clothes that I could wash."

"No, I don't, Grandma."

Once Jason's grandmother left the room, he closed the bedroom door and continued with his search.

"That's what the fuck I'm talking about!" Jason said out loud with a sigh of relief after finding Doc's coke. He had been so stressed out after finding out that his supposed wifey, Camay, was giving up the pussy to niggas in the streets, he wasn't thinking clearly. Jason planned to keep fattening up his pockets and worry about fixing the sheisty-ass bitch Camay, and grimy, disrespectful Doc, later.

CHAPTER
TWENTY-NINE

Goldmine watched carefully as Jason walked back to his car with his teeth and fists still clenched, thinking that Doc made a grave mistake in letting the man leave like that. She knew many a man had died in the ghetto fucking around with a guy's girl and his pride. In this particular case, Doc did both, humiliating the young guy in front of everybody, and totally underestimating his frame of mind.

"Come on, girl, get your fine ass in and let's roll," Doc said, smacking Goldmine on the butt with a rough hand. She did as she was told, climbing into the truck's back seat, her thin Valentino summer dress slightly lifting into the air by an afternoon breeze, causing a car horn to beep after the driver caught a glimpse of her G-string. Doc's driver got behind the wheel as Doc talked for a few minutes outside, giving the guy from the barbershop some money for cleaning the SUV.

The trio pulled off, with Doc conducting business on his cell phone while Goldmine sat in the back, feeling bored. They soon pulled up to a house in an expensive part of town. Doc and his driver got out and met with another man, who stood next to a crisp black Beemer coupe. Goldmine couldn't make out what the men were saying, but she knew the conversation could only be about the dope game.

After Goldmine finished her third Newport, Doc told her to get out and get into the front seat. They both jumped back into Doc's BMW and sped off.

"What we gonna do now?" Goldmine asked, rubbing on the man's leg.

"I got to meet some of my folks in a little while. Something came up. I'm gonna have to get with you later," he answered.

Goldmine knew that in the busy, hectic business of drugs, later could mean anything from a couple of days to a week. She also knew that any guy in the hood who was making major moves like Doc always had a plentiful supply of willing women to do just about anything to get next to him. Goldmine had to admit to herself that she was one of them.

"I thought we was gonna spend a little time together. You know I've been thinking about da last time we chilled," Goldmine stated in one of her sexy voices that she often used to get bigger tips at the club.

"You know I want to tear that ass up again, but paper always comes first," he stated. Goldmine knew for a fact that when he started running from A to B, he would most likely bump into a chick with dollar signs gleaming in her eyes who would, without a doubt, throw the pussy at him with full force. As Doc slowed down for a red light, Goldmine smoothly unzipped his pants and delicately squeezed his balls.

"Come on, baby, you know what I want," she said with a knowing smile.

"Damn, I shouldn't have laid the pipe game on you so

strong," he replied, not resisting as the eager woman milked him to a hardness that was unparalleled to any erection he had ever had. As soon as Goldmine's soft, red lips touched his penis, he quickly pulled into the back of a Krispy Kreme parking lot.

"Yeah, bitch, I know you want this," Doc groaned, not worrying about anyone spotting the sex act because of his mirror tints.

"Daddy, please cum in my mouth," Goldmine said, looking up at him, her eyes begging. Goldmine was giving Doc her special dick-sucking flute technique move that she saved for only the high-paying customers in the VIP room at the strip club. She knew one other woman, a Brazilian, who had mastered the flute technique and practically became rich because of it.

Just when Doc was about to cum, there was a loud thump on the driver's side window, followed by a crash. The window was completely shattered, spraying the couple with shards of glass. The next thing Doc knew, he had an arsenal of guns pointing in his face.

"Don't move, you fucking scumbag," the plain-clothed officer yelled, his breath smelling like stale coffee. Meanwhile, Goldmine was too stunned to even move, still holding on to Doc's still rock-hard dick.

"Get the fuck out the car, you fucking whore," another officer screamed, snatching the woman out of her once-comfortable seat and roughly throwing her to the ground. It seemed that a whole police regiment had the BMW surrounded. They had Doc lying handcuffed in a small puddle of dirty water with his pants still open. Other cops were busy searching the car as sergeants in white shirts watched over them.

"What the fuck is this bullshit?" Doc asked.

"Shut the fuck up, boy, before I kick in your spleen," a potbellied detective growled.

"Fuck you and the rest of these pigs. I'll be out in an hour," Doc responded. The officer's face tightened up as he prepared to carry out his threat. Another cop quickly bent down and patted Doc all over, halting his partner's illegal assault. The officer stepped in between the near beating, not because he believed in a suspect's fundamental rights, but because his partner already had a long list of civilian complaints and was on the verge of getting suspended.

"The car and the woman are clean, Sarge. What do you want me to do with her?" a uniformed cop asked his superior.

"Give her a citation for public lewdness and let her go," the sergeant ordered. He then walked over to Doc, who was now sitting cross-legged, but still on the ground.

"What y'all arresting me for? What you said I supposedly did?" Doc asked, knowing he was now speaking to the man in charge.

"You'll find out everything when we get down to the station. Do you want us to release your vehicle to the young woman, or impound it for you?" the cop asked.

Doc didn't want to have his luxury car towed away and stored in some dusty impound lot. The last time the Atlanta police impounded one of his vehicles, some jealous, low-paying officers scratched and dented his Lex, saying it was like that already. He'd rather take his chances with Goldmine, even though he hardly knew her. He wasn't worried because he knew she respected his gangster.

"Yeah, give her my car keys," Doc said. Once the keys were in Goldmine's hands, Doc yelled out instructions.

"Go take my shit and drop it off by the barbershop. They'll know what to do," he called out as the police stuffed him into the back of an unmarked car.

Goldmine was still shaken, thinking she was going down

for whatever Doc had gotten himself into. She put on her seatbelt, something she never did, and slowly pulled out of the parking lot.

"Damn, I need some weed," she said to herself as she headed in the opposite direction of Blazen Cuts.

CHAPTER THIRTY

Chase, Head, and two thick, pretty ghetto bunnies were relaxing in the house, playing cards while smoking some high-potent chronic.

"I saw you, Chase. I peeped you slide that ace from under the table," a girl who sported a waterfall hairdo said, as she giggled hysterically at her own comment.

"Nah, shorty, you just imagining things. I won fair and square. You know da rules," Chase replied, cracking open an ice-cold forty and taking a long guzzle.

"Come on, Head, you saw how he cheated. You both just want to see my titties," the girl replied while sliding her belly sweater over her head.

"Who you trying to fool, Trish? Even if you woulda won every hand tonight, you still would have found an excuse to take your clothes off," the second girl said, laughing in a good-natured tone of voice.

"Look at you. You been sitting in your bra and panties since the last two hands," Trish shot back, looking at her good friend, who wore a satin bra two sizes too small, causing her full, sturdy breasts to spill out from all sides of the weak material.

Meanwhile, Head sat in an extra-white wife beater, showing off his solid, chiseled form. At this moment Head couldn't care less if both women were buck naked, climbed on top of the table, and began freaking off with each other. His mind was on how Chase was inciting an all-out war with those New York cats. He had told Chase that committing senseless murders was bad for business for everyone involved.

"Fuck dat! We got to let everybody know dat they just can't come down here and set up shop like we invisible or something, especially outta towners," Chase had responded, walking around the room with his gun in his waistband.

"So what's going on? How's everything looking out there?" Chase asked into his cell phone after it went off. One of their workers on the other end had informed him that business was flowing as usual and that Knowledge's crew was quiet as church mice. "Ha ha ha, I knew dem niggas had no heart. They probably somewhere back in Brooklyn, or Queens, or wherever they're from," Chase said to no one in particular.

"Yeah, they probably shook," Head added, not challenging Chase's ghetto reasoning, mainly because he knew it would fall on deaf ears. In Head's mind, he knew that in the lethal drug game, Chase was making the fatal mistake of underestimating his enemies. When you fuck with a man's pockets, they're liable to do anything to the fullest extreme.

Both couples smoke, drank, and cracked jokes until about three in the morning, when Head took his shorty and bounced.

"Ain't you coming in?" the girl asked after Head pulled up in front of her house and she noticed that he made no attempt to get out with her.

"I gotta make a power move. I'll get with you later," he answered nonchalantly.

"Oh, so now you tired of being with me? What, you breaking out to go fuck one of them stank College Park girls in the ass?" she shouted, leaning in the window of the passenger's side door.

"Bitch, who the fuck you think you talking to? I just met your ass a month ago and now you trying to be up in mines. I know you a little bent from the Henny, so I'll let it slide this time. If you say another motherfucking word, I'm gonna say fuck my business and tear into that ass," Head said, glaring straight at the young woman and meaning every word he spoke. She decided to say she was sorry, but quickly changed her mind, remembering Head's last comment and not wanting to take any chances.

Head finally drove off and located an isolated payphone.

"Is this Detective Summerset?" he asked into the spit-covered receiver.

"Yes, who is this?" the voice asked.

"That's not important, but what is important is a young girl's body buried under a wreck in the vacant lot on 63rd Street," Head stated.

"Is this a confession?" the detective asked.

"No, asshole, but the person who did it goes by the street name of Chase. I'm sure you have his government name on file," Head replied before hanging up.

Head then drove off, not giving it a second thought that he had just set up his childhood friend for a murder Chase didn't even know existed.

CHAPTER THIRTY-ONE

Pumpkin was on her way to the Warehouse. She was thinking about how Goldmine was acting very nervous and strange the last time she came into the apartment. This was the first time she didn't say anything slick or mention anything about money. When Goldmine quickly changed and jetted back out the door, Pumpkin crept outside to see what she was up to. The only thing she saw was Goldmine peeling off in a brand new, series seven BMW. It registered in Pumpkin's mind that Goldmine couldn't afford such a car and that she had to be up to something, *but what*, Pumpkin wondered.

Pumpkin arrived at the Warehouse late, mainly because she didn't want to be up in there, but she had no choice. She needed paper if she hoped to bounce from sneaky Goldmine's place.

"Oh shit, Chi-Chi! What's up? Where you been hiding at? I haven't seen you up in dis place since I started," Pumpkin said after seeing her friend bending over, talking to some guy in a car.

"I'm all right. I'm just trying to do me. You know how it is," the woman responded.

"So you working tonight, or what?" Pumpkin asked, paying the cab driver, who was tired of waiting for his fare.

"Nah, I don't work up in there no more. I met this dude who be finding me private parties to dance at. The pay is crazy good without all the hassle of a club environment," Chi-Chi answered, looking down the street as if she was waiting for someone.

"I feel you," Pumpkin stated, still wondering why Chi-Chi was standing outside, wearing a skimpy dance outfit.

"Anyway, what's up with you? What you been up to lately?" she asked Pumpkin, who was about to go inside her place of business.

"I'm trying to find a new place to rest my head. My roommate been on some real ra-ra shit from day one. Dat's why I'm trying to stack dis dough so I can bounce," Pumpkin said.

"Word! I'm fixing up my basement so I can rent it out. You can have first dibs on it. And if you want to get into some serious money, I could introduce you to the guy who put me on. He's mad cool and understanding," Chi-Chi said. She then handed Pumpkin a business card that showed a full set of women's lips painted candy red with a couple of numbers underneath it. Pumpkin stuffed the card in her bag and told Chi-Chi she would think about it. She didn't want to rush into another fucked-up situation until she investigated the details further.

Pumpkin went to work, going through the motions and having a few stiff drinks before changing into her dance attire. The place wasn't really jumping, so Pumpkin just entertained herself by watching a couple of the other girls perform. A dark-skinned stripper came out with a tight, black, fake leather outfit, trying to be as seductive as possible. A Ying Yang Twins joint banged throughout the room, but the dancer couldn't seem to get her rhythm to-gether. Her long, flat titties resembled fried bologna flap-ping in the air, and they didn't seem to help her case either. When Pumpkin spotted what seemed to be ciga-rette burns in her cheap skirt, she just couldn't hold it any longer, busting out into an ear-piercing laugh. Pumpkin didn't seem to care that she let everybody, including the stripper, know that she was laughing at her personally. The embarrassed girl just shot sharp daggers at Pumpkin as she gathered what little sympathy dollars were thrown her way and headed off the stage.

Pumpkin performed a couple of lap dances, not really into her performance. She kept thinking, *Where da fuck is everybody at?* She hadn't heard from Dallisha in a while. She kept telling herself that she would drop her a letter and was sure to mention what her own sister said about her. Knowledge's cell phone just kept going straight to voicemail whenever she called. *Niggas got to make dat money just like anybody else,* Pumpkin thought. Then there was Ju-nior, who she let fuck her raw. She didn't regret what went down between the two of them, but she wondered why he hadn't called since that night. He had to have lost her number or something.

Pumpkin was deep in thought, giving some guy a wall dance, when he broke her concentration.

"At least act like you wanna make some money," he blurted out.

"Motherfucker, I don't have to act like shit. Keep your money and buy a clean shirt," Pumpkin spat out, upset that she knew she wouldn't be making any money that night, but even more fed up with the whole stripper scene in such a short period of time.

Pumpkin arrived back at the apartment, going straight to the bedroom, glad that Goldmine wasn't home. As soon as she got undressed and climbed into bed, she heard the front door being opened. Her young, keen ears picked up a couple of voices talking in hushed tones. For some reason Pumpkin's instincts kicked in and she pretended to be asleep. She heard the door crack open and Goldmine say, "Pumpkin, Pumpkin, you asleep?" Pumpkin kept quiet as the woman slowly closed the door and crept back toward the living room. Pumpkin slowly got back out of bed and pressed her head against the thin door to find out what the fuck was going on.

CHAPTER THIRTY-TWO

Goldmine tiptoed back to her living room where Doc's bodyguard/driver was sitting on the sofa, drinking a full glass of the ghetto concoction the Incredible Hulk.

"Everything's cool. She's knocked da fuck out," Goldmine stated, flopping down next to the beefy man and taking a long sip of his mixed drink.

It'd been a long two days for Goldmine. After the police had snatched up Doc, she got high to calm her nerves. She then drove around in Doc's luxury car, praying that the cops wouldn't come back for her later, thinking that she had something to do with whatever Doc got trapped up in. She later called the police station from a payphone, pretending to be a frantic sister calling to see how her big brother was doing. The desk sergeant informed her that Doc, real name Kenneth Simmons, had been secretly indicted and charged with conspiracy to distribute cocaine, running a criminal enterprise, manufacturing illegal substances, and delivery of a controlled substance.

Goldmine then acted like she was on the verge of tears and asked if her brother had a bail. The answer was a rude no. Goldmine, being around hustlers all her adult life, knew that with those type of charges leveled against Doc, the federal government would soon get involved if they weren't already.

It's a wrap for that nigga, Goldmine thought as she jumped back in Doc's vehicle.

The next night, when she arrived back at her apartment, she spotted Doc's gold Expedition parked in front of her building, with his driver waiting for her.

"Why didn't you bring the car by the barbershop like he said," the driver asked with an angry expression covering his face.

"I was, but I was so nervous, thinking da police might be following me or something. I didn't want to take a chance, so I laid low for a while," she responded, speaking in half-truths. In reality, Goldmine was shaking like a hot game of cee-lo, but at the same time she was thinking about how she could keep the BMW, especially after finding out that Doc probably wouldn't be touching the streets no time soon.

"Fuck all that other shit. I got to get the shit out the car," he replied, taking the car keys from the woman. Goldmine knew right away that Doc had some product stashed in the car. That was why he had wanted her to bring it by his shop right away.

"Let me help. I feel bad dat Doc got knocked off," she said, slightly caressing his arm while thinking about how to flip the situation in her favor.

"Well, come on, I gotta make moves," he stated, waving Goldmine to climb inside the car.

He then drove around the back of the projects, away from prying eyes, and parked behind a green, smelly dumpster. He expertly removed a specially made hidden door located in the trunk, pulling out package after package of top quality Nigerian heroin.

The idea that she was riding around with so many drugs never entered Goldmine's mind. She could have gotten twenty years if the police somehow knew that she was riding dirty. But now her mindset was on how she could get a piece of that pie.

"There goes the DTs cruising by. They gonna turn around, thinking we up to something being out this late at night. Let's go upstairs until things cool down a bit," Goldmine said, lying after seeing a dark, four-door Crown Victoria drive by.

Goldmine and Doc's driver were now upstairs in the apartment.

"Is that your roommate in the other room?" he asked.

"Yeah, but not for long," she answered, moving closer to the man. "So how long you been driving for Doc anyway? I see you more as a nigga dat makes things happen," Goldmine said, trying to relax the atmosphere and at the same time playing the ego trip game.

"I met him at the club a couple years ago. Shit jumped off and he liked the way I handled my biz," he answered.

"Lord, I wish I could have seen you in action," she said, laughing while gripping his bulging biceps. He soon stood up, finishing his drink.

"Yo, I gotta go. It's been like twenty minutes already. I'll send somebody sometime tomorrow to pick up the other car," he said. Goldmine had to think quickly before the guy and that big bag of drugs walked out the door.

"Chill. You can't just walk outside with a filled up trash bag. You'll look mighty suspicious, especially in a neighborhood like dis. Let me go get you something dat looks a little better," Goldmine said, walking back to her room. Goldmine came back moments later carrying an Elaine Turner leather duffel bag and wearing a short, see-through, pink nightie, walking barefoot to show off her pedicured feet.

"I hope you don't mind, but I had to get out of those

sticky clothes. Dis bag should be big enough," Goldmine said while bending over and giving him a full view of her round, braless titties as she started putting the packages of heroin into the expensive bag. The sexy woman was almost finished before the lusting man stepped back and started helping her with the remaining bags.

"Before you go, I want to ask you a question," she said, sitting with her legs crossed and letting the driver roam his hungry eyes over her light-skinned, flawless thighs. "It's obvious dat you're an intelligent man who knows his way around da hood. Why Doc only got you being his chauffeur when, from my point of view, you could be easily handling some major shit?" Goldmine asked, looking him straight in the eyes like she had never been more serious in her life.

"I'm just waiting for my time to shine," he meekly answered, now embarrassed on how he earned his paper.

"Fuck dat! Your time is now. Doc not gonna be making any moves anytime soon, and if he was to come out trying to set up shop again, niggas gonna think he's snitching. You know da rules," she said, pouring some Hennessy with Hypnotiq for the man, who was now deep in thought.

"So what you trying to say?" he asked.

"All I'm getting at is dat you put your work in already. Since Doc gonna be laid up for a minute, it's time for you to step up your game." Goldmine saw the man thinking, but she didn't want him to think too much, so she kept up the verbal gymnastics. "With dis much shit, if you know what you're doing, and I know you do, you could easily flip it about ten times and retire. No need to be greedy. Not to kick mud on Doc's style, but da nigga made mad shit but dat wasn't enough. He wanted it all. After a while it gets to a point where ballers be thinking they're untouchable. I guess dem white folks proved him wrong." He knew that the woman was spitting out the truth, but he wondered what her stake in all of this was.

When he didn't reply, Goldmine continued.

"I know he wants you to drop da drugs off with another nigga. Fuck dat! It's in your hands now. Matter of fact, you can tell Doc da police took da car, or it got stolen, or something. Yeah, he might be heated for a minute, but when da district attorney starts talking about life without parole, dis here shit is gonna be da last thing on his mind," Goldmine said as she stood up, looking him dead in the face.

"You're right. I gotta get mine while I can. I know some people I could make some moves with," he stated, thinking how he was gonna have someone drive him around, like Doc used to do with him.

"Nah, your folks might know Doc's peoples. I know some straight-up niggas who don't bullshit. We could sell shit at cut-rate prices and then have niggas beating down our door," Goldmine stated, also dreaming on how she was finally going to get out the hood.

"OK then, our deal is set. Let's say we finalize the plan in a more private setting," the grinning man said, letting his eyes do most of the talking. Goldmine knew what time it was as she took him by the hand and led him into the bedroom.

The next morning, Goldmine was in the kitchen chopping up some mushrooms and green peppers for an omelet. Her pussy was sore from fucking all night.

Damn, da way that nigga was acting, it was like he just finished doing a bid, the stripper thought. Just then Doc's driver walked into the kitchen butt naked and went straight to the refrigerator.

"I was just about to fix you my special breakfast. After we eat, we could make those moves we talked about last night," she said, hoping he didn't want some morning pussy. He finished drinking straight out of the orange juice carton and then responded.

"Nah, I think I'll roll alone. I'm gonna fuck with my peoples."

"I'm telling you, dat's not a good idea. Let me make a phone call right now," Goldmine quickly threw in before he could change his mind again.

"Don't waste your time. I'm not fucking with you or your peoples," he said. Goldmine stood there, looking as if her best friend had betrayed her.

"What, you thought I was gonna flip the script on Doc just because you gave me some pussy? I would have fucked you sooner or later. Doc always gives me his leftovers. Anyway, you must be one dumb bitch if you thought I needed your help to get off this heroin," the man said, smiling a wicked smile and then turning his back to look inside the refrigerator.

Before Goldmine knew what had happened, a sudden rage overcame her and she plunged a butcher knife into the man's back. The shocked guy turned around, holding on to his wound as Goldmine's face showed regret.

"You fucking ghetto bitch," he shouted, rushing forward and clamping his oversized hands around the girl's delicate throat. The next thing Goldmine realized was the beefy man slipping onto the cold kitchen floor, as gray intestinal matter and dark red blood pooled around her feet.

"Oh shit!" a voice yelled, causing Goldmine to snap out of her trance as she looked down at her victim, who seemed to have at least a half dozen stab wounds to his mid-section. Goldmine was so full of pent up rage that she momentarily blacked out, forgetting that she had stabbed the man a few more times.

Pumpkin was standing at the entrance of the kitchen, holding a toothbrush in one hand and covering her mouth with the other hand.

CHAPTER
THIRTY-THREE

Jason was sitting in his car, smoking some weed sprinkled with a good amount of Arabian red hash, giving the blunt a more potent high while he listened to some Young Jeezy.

Jason had found out through numerous people connected to the foul drug game that Doc had finally slipped up big time. From bits and pieces of information he gathered from the hood, Doc was out for the count and wouldn't touch the streets for a minute, being that the Feds were involved. With the case he caught, Jason knew that anything was possible when the state or government had a man firmly by the balls. Most of the time they snitched on niggas higher up the ladder or became a straight-up confidential informer, wearing a bitch wire just to have the chance to walk the streets again. Jason just had to play out his hand and flip the situation in his favor. People told him that Doc was being charged with the Kingpin Statute, which carried an automatic life sentence.

Jason knew that the wannabe gangsta Doc wasn't built

for any type of jail, much less the federal penitentiary, where so-called thugs ended up wearing glass slippers.

"Fuck his coke! Fuck Doc! And fuck Camay! Let her run up and go see his old ass for the next sixty years," Jason said to himself as he sat smiling, thinking about all the product he had in the truck. Jason planned on deading his boss on the drugs and keeping everything for himself. "He took my chick and now I'm taking that nigga's coke! Fuck it! Everything is everything," Jason said to himself as he took another pull of the blunt

Jason finally found the house he had been looking for and was soon knocking on the back door.

"Who is it?" a voice asked from behind a thick looking steel door.

"It's Jason, Free's little brother," he answered. A couple of latches were taken off, along with heavy beams that helped fortify the entrance. An old-school dope fiend in his mid–fifties, whose face looked like it had been through hell and back, opened the door.

"Come on in," the man said as he looked from left to right, then slammed the door shut, putting the security measures back in place.

"So you got everything set up?" Jason asked the man, who he was told wasn't into any small talk.

"Yeah, let's get started. Let me see what you working with," he stated, looking at the much younger man with eyes that said he done it all, seen it all, and wouldn't mind doing it again if his hand was forced.

Soon the man, who was known throughout the hood as one of the best drug cooks around, sniffed up a few grams of coke to see exactly what he was dealing with.

"Yeah, I can work with this," he said as he started preparing to transform the high-quality cocaine into some kick-ass crack rocks. As the much experienced man began precisely measuring his ingredients, Jason sat back, intensely watching every hand movement. He knew fiends were like magicians when it came to the drugs they craved morning, noon, and night. A moment of distraction was all the man needed to swipe some ounces of the coke with his panther-like reflexes.

Much, much later, the man was finishing cooking up the cocaine, leaving beige-colored, thick, dinner-sized plates of crack rocks to dry. He had oversized table lights strategically placed to help speed up the process. Jason kept a medium-sized bag of coke to himself, because he still had a few customers who preferred blow.

When the newly-made crack rocks were 90 percent hard, he gave the cook a nice-sized crack cake and broke out.

Damn, this shit is heavy, Jason thought as he tossed the weight in his trunk and carefully pulled off. He stopped by the twenty-four-hour smoke shop on the West End, picking up some razor blades and little plastic baggies. The smoke shop was popular in the hood because it was open twenty-four hours a day and held every kind of drug paraphernalia available on the market. The Guyanese family who owned the store sold everything from rose-colored crack pipes to pocket-sized scales.

After copping what he needed, Jason jetted over to the hotel, where L.B. had been waiting for more work. He and his worker cut up the two large rocks and placed them in two piles of five- and ten-dollar hits. They took a short break and ordered pizza. L.B. told Jason his cousin wanted to get down with the program.

Jason was soon out the door, feeling tired but leaving L.B. with roughly $10,000 worth of work. He planned to start out early tomorrow to get his own sling on, once he stashed the other cakes in a good spot. He still had to be on point, not knowing who was going to show up looking for all the coke that Doc had given him on consignment before the police had snatched him up.

CHAPTER THIRTY-FOUR

Knowledge and Daquan sat in the Suburban in front of their spot, sipping on Hennessy and discussing what their next move should be. Knowledge had received a phone call last night from a fiend, telling him that Chase and his peoples had some dealing with some white boy whom they got some ill fire power from. Knowledge wanted more information on him, like where he rested his head. The only thing the fiend said he knew for sure was that his name was Danny and he pushed some kind of classic, hooked-up car.

"Dem niggas rolled up on us twice. We got to let these motherfuckers know NY ain't nothing to fuck with," Knowledge stated.

"I feel you. Now everybody gonna think we some fronting-ass niggas, letting Chase get away with what he did," Daquan responded, taking a drink and then looking down the street to see who was approaching.

"Now they want to meet with us like they want to squash da beef or something. Fuck dat. I say we just make a power move and end all dis bullshit. Did you find out when da other guys are heading down here?" Knowledge asked.

"Yeah, they gathering up the squad and should be here in a week or so," Daquan responded. "Chase must know that, since he set shit off. He figures we gonna touch everything moving on this side of town, and say fuck it and set up shop somewhere else," Daquan added.

"I say we contact dat bitch nigga Chase and set up a meeting place. We make him think we don't want it, and rock his ass to sleep," Knowledge stated, giving his partner some dap while smiling a sinister smile.

Knowledge sent word that he would meet with Chase to work out their differences. All parties involved agreed to meet at the local elementary school playground early one morning. Knowledge arrived with Daquan and the hotheaded young Reese, who didn't give a fuck about no meeting. He felt it was just a waste of time. Head was already there, waiting with a guy who looked like he did bench presses every morning before he came out.

"So which one of you is Chase?" Knowledge asked, looking at both men carefully.

"I'm Head. Chase is out the picture for now. I'm the one who decided we should kick it like real men," Head answered with his eyes never blinking.

Homicide detectives had picked up Chase in his truck on suspicion of murder for the young, unidentified black girl they found in a vacant lot. Head knew that Chase was a good candidate for a prime suspect, due to his two prior arrests for aggravated battery and aggravated felony assault on young girls when he tried his hand at pimping. One used to be a pretty girl. She was caught talking to another pimp, a lawbreaker in the skin game. Chase flew into a rage and smashed every bone in the child's face with a taped-up lead pipe, permanently disfiguring her. He kept her in his house for a whole day without medical attention until she passed out from the excruciating pain. Hospital staff notified the authorities, who promptly arrested Chase on a variety of charges, including kidnapping and attempted murder. The young girl refused to testify at the last moment, opting instead to go to jail for a year for contempt of court. After that incident, Vice, as well as the district attorney's office, had their eyes on Chase. To make sure Chase didn't maneuver his way out of a murder indictment, Head had secretly placed a small-caliber gun that he was sure had at least one body on it, in Chase's vehicle.

"So whatcha want to talk about? Your guns did all the talking already," Knowledge said.

"Yeah, a couple of your peoples got rocked, but that wasn't my decision. I'm in charge now, and as you probably already know, business slowed up with the po-po asking questions like they were the Feds," Head stated.

"You think we supposed to forget you spread some of our boys out? Who the fuck you think you are?" Daquan asked, making the air a little thick.

"Yo, all I'm saying is that that's part of the game. Niggas gonna always be leaking when it comes to dough. We still here, so I say we all still gonna eat, no matter what," Head responded.

"Fuck this nigga and his weak-ass crew. Let's finish this shit right now," Reese shouted, reaching under his Theisman throwback and producing a Desert Eagle gun. Instantly everyone started reaching for their shit, but Knowledge stopped everyone.

"Hold up. Put dat shit away. I got dis," he told Reese. Reese lowered his weapon as Head told his own boy to relax.

"Whatcha doing, Knowledge? Look at those clowns. They think we some soft-ass niggas," Reese stated, his heart pounding faster now, praying for a jump off.

"He's right. We keep dis little bullshit war up, and nobody gets paper. And like he said, Chase is out the picture now," Knowledge responded.

"What! Fuck all this truce shit. That's my little man, laid up in the hospital. Now you acting like a fucking old lady who, once she sees a little blood, wants to lock herself in the house," Reese said, not realizing what he was saying. Before anyone could say or do anything, Knowledge grabbed Reese by the shirt as Daquan quickly snatched the gun out of his hand.

"Nigga, you think I'm some wannabe thug? I'm about business and dat paper," Knowledge said, then slapped Reese and pulled out his own gat, pressing it against Reese's eyeball. "A young, stupid nigga like you will have everybody broke and in jail. Before dat happens, I'll have you sent back to New York in a fucking box," Knowledge said. Reese just kept quiet as Head spoke.

"Yo, you all work that shit out amongst yourselves. Knowledge, you know how to contact me." Head and his boy then hopped in their own ride, but not before Head winked at Reese as if to warn him to stay in his place.

The remaining three men climbed back in the Suburban with Reese thinking about the fastest and easiest way to murder everybody, including faggot-ass Knowledge.

CHAPTER
THIRTY-FIVE

"He tried to rape me! You saw I was just defending myself!" Goldmine shouted as soon as she saw Pumpkin standing there, gawking at the whole brutal scene.

"Yo, we gotta call da police," Pumpkin said, walking back toward the living room and heading for the phone, even though she knew there was no type of rape involved.

"Wait a minute. Hold up! We got to think dis thing through," Goldmine said, rushing up behind Pumpkin while still holding the blood-smeared butcher knife.

"Whatcha mean? Think what through? There's a dead guy on the kitchen floor. We gotta let someone know what jumped off," Pumpkin said, looking at Goldmine like she was crazy.

"Now if the jakes were to come, they wouldn't believe our story, being dat we strippers and all. You know, Pumpkin, how everybody think we some fucking whores just out for the buck," Goldmine explained as she put the phone back on the hook.

"What do you mean, our story? I don't have nothing to do with dis here shit. I'm outta here," Pumpkin said while walking back to the bedroom. Goldmine quickly followed her.

"What you think you gonna do? Just break out like nothing happened? You know very well how these white cops get down. They gonna start asking all kinds of questions like who I live with, and when you're not here, they gonna start wondering why you left in such a hurry," Goldmine stated, causing Pumpkin to slow her movements.

"I'll just tell them the truth. I woke up, went to da kitchen, and I saw a dead man on da floor. Dat's it," she said, looking at the older woman and hoping that would be enough.

"First off, they gonna wanna know who he was and what he was doing up in here butt naked. They might switch shit around like we both met him at da club, took him home, and killed him for his loot." Goldmine paused. Once she realized she had the young girl's full attention, she continued. "I say we just get rid of his ass and say, fuck da police."

"Oh, hell no! First you tell me I shouldn't call nobody, den you want me to help you dump a body? You gotta be high off some shit if you think for a minute dat I'm gonna help you!" Pumpkin shouted.

"OK, you wanna play it like dat? You call the police and when they get here, I'll say it was all your idea to rob him and things just got outta hand. I see you're looking at me like they gonna believe you. You think dem white motherfuckers care about locking up two black bitches? I don't give a fuck anymore. I go down, you go down. So what you gonna do?" Goldmine asked with her hands on her hips.

This was the first time that Pumpkin felt pure, uncontested hatred for anyone or anything in her life. Goldmine was dragging her in on her bullshit on purpose, and she knew she was trapped like a nigga that just blew trial. She had heard stories on how when somebody got wet up

in the streets and a crowd gathered around the yellow caution tape, sometimes the detectives on the scene would
snatch a guy out the crowd at random, saying someone
ID'd him from earlier. They would pressure him for information. Since he was black and from the so-called hood,
he must know somebody who knew somebody who perpe-
trated the crime. If they didn't receive the information
they were looking for, they would threaten the bystander
with the murder charge.

"So how you want to do dis?" Pumpkin asked, deciding
to take her chances with a dead man rather than the police.

"Thanks, I knew I could count on you," Goldmine responded like she had asked Pumpkin for a simple favor,
like picking up her clothes from the cleaners or something.

Both women went back to the kitchen after changing
into some old clothes. Pumpkin almost stepped in the
blood that had run toward the entrance of the kitchen.
Goldmine went under the sink and retrieved some cleaning supplies and rubber gloves as Pumpkin just stared at
the nude, dead man, gutted like a hog. His face held a
frozen expression, like he couldn't believe this was actually happening to him, especially by a woman.

"Dis nigga too big. Let's drag him into da bathroom,"
Goldmine said when she tried to move him a little so they
could clean the blood up around him. Both girls then
struggled to drag the two-hundred-plus-pound man into
the bathroom, with each one grabbing a leg.

"Come on, Pumpkin, pull dis fucker," Goldmine shouted,
breathing a little harder.

"I'm trying, but I think he's stuck on something." Both
women then braced themselves and pulled with all their
strength. Unknowing to the struggling girls, a medium-
sized nail in the floor had snagged the dead man's nut

sack. The combined force of Goldmine and Pumpkin caused the iron nail to tear into his dead flesh.

"Oh shit! What da fuck!" Pumpkin said when she noticed a testicle roll out from under the man, hanging loosely by a thin, bloody artery.

"Come on, I don't have time for dis shit," Goldmine said, pulling even harder and ripping away the remaining soft tissue.

They finally got the heavy corpse into the bathroom and inside the tub. After taking a breather, Pumpkin asked what was next.

"Pumpkin, you know there's no way we could get him downstairs and into da trunk by ourselves."

"So what you trying to say?" Pumpkin asked?

"We got two choices. I could call somebody else over to help move his big ass and take da chance on dat person either snitching on us or trying to get dough out of us for keeping quiet, or we could just cut him up so it would be less weight to move," she answered.

Dis bitch gotta be insane, but she's right. We got to lighten the load if we expect to be able to move him, Pumpkin thought, so she agreed to the cutting. Goldmine put on her coat and went to see the old handyman that did odd jobs for people around the projects, when the regular maintenance guy couldn't get to them in time.

She came back with a rusted but sturdy-looking saw. Pumpkin thought she must be in a horror movie as Goldmine positioned the saw for its grisly purpose. As soon as the hard, steel teeth ran across the man's leg, blood sprayed the wall tiles. Pumpkin threw up right on the guy's chest, causing an even bigger mess than before.

"I can't do dis," Pumpkin stated, wiping her mouth with her sleeve.

"Fuck it, I'll take care of dis. You go clean up da kitchen and da living room.

Hours passed with Pumpkin scrubbing the floors from top to bottom, not taking any chances on any forensic evidence being left behind after she had watched too many shows of *CSI*. Goldmine had neatly cut off the arms, legs, and head and placed them in large Hefty bags. She then placed the bags in a couple of wide duffel bags by the front door. Pumpkin went into Goldmine's bedroom and peeped what looked like a coldhearted grave robber rifling through the dead man's pockets.

"I was just looking for the car keys," Goldmine said when she noticed the disgusted look on Pumpkin's face.

They both changed into fresh clothes, putting the soiled, bloody ones in one of the duffel bags. They then carried the body parts outside, placing them in the jeep and laughing and talking like they were going on a trip, just in case some nosey neighborhood resident was bored and curious.

After they safely had the dismembered driver tucked away, Pumpkin asked what was next.

"I know dis guy who works out of a junkyard. He'll take da whip and crush it up for us, no questions asked, for a little dough, of course."

"Do I mention your name?" Pumpkin asked.

"Hell no! Just give him dis money," Goldmine said as she gave her a hundred-dollar bill.

"What you gonna be doing, when I'm running around with a chopped up nigga in da trunk," Pumpkin asked.

"I'm gonna take the other whip to dis chop shop I know and pick up some quick cash," she answered. She gave Pumpkin the address and then peeled off.

Pumpkin climbed into the Expedition, almost having a nervous breakdown with the thought of being pulled over. *Miss, could you please exit the vehicle?* she kept hearing over and over in her head.

Fuck dat shit. I'm not going to no junkyard, talking to a guy I never met before. Da first thing he's gonna ask himself is why I want to smash such an ill truck. Den he starts to get curious and it's a wrap for me, Pumpkin thought. She turned around and a half hour later, she had the Jeep parked in long-term parking at the airport. She then jumped on the train and headed toward the police station to tell them everything.

CHAPTER THIRTY-SIX

"It's on now, kid! Now you rolling with some real mother-fuckers," Head stated, giving Jason some dap.

"Yeah, I've been waiting to get down with y'all, but I had to tie up some loose ends. You know how that goes," Jason said.

Jason was kicking it with Head in the spot, while a young kid in his teens bagged up healthy bags of crack. Head had wanted Jason to get down with them, when he first started working for Doc.

"Fuck that old timer. He's past his time. That nigga was just hustling to ride around and bag the young bitches around the way," Head would say when he visited his aunt and uncle, who stayed on Jason's grandmother's block.

"So what's up with this Chase I've been hearing about?" Jason asked.

"He got caught up in some real foul shit. I think he's out for the count. I'm still trying to find out more info through his peoples," Head responded.

"Does it have anything to do with that little beef I've been hearing that y'all been having up here? Anyway, what's up with that shit? Is shit still on, or what?" Jason asked, wanting to know more fully what he was getting himself into with dudes he knew by sight only.

"From what I know so far, Chase got mixed up in some wicked shit that had nothing to do with this here business. And about that petty drama, you know how we get down in the 'Nam. Once the hot lead started tearing in the ass, niggas all of a sudden wanna work something out," Head replied, puffing his chest out.

"Well I gotta bounce. I'll get with you later," Jason said, getting up and preparing to leave.

Soon Jason was heading to his other drug location that his worker, L.B., had on lock at the hotel. The money was coming in steady waves, but he really wanted to have his foot firmly planted in Little Vietnam, which seemed to have an endless army of walking dead fiends carrying five, ten, and twenty-dollar bills.

"Yo, L, how many times I told you to keep the door locked? Don't say nothing when niggas run up on you," Jason said when he noticed the hotel room door was slightly ajar. His good-natured smile turned to a suspicious frown when he walked into an empty room.

"Yo, L.B., where you at? Stop playing fucking games. We got shit to do," he shouted, still not sure what was going on, so he took out his gun as a precaution.

Jason noticed that the room was more messy than usual, with the mattress lying halfway off the bed and the room's television set looking as if someone had purposely ripped the metal guts out, hoping to find something. That made Jason even more leery as he carefully crept toward the bathroom with his weapon now cocked, holding it straight out in front of him. Before he even flicked on the hotel's bathroom light, his nostrils were bombarded with the grim, unmistakable odor of death. The dim light bulb revealed a man tied to a chair with a plastic bag tied to his head and a long strip of cloth secured firmly around his neck. Jason couldn't make out exactly who the victim was because it seemed that whoever did whatever they did, once they were finished they repeatedly smashed the man with some kind of blunt instrument. The heavy blows caused the contents inside the bag to resemble some kind of mixed soup. The plastic bag was so tightly fastened that a sickening, repulsive mixture of stale blood, mucus, brain matter, and some other unknown elements were floating around inside. The only way one could tell that the thing used to be human was the chipped teeth and snarled up lips frozen in a painful grimace.

Any other person viewing the unnatural spectacle wouldn't have any idea who the unlucky person was, but Jason knew it was L.B. because he was stripped down to his boxer shorts, revealing a jailhouse tattoo on his chest of his baby's mama's name, with a crude heart surrounding it. L.B.'s unprotected knees were also ruthlessly battered, causing shards of jagged bone to pierce through his brown skin, leaving a trail of dried blood down his legs.

Jason didn't need to look anymore to know what exactly had transpired between his worker and the unknown assailants. They were looking for more drugs and money to add to the stash they had already taken. Not believing him or just desperate, they tortured him and enjoyed it from the look of things.

Stupid motherfucker! I told him to stop tricking with them sheisty-ass bitches, Jason thought as he closed the front door with his shirt and then jumped into his car. Jason wondered whether Doc's people had something to do with his worker's demise, or if some hood rat chick set him up, thinking he was the main man holding the weight. Something clicked in Jason's brain that told him to head straight home, so he floored the gas pedal.

Jason knew something was definitely wrong when he

saw his grandmother standing in front of the living room mirror, adjusting her best Sunday hat.

"Grandma, where you off to? You know today ain't Sunday," he stated, wondering what she could be up to now.

"Oh, Jason, something terrible has happened to your sister. Policemen have been calling all day wanting someone to come down and talk to them about Tiffany."

"Don't worry, Grandma, I got this," Jason replied after taking the piece of paper with the detective's name on it.

All kinds of things circulated in Jason's mind as he sped off towards the police station. *Did she start selling drugs to keep up with the older local girls and got robbed? Or maybe she got caught carrying a gun while hanging out with some of their wild cousins.* Jason felt stupid, not following through on locating his sister after not having seen her for days now.

He finally made it to the police station and eagerly asked where he could find Detective Summerset. His mouth nearly dropped when the detective turned out to be the same officer who had pulled him over and humiliated him in front of his used-to-be wifey, Camay. The detective showed no sign whatsoever that he recognized the young man, causing Jason to suspect that he often did such things to other black guys from the hood, thinking they all looked the same.

Jason momentarily put his feelings aside to find out what was going on with his sister, whom he had promised always to watch over. The red-faced man showed Jason a couple of Polaroid pictures of Tiffany, lying somewhere in a littered, cluttered lot, naked except for her sneakers and socks. Once Jason ID'd the body of his young sister, Detective Summerset unsympathetically asked him if Tiffany had any type of history with prostitution. When Jason angrily answered no, the cop made Jason even angrier with his next comment.

"Usually when we find young women in that part of

town, nude and abused, most of the time it was a pissed-off or disgruntled john." Then the cop started asking the shocked Jason if she was involved with drugs or gangs, never giving it a second thought that a black girl could be an innocent victim without her having to be mixed up with something illegal. When Jason tried to ask questions about where his sister was found and if there was already a suspect, Summerset rudely stated that he couldn't say anything at that time because the "investigation was still ongoing."

"And another thing," the detective added as Jason was leaving, "stay where I can reach you. I might have further questions for you," implying that Jason might have something to do with his sister's death, or that he wasn't telling the whole truth surrounding the circumstances. Not only was Jason grieving the death of his baby sister, but this obviously racist, fat cop was disrespecting the memory of Tiffany by insinuating that she must have been walking the streets or she wouldn't have been found in her predicament.

He dissed me, and now he's dissing my sister like she's a whore or something. If it's the last thing I do, I'm gonna teach that piece of shit a lesson, Jason thought to himself as he tried to make it out of the station without flipping on somebody.

Jason rushed outside to clear his head, thinking about how he was going to let his older brother know what had happened when Jason had made a blood promise to look out for Tiffany.

Jason's thoughts were so filled with the two deaths he had experienced in the last couple of hours that he ran smack into a girl standing outside the police station.

"Pardon me. I didn't see you there," he said, looking at the extremely pretty woman.

"No, it's my fault. I shouldn't have been daydreaming

out in the open like dat. Are you all right?" Pumpkin asked when she noticed the pained look on Jason's face.

Before he knew it, Jason was telling this complete stranger every detail about his sister's death as they sat in a quiet restaurant. He also told her how the detective treated him and his sister like black trash. Pumpkin told him her ghetto story, from how her own flesh and blood flipped on her and how she had wanted to get out of dancing because of the shady people involved. She felt good telling someone her problems and getting the load off, but she left out how she had just finished disposing of a dead body not too long ago.

They talked throughout the rest of the evening, promising to hook up again once Jason took care of Tiffany's funeral arrangements.

CHAPTER
THIRTY-SEVEN

Doc was in Atlanta's pre-trial detention center, currently being escorted from a visit he just had with his high-paid attorney. Doc knew that it wasn't looking good for him, since the Feds were now firmly implanted in his case. His lawyer was still hard at work, trying to get him some kind of bail; and even if he succeeded, he was informed that he would have to go to a bail source hearing. That meant that if somehow the judge granted him some bail, which would be ridiculously high due to the nature of the charges, he would have to prove that the money came from a legitimate source. The Atlanta courts were cracking down on suspects, especially alleged drug dealers, who were posting bonds and then continuing their enterprises, intimidating witnesses and sometimes even murdering them. The district attorneys were even requesting bail source hearings for petty street dealers, tying up the courts even more for the so-called war on drugs. Even if, by chance, Doc's lawyer was to use his contacts and make it through the hearing, he was practically broke since the federal government had frozen all his assets, giving his wife and daughter just enough money to survive.

Doc was soon back in his cell by himself, which he had arranged for, even though the jails were so overcrowded that inmates had to sleep on the floor with their bare, flat mattresses. He was going through some legal paperwork when he heard a light tap on his metal cell door.

"I have a message for you," a correction officer whispered through the crack. Doc quickly stopped what he was doing and went to the door. "Mooka says you have one week to make payment," the guard said, taking a toothpick out of his mouth while flexing his biceps through his tight, rolled-up uniform shirt. He then walked away, not even giving Doc a chance to respond.

Doc watched the man casually walk away, not even sure if he was really a corrections officer at all. Doc knew the African drug kingpin Mooka had eyes and ears everywhere, so it wasn't a big surprise to him that Mooka had reached Doc in jail. He knew exactly what the message meant. Even though Doc was in jail, that meant nothing concerning the game at this level. Paper still had to keep flowing and Mooka let it be known that he still wanted his money. Mooka had fronted him all those kilos of heroin on a consignment type of deal with the promise that Doc make regular payments. He could maybe get up the first payment, which was no joke, but what about the others since the Feds had snatched up his money.

But what was a slight surprise to him was that his most trusted bodyguard seemed to have disappeared off the face of the earth. Doc's peoples told him that they hadn't seen him, or the Beemer coupe that held the crazy stash of heroin that he was supposed to pick up right away, after his arrest. Doc knew very well that when it came to money anyone could be turned out, flipping the script in a heartbeat. At least Doc still had a backup plan, which he would use as a final option only.

*   *   *

Meanwhile, not far away, Chase sat in his cell, smoking a cigarette that had been smuggled in by one of the trustees.

"That's what I heard. New York niggas are getting their grind on, trying to take over Little Vietnam. And I heard your man Head got so shook since you left, that he's letting niggas run around like they lived there their whole lives. Word!" A guy was telling Chase what rumors he was hearing.

"Nah, I don't believe no shit like dat. I don't roll with no soft-ass cats. All my peoples gets gully or they wouldn't be repping the Folks' flag," Chase replied, after hearing the same rumor from someone else.

"I'm just telling you what the streets are saying," the guy added, hoping to get a drag off the Newport.

"Da only niggas dat's saying dat wack shit is probably da same motherfuckers I ran off before," Chase replied in a voice that let his cellmate know he was done with the conversation.

Chase was deep in thought, wondering why he hadn't heard from Head since he was on lockdown. No visits, no kites, nothing. He wasn't really concerned with his case, for the simple fact that he knew he didn't body some unknown hood rat. He might sit for a minute until he proved he didn't have anything to do with it, but by that time he would hope to cop a plea for time served for the gun charge for the gun found in his car, which he had no idea how it got there.

Something is definitely wrong with both these cases seemingly coming out of thin air. Could dem New York dudes have something to do with it? Chase wondered, waiting for tomorrow to come so he could use the phone again, to find out what the fuck was up with his boy.

CHAPTER THIRTY-EIGHT

Reese turned the corner sharply on his newly acquired Ninja 600 bike, as he traveled to one of his groupie's houses to show it off. He had large white socks covering half of his suede, winter gray Timberland boots so he wouldn't mark them up while riding.

"So I'm doing it up or what?" Reese asked, smiling while sitting on his bike.

"Hell, yeah! Come on, let's go for a ride," a short, thin, red-boned girl squealed as she attempted to get on the backseat.

"A little later. I just picked up a fat bag of some ill chronic. Let's get our smoke on first," he answered while getting off the Ninja. He then grabbed her hand and led her back toward the house.

Moments later, Reese was inhaling deeply from a tightly rolled, swollen blunt.

"So when are we gonna go on that cruise to the Bahamas, like you said?" the girl asked as she got up and sat on his lap, taking the blunt from his mouth.

"I'm just waiting for my pockets to get a little deeper.

You know how that go," he said, adjusting her ass so it was directly on top of his dick.

"That's fucked up! You should be rolling just like your boy Knowledge. Me and my girls peeped him the other night up in the club, popping champagne and all that other good shit," the girl stated, trying to amp Reese up.

"I know, and plus he just copped an iced-out piece that probably cost the same as my bike," Reese responded, growing a little irritated.

"A nigga like you, with heart, should be running things, or at least getting what's due you," she spat out with as much sincerity as possible.

"Fuck that soft and let's-make-peace shit! We shoulda been had this whole area on lock, but niggas wanna squash shit. I got something for their asses," Reese shot back, standing up and pulling out a heavy chrome, sixteen-shot nine from his baggy Akademiks jeans. "Them punk motherfuckers gonna know it's real when these rhinoceros bullets start ripping through shit," he said, taking the clip out and putting it back in again.

"What's that?" she asked.

"It's some secret special military shit. When you get hit with one of these, it explodes into a thousand tiny pieces all throughout your fucking body. You know how when a nigga get shot in the arm in the movies and they be all right and shit? Well, if I was to blast you in the arm, you can forget about it. It's a wrap," Reese replied, wanting to see firsthand if what he was told was accurate.

Reese was now feeling powerful as well as dangerous, which made him a little horny.

"Shorty, you know what time it is," he stated, placing his hand between the girl's thick thighs, which were covered with a pair of tight, Baby Phat jeans. The weed and the alcohol she consumed earlier made her a little sluttish as she put her little brother in the other room to finish watching cartoons. She arrived back in the living room, going straight to Reese's zipper, pulling out his dick, and doing what she did best with her gold ball tongue ring.

Later on that night Reese rode his bike, thinking about what the girl had said.

Yeah, she was right. I should be running shit instead of taking orders and being told to chill out every time I wanna let niggas know we for real, he thought as he rode deeper into Head's territory. He slowed his bike as slow as he could when he spotted a couple of guys standing by a van.

"Oh, shit," Reese said out loud when he saw that one of the men was Head himself. Without a moment's thought, Reese pulled out his weapon and fired at the two unsuspecting figures. As soon as the gun barked, Head instantly hugged the sidewalk as his partner made the fatal mistake of looking up toward the sound of the gunfire. The first bullet tore through the partner's soft neck tissue, severing his vocal cords and not giving him a chance to even cry out in pain. That shot was followed by a second bullet that hit the guy in the jaw, causing teeth, blood, and bone marrow to splatter the side of the van. Head screamed, thinking he was hit as a bullet hit the side of the van and caused a piece of sharpened metal to ricochet into his delicate eye socket. Reese drove off laughing, thinking he had just committed his first two murders.

* * *

"You heard what happened? Somebody tried to put a toe tag on Head about an hour ago," Daquan said to Reese when he entered the spot.

"I know. It was me. Are they dead or what?" Reese asked as he sat wiping his gun with his leather gloves.

"Whatcha talking about?" Daquan asked.

"I said, it was me. If that nigga Head lives, which I don't think he will, he's gonna be on our dicks from now on. Now we gonna make some real dough with him probably packing up and breaking out," Reese said with a chuckle as he finished the last of his forty ounce.

"You stupid, young motherfucker! From what I heard, Head didn't even get touched. I told you before that Knowledge had some shit set up for their whole crew. Now you went and did some dumb shit," Daquan shouted, standing face to face with the younger and shorter man.

"Knowledge gonna give me props for at least hitting Head and his boy. I know for sure I wet up at least twice. I say we finish them off tonight," Reese replied, gripping the nine and letting Daquan know he was still down for whatever. Daquan grabbed Reese by the shirt, yanking him forward.

"You started some more unnecessary beef, which is gonna fuck up our money flow. After I kick your little ass, Knowledge just might body you," Daquan said.

Reese lost it when Daquan put his hands on him like he was some kind of bitch. He immediately broke Daquan's grip and fired a shot point blank range at the man's chest. Daquan stumbled back, blood spreading across his crisp, white tee as the slug bounced off his rib cage and splintered off in many different directions. The pieces tore into his major organs like a knife slicing butter, shredding them like they never existed. Daquan coughed one time and fell backward with blood leaking out his mouth and nose—dead.

"I told you I wasn't the one to fuck with. I told you! Now look at you, staring up at the ceiling, wondering what the fuck happened," Reese yelled. He paced the floor, tapping the gun on his leg and thinking about what his next move should be.

CHAPTER
THIRTY-NINE

The whole day after Goldmine murdered the body-guard, Goldmine and Pumpkin stayed holed up in the apartment, not going out for any reason. Goldmine was especially paranoid, thinking that someone was going to come busting through the door looking for the large amount of missing drugs. She stopped answering the phone and when someone knocked on the front door, she would freeze, signaling Pumpkin to be extra quiet until she looked through the peephole to make sure who it was.

Pumpkin, on the other hand, was handling things all right in the beginning until Goldmine's increasing para-noia started taking effect on her.

"You got rid of dat truck like I told you to? You know how da police got all kinds of crazy forensic tests and shit. They could easily find some hair or a piece of fingernail and lock us up for life," Goldmine said over and over. So then Pumpkin began to jump every time the phone rang or someone knocked on the door. Both women ordered takeout Chinese food, pizza, and other fast food that could be delivered, making extra sure it was their order before cracking open the door.

Goldmine and Pumpkin were in the living room, puffing on some weed to relax their frayed nerves, when a thunderous knock sounded at the front door. Both women looked at each other, knowing that neither one of them had placed an order so early. The knock came again, only harder, which caused Goldmine to tiptoe to the door and quietly place her ear to the wooden structure, hoping to find out who it could be.

"Come on, open up. I'm tired," a female voice said. Still the women in the apartment kept quiet, thinking it was some kind of trick. "Stop playing. It's me, Dallisha," the voice said. Goldmine carefully opened the door with the chain still attached and peeped out into the hallway. Once she was satisfied that it was indeed her sister, she unlocked the chain and practically snatched her younger sister inside the apartment.

"What the fuck is going on up in here?" You act like I'm the sheriff or somebody coming to evict everybody," Dallisha jokingly responded, looking around to see what was really up. "Oh shit, let me hit that," she said when she saw Pumpkin holding the half smoked blunt in her hand.

"Here. Do you. When did you escape?" Pumpkin asked, handing her friend the joint, relieved to see a friendly face.

"I got out this morning. So what's everybody been up to since I've been on vacation?" Dallisha asked, taking a good pull of the blunt. Before Pumpkin could respond, Goldmine jumped in.

"Nothing. Dallisha, let me holler at you in the other room," she said, all the while glaring at Pumpkin, making it clear that Pumpkin was not supposed to mention anything about the body.

Both sisters went into the back bedroom, with Pumpkin

wondering what sneaky Goldmine was up to now. Pumpkin knew Goldmine still had no idea that she had overheard Goldmine and the guy talking about what seemed
like a large amount of drugs right before he was brutally
murdered. Pumpkin played along for the meantime, letting Goldmine think she believed her unconvincing story
that he had tried to sexually assault her.

Goldmine and her little sister finally came out of the
room after an hour of whispering in hushed tones. Goldmine was fully dressed, like she was going out.

"Pumpkin, I'll get up with you later on. I gotta make a
couple of moves," Goldmine said as she snatched her car
keys off the table.

Both women quickly left the apartment and jumped
into the Mustang. Goldmine had taken Doc's BMW to the
local chop shop and got three thousand dollars for the
$85,000, high-performance car. She then used some of
the cash to pay back her overdue car notes.

Pumpkin took a long, hot shower, thinking that Goldmine was going to get Dallisha mixed up in some of her
bullshit. Sitting in a pair of sweat pants and an oversized
T-shirt, Pumpkin decided to turn on her cell phone. She
had it off for a while, not really in the mood for kicking it
with anybody. She wanted to call Jason, the guy she met in
front of the police station, but decided against it, figuring
that he must have been busy handling his little sister's
death. She was just about to get dressed when her cell
phone went off.

"Hello?" Pumpkin asked.

"What's up, shorty? Dis is Knowledge. What's popping?"
he asked.

"Nothing. I just came out da shower. What's good with
you?" Pumpkin asked.

"It's been mad hectic. You know how it is when you trying to stack dat paper. I'm coming to scoop you tonight so

we can chill," Knowledge said and then hung up before the girl even had a chance to respond.

For the first time in a while, Pumpkin produced a sincere smile. She definitely needed to get out and breathe some fresh air, plus get her mind off everything that'd been swirling around her and Goldmine. She liked the way Knowledge just seemed to take total control of any situation in which he was involved.

Pumpkin planned on going back to dance at the Warehouse because she was flat broke. She didn't even have the change for a pack of Newports, but she decided to do her thing tomorrow night after she hung out with her New York friend.

CHAPTER
FORTY

Knowledge cruised through Little Vietnam, playing a Mike Jones CD and drinking straight Hennessy out of a small plastic cup. He felt things were finally starting to smooth themselves out. The police had stepped down their presence since the killing of some of his boys. He knew how Reese felt, wanting revenge on Chase and his crew, but the timing was way off.

Dis part of town is raking in mad dough. Once I have shit on lock, I'm taking da whole set out, and I'm personally gonna push Head's wig back, Knowledge thought to himself as he re-filled his cup.

He stopped at a small, damp, windowless basement and picked up a knot of cash, dropping off another load of crack and weed for the worker to get off for him. Knowledge made several more identical stops before he ran out of product and was left with just a bundle of blood money. He then called Daquan twice on his cell phone to see if he had picked up those four kilos of cooked-up coke. The voicemail just kept popping up, so Knowledge decided to go scoop up Pumpkin, but then his own phone rang.

"Yeah, what's up?" Knowledge asked, recognizing Reese's number.

"Yo, you need to hit the spot right away," Reese said into the phone.

"I was on my way to take care of something. Whatever it is, if you can't handle it, try hitting up Daquan," Knowledge responded.

"This is some shit I can't say on the phone," Reese quickly shot back.

"OK, I'll be there in fifteen minutes," Knowledge replied, hoping it wasn't nothing serious. He wanted to take Pumpkin to a motel and lay the pipe game on her something serious. Ever since he chilled with this young firecracker when she wore that short-ass dress, he had imagined himself blowing her guts out while he had her bent over a couch.

Knowledge cautiously pulled up to his shop, double-checking to make sure he had his gat close by if anything was to ignite. Everything seemed unnaturally quiet as he walked around the back of the house and walked inside. Reese had his back turned toward him and was leaning over someone, doing something. Knowledge stepped on a soda can, causing Reese to jump up and point his gun directly at Knowledge.

"Whoa! Slow down. It's me," Knowledge shouted, staring down at the barrel of the gun. Reese had his finger tightly pressed against the hair trigger. For a split second, Reese thought that all he had to do was apply a little more pressure and Knowledge's whole operation would be his. Then he thought that he would have to finish what he started with Head, and Little Vietnam would then belong to a true thug.

Knowledge spotted a look of hesitation in Reese's eyes, and he knew that was a bad sign.

"What da fuck is wrong with you? What, you're trying to

mark me or something?" Knowledge yelled, walking toward Reese and snapping him out of his unrealistic fantasy. Reese lowered his weapon. Just then Knowledge noticed Daquan on the ground with a large bloodstain across his chest.

"What happened to Daquan?" Knowledge asked.

"I was just pulling up on my bike when I heard some gunshots and peeped Head and some other niggas pulling off. I'm not sure if I hit any of them, but that's when I noticed Daquan on the sidewalk leaking. I took him inside and then I called you," Reese said.

"Are you sure it was Head?" Knowledge asked, staring at the dead body of one of his partners, and his best friend.

"Yeah, I'm 100 percent positive. I know that big waterhead nigga anywhere. Whatcha wanna do? You want me to call the other guys?" Reese asked, hoping for more gunplay.

"Chill! First we gonna see if Daquan had a chance to pick up da work."

Both men walked out to the recently deceased man's car, and after checking it out, they went back inside the house. Knowledge looked around the room and spotted a Rough Trail backpack over by the door on the floor. He quickly snatched it up and dumped the contents onto the round wooden table that was used for chopping up product.

Reese was shocked at seeing the bag full of drugs that had been no more than a couple of feet away from him the whole time. After making sure all the work was there, Knowledge went over to Daquan and began searching his pockets. Then he noticed that Daquan's platinum, diamond-encrusted chain was missing, along with everything from his pockets.

"They must have robbed him," Reese said after he saw the look that Knowledge threw at him.

"Why would they take his shines, and not da bag, and

how did it get back inside the house?" Knowledge asked, not really talking to the other man, but instead beginning to question the whole situation.

"They must have got shook when they saw me, or they didn't know what was in the backpack," Reese added, still not explaining how the bag ended up back inside the house.

"Fuck it. At least we got dis weight. Come on and help me get Daquan to da truck," Knowledge ordered. Soon they had Daquan in the Suburban's backseat. Knowledge continued sipping on his Hennessy, thinking everything over.

Meanwhile, Reese didn't know what the quiet man was thinking, but he was prepared for whatever. They finally arrived at their destination—Grady Memorial Hospital—and rolled Daquan out in front of a smaller building. On their way back to the spot, Knowledge made a call.

"I need to see you tomorrow morning, right away," Knowledge said into his phone as the curious Reese started wondering who the hell he was talking to.

CHAPTER
FORTY-ONE

Jason was pushing his brand new Infiniti QX56, moon-colored truck with deep pockets, sitting on twenty-four inch rims that he had just copped the other day. Since the death of his little sister, he had pursued the game more vigorously than ever, more for the sake of keeping his mind off the sordid details of Tiffany's murder. Family members came and went just as quickly, tired of attending a senseless funeral of another young person lost to the clutches of the streets. His older brother, Free, was granted special permission to attend the services, accompanied by no less than six sheriff's deputies. Free stood solid as a stone statue with heavy ankle, waist, and wrist chains hanging from his body, as he threw hurtful glances at Jason, his eyes silently asking how Jason could have let this happen.

Jason's mind then wandered to his boy, L.B., and how he found him in the hotel spot, apparently beaten to death. He was lucky that the police didn't connect him to L.B.'s murder, even though he didn't have anything to do with it. The police, especially the ones in Atlanta, were quick to label you a suspect just for knowing the victim. In

some counties, if they knew you had a strong connection
to a murdered victim and the detectives working the case
were lacking suspects, they would most likely arrest you.
Their tactic was to have you sweat it out in jail until you
would help them with valuable information on that particular case.

Jason heard through the streets that the police had a
theory that L.B. was probably killed by some crazy, doped-
up prostitute, for the simple fact that he was known to
trick with crackhead females who still had a little body left
on them. In the back of his mind, Jason still thought that
Doc was somehow tied to everything.

A little while later, Jason was walking in the house after
Head made sure it was him.

"I got your message. You all right, playboy?" Jason asked,
taking a good look at the wounded man. Head was sitting
in a cushioned sofa chair, wearing a dark gray Von Dutch
jeans suit, with his hair looking crazy. The right side of his
face was grotesquely swollen and he sported an off-white
eye patch.

"You know me. I'm like cream. I always rise to the top,"
Head replied, motioning for Jason to take a seat. "I feel
for you. I heard about your sister. I know you heard that
them New York niggas tried to take a nigga like me out,
but as you can see, them faggots can't even shoot straight,"
Head said, taking a freshly rolled blunt from one of his
boys and sparking it up. He took a strong pull and then
continued. "I squashed the beef before, because it was bad
for business with the jakes floating around trying to lock a
motherfucker up for anything. Niggas wanted to bring it,
but now we gonna show 'em how we do it up, Dirty style.
Yeah, after we lay the murder game down, the heat's gonna
be on for a while. But after shit die down, we gonna have
enough dough stacked to the fucking ceiling," Head finished, passing the cigar to Jason.

Just then there was a knock on the door, interrupting their conversation. Head reached for his Taurus .357 long-barrel Magnum that was on the table, and told his boy to go see who it was. Seconds later, a boy in his early teens walked in with a girl only a few years older than him.

"Head, I got somebody who has something important to spit at you about," the young guy said. Head looked at his loyal worker with his good eye, hoping it had nothing to do with the dead girl's body the young boy told him about, which he later had Chase take the fall for.

"So what's the deal?" he asked, looking at the girl and then back at the boy.

"She says she knows for sure who shot at you the other day. Go ahead and tell him what you told me," he said.

"I was messing with this nigga who's down with Knowledge. I mean, I really don't mess with him 'cause he's cornball-acting like he's making major moves—" Before the girl could finish her sidetracked story, Head interrupted her.

"Get on with it! I don't have all fucking day," he said.

"Well anyway, he's always bragging on how ill he is and then he told me that he was gonna spray you and your crew. At first I thought he was bullshitting just to impress me, until I heard about the shootout on the news," she said nervously. Head unconsciously touched his shattered bad eye, thought for a second, and then spoke.

"That's good you came to me. I want you to hook up with this nigga in a couple of days so he won't get suspicious. Act like you want to give him some pussy or whatever, and then give me a holler, letting me know where you at. Now repeat what I said," Head stated as he stared intensely at the girl.

After the girl repeated what Head had said, he gave her a piece of paper with his number on it. Head then noticed that the girl was still standing around like she had something else to say before he realized that nobody in the hood would give up anything without wanting something in return. Head reached in his pockets to give the girl some money when she stopped him.

"If you have some weed, I'll take that and you can give me some money later on." Head then gave the grinning girl a Ziploc bag filled with Jamaican sugar haze as she was escorted out the door.

As soon as the girl was gone, the phone rang and Head picked it up. It was Chase, calling on a three-way line from jail.

"Don't worry, I'm holding the fort down. I said I got this. Yo, I gotta roll out, Chase."

"What's up with Chase?" Jason asked as Head hung up the phone. "He gonna beat his case or what?"

"I don't think so. I didn't want to tell you this before because I wasn't sure, but the police got him on lock for killing your sister," Head replied.

"What! What the fuck you trying to say?" Jason yelled, standing up now.

"I didn't want to believe it either at first, but word is that he bodied her, saying that she stole some drugs from him. But to get down like that with a little girl, that's some real foul, grimy, off-the-wall shit," Head said with a hidden smile. Jason was just too full of rage to say anything as the young boy stood by, wondering what the fuck was really going on.

CHAPTER
FORTY-TWO

"So when is he supposed to be dropping by?" Goldmine asked the woman, who was eating a big bowl of soggy Cornflakes.

"Don't worry, I got this. He said he'll swing by when he finishes up what he was doing," the girl said between mouthfuls of food that caused milk to dribble down her chin.

Goldmine and Dallisha were inside Dallisha friend's house, waiting on some guy that she said she knew would give them a good deal on some of the dope that the sisters said they had.

"Yo, Ronnie, tell her how you bust that bitch upside her head with that hard-ass dinner tray for running off with the lip," Dallisha said with an admiring smile.

"It ain't nothing. You know how I handle mine, both ways," Ronnie stated, looking at Goldmine and throwing a hidden curve in the meaning. Ronnie sat there, eating her cereal and making slurping sounds, all the while staring at Goldmine's figure to see if she was with her program. She had gotten out of jail three weeks before Dallisha did, for slashing her next door neighbor in the face with a GEM razor blade for calling her a bull dyke man bitch. Just by looking at her, you could tell that she wasn't a stranger to the prison system. She had freshly done, thick cornrow braids that were tied together in the back with a rubber band. She wore a tight wife beater that revealed muscular arms and a few jailhouse tattoos that seemed to have been sloppily done.

After a couple of hours and a big bottle of imported Dominican rum, the phone rang and Ronnie quickly snatched it off the hook.

"OK, I got you. I'll be right here," Ronnie said before hanging up.

"So what's up? I'm not gonna be waiting all day for some nigga," Goldmine spat out, growing impatient.

"Chill out! Dat was him on da horn. He couldn't get away, so one of his chicks is on the way to check out what y'all working with," she answered.

Twenty minutes later a slim, pretty, white woman wearing an evening gown with a long slit down the side, walked through the front door. She seemed totally out of place in this type of neighborhood. All eyes were on her as she introduced herself.

"Hi, I'm Anne, but everyone calls me Anne Sprinkles."

"Why they call you Sprinkles?" Ronnie asked, practically running over to the woman like a dog in heat.

It's been a long time since I had a white girl of this caliber, Ronnie thought.

"Well a lot of guys were asking me to pee on them. At first I thought it was disgusting, until they started throwing all this money at me. So I said fuck it, drunk a bottle of Chardonnay, and you couldn't stop me from sprinkling them. So the name just stuck with me," the white woman said with a voice full of enthusiasm, like she had accomplished some major goal in her life.

"Fuck all da bullshit small talk. Let's get on with it," Goldmine said, loud enough so Dallisha could snap back to business.

Minutes later the white girl was at the kitchen table with the remaining three women standing up around her. Anne took a little black pouch out of her handbag and unzipped it. She took out a set of clean "works" that dope fiends used to shoot up with. Once the Nigerian heroin was properly prepared and a popped-out vein was awaiting its pleasure, Anne plunged the needle deep into her milky white arm. The drug took effect almost immediately as the user threw back her head and let loose a loud, rumbling fart.

"Dat must be some ill shit. Look at Miss High and Mighty," Goldmine said loud enough so everyone in the room could hear.

By now the white woman was sitting on the floor getting the most out of her high with her legs spread far apart, letting everyone know she wasn't wearing any panties.

"Oh yeah, y'all niggers always have the best shit. No wonder motherfuckers in the hood always stay fucked up," Anne Sprinkles stated, thinking that she was giving the black race some kind of compliment.

"OK, I told you I had some bomb-ass shit. Now tell your peoples I want to work something out," Goldmine said, already hating this stranger she only met a short time ago. She then signaled for Dallisha to get ready and bounce as Ronnie looked as if she wanted to crawl up between the still-out-of-it woman's thighs.

"I don't trust neither one of dem bitches," Goldmine said to her sister as they were pulling off.

"I don't know about white shorty, but my homegirl is straight up some fo' real shit. She looked out for me, and plus everybody in jail said she was 'bout it 'bout it," Dall-isha answered, wondering what her friend was going to do with the white girl once they left the house.

Goldmine had given Anne a sample and her number. Anne, saying over and over that Goldmine's dope was some of the best she ever had, told Goldmine that her peoples would get back to her within a day or two without a doubt.

CHAPTER
FORTY-THREE

Doc was preparing himself for a visit, wondering who the hell could be visiting him. His lawyer or his wife usually let him know in advance when they planned to come see him. He took his neatly folded pants and cotton, button-down shirt from under the mattress and carefully put them on. He then looked in the scratched-up wall mirror, smiling to himself on how the weight of the thick mattress, combined with the straight, heavy, iron bed frame, produced almost perfect jail creases.

"Mr. Simmons, are you ready now?" a solid, built, white CO asked him. Doc quickly put on his Azure frames and took one final look at himself.

"Yeah, let's roll." Halfway toward the visiting room Doc's curiosity got the best of him again, so he turned to the black corrections officer who was also accompanying him, and tried to get some information. "Yo, man, who came to see me today?"

"I don't know. I guess you just gonna have to wait to find out," he answered like he was holding a hidden secret of some sort. A few minutes later the three men approached a room that had newspapers completely covering the window on the steel, pale green door.

"Why we going up in here? This ain't the door to the visiting room," Doc stated with the authority of a man who was used to always having people answering him quickly whenever he spoke.

"We were given specific orders by our supervisors to search you before and after every visit. Don't ask me, 'cause I don't know," the brutish-looking white guard said while grabbing Doc by the arm, to let him know that they were just doing their jobs. Doc knew that it was standard procedure for the jail to have all inmates strip-searched after each visit to control the flow of contraband, mostly drugs and weapons. He figured someone high up had ordered him to be double-searched, probably because of who he was and the crimes he was charged with.

Doc now stood naked in front of the two solemn-faced guards, wondering when they were going to go through his clothes. He then happened to look down at their feet and noticed that they were wearing regular street footwear instead of the all black, hard-toed boots that were mandatory for all the COs to wear while on duty. In the split second that it took for Doc to realize something was definitely wrong with the whole scene, both men rushed him. Within moments they had him up against the cold wall with his face pressed painfully into the concrete material.

"What the fuck is this all about?" Doc barely managed to say, trying his best to control the situation when he knew that he was up against losing odds.

"You fucking *acota*! You know why we're here and what for," the black man stated, his voice now taking on an unmistakable West African accent. His partner laughed while twisting Doc's arm up to his neck.

"Acota?" Doc asked.

"You know, black American cotton pickers," the African

guy replied. Doc was about to say something when the African pressed a calloused thumb into a spot behind his ear and gradually increased the pressure. Hot white pain shot through Doc's head, nearly causing him to pass out. He finally managed to speak.

"I was gonna send word that I would have his money in a couple of days," Doc muttered. The slim African grabbed Doc by the throat with a grip of steel, cutting off any words he might want to add to his plea.

"This is just a reminder so we're sure you won't forget," the African stated. His white partner twisted Doc's arm a little more just before the breaking point, and then kicked Doc's legs apart. Out of the corner of his eye Doc saw the African take out a long, thick police baton and smile sickly. Doc's worst fears were confirmed as he felt the nightstick against the entrance of his asshole. Physical limitations were being horrifically altered as the baton started doing its evil job.

Before his abuser could do any serious damage to Doc's virgin sphincter, a high-pitched alarm went off throughout the building. The next thing the terrified Doc knew was that he was roughly thrown to the floor as the two fake corrections officers quickly exited the room, slowly closing the door behind them. Doc crawled halfway under a metal chair and started trembling uncontrollably so that to the average spectator it might seem that he was going through some kind of seizure. He covered his face and started crying like a newborn baby, wishing that he had listened to his dead mother's advice and stayed in college, instead of wanting to be the man on the streets.

* * *

At the same time Doc was being assaulted, Jason's brother, Free, was being handcuffed and shackled down in another part of the jail, causing the riot alarm to sound off.

DeJon

"Yeah, nigga, you thought you was gonna be safe in jail for murdering my sister," Free was screaming as a CO threw a knee into his back. The other guards were shaking their heads, standing over the fallen Chase. Just minutes ago Free had asked him if he was the Chase who ran Atlanta's Little Vietnam.

"Yeah, why, who you be?" were Chase's last words before a heavy, wooden, three-pound scrub brush connected into the middle of his forehead. More brutal blows followed, and Chase's wrist bone was shattered in two as he tried unsuccessfully to block a thunderous blow.

"If this guy makes it, he's gonna be no smarter than a turnip," a guard stated, referring to Chase, as he and his fellow coworkers led the still shouting Free away.

CHAPTER
FORTY-FOUR

Pumpkin and Jason were just cruising around in his Infiniti truck, enjoying each other's company. Jason was still having mixed emotions about what his brother's lawyer told him the other day.

"It seems that your brother got himself caught up in some sort of violent altercation in jail," the lawyer told him. Jason knew exactly what went down, but played it off anyway.

"What! Is Free all right? What happened?" he asked in a very concerned voice.

"Calm down. He's fine. The other fellow got the worst of it with the run-in. From the limited information I've been told, a Mr. Chase Miller has been severely beaten about the head and upper body. He's in and out of consciousness, due to some minor swelling of the brain. Free is about to be formally charged with aggravated assault, and if the young man should die, expect Free to face manslaughter charges some time in the near future."

Jason knew that the attorney was just building up to say

that due to the new circumstances, he would need more cash.

All lawyers are the same. A black person as a suspect with some money was seen merely as a paycheck to help maintain their lifestyles, whether or not their clients were found guilty. The white lawyers would especially think that the animals were slaughtering each other off in record numbers, so why not make a little money in the process, Jason thought to himself about Free's lawyer, who was now telling him that he needed a lot more money so he could hire an investigator to prove that Chase had a long history of violence in and out of the penal system.

The lawyer went on to say that he would prove that Chase Miller was prone to future anti-social behavior toward his fellow man, and on the date in question it was no different.

"Your brother was just acting in self-defense," the lawyer explained. Jason responded by saying that he would get back to him about the money.

Who that motherfucker think he is, trying to gas me up on a tank that's empty? He don't know nothing about Chase or why shit jumped off, Jason thought after hanging up the phone.

"Is everything all right? Pass the yak," Pumpkin said when she noticed the faraway look in Jason's eyes. She knew he'd been going through some shit about his sister, brother, and the general stress of street hustling.

Pumpkin liked Jason because she felt that he was a little more open than most guys she dealt with, so the other night, when he reached over for condoms, she told him she wanted to feel all of him and be closer with him too. Pumpkin felt at ease with Jason, especially with Goldmine and Dallisha creeping around so secretively like she was a complete idiot who didn't know that they were trying to get off the dope that Goldmine had stolen and killed for.

"Here you go. I was just thinking about this outfit I

peeped that would look ill on you," Jason said, passing her the bottle of expensive, strong cognac.

"You know me. I'll never turn down some free gear," Pumpkin said with a flirty smile.

"Fuck it. Let's make moves. I wanna see how your fat ass fills it out anyway."

Once they were parked and put some quarters in the meter, a voice yelled out to Jason.

"Oh, I thought that was you pushing your new shit."

"What's popping? What you doing down here?" Jason asked the young kid. The last time he saw him was when they were all in the house, right after Head came home from the hospital.

"I'm just cooling down here with my auntie. Anyway, I need to holler at you on some real shit," he said.

"OK, what's up?" Jason asked, stepping closer to the boy as Pumpkin took the hint and started to do a little window-shopping.

"You remember when Head told you Chase had something to do with your sister being killed? Well, Chase was arrested for it, but I know for a fact that he didn't do it," the kid stated.

"If he didn't do it, then who did, and why would Head lie about it on his right-hand man?" Jason asked, studying the guy more closely now.

"I don't know what Head and Chase got going on between them, but I seen a white boy toss a body over in that vacant lot with all those old junk cars. When I told Head what I saw, he told me to keep it on the low-low and the next thing I know, Chase is locked up for some bullshit that he didn't even do," the guy said.

"Why you telling me this? What's in it for you?" Jason asked, trying to piece together everything he had just heard.

"I don't want nothing, don't need nothing. I feel it's some foul shit what Head told you. Chase looked out for me when my moms didn't even have a jar of mayonnaise in the fridge, and when our lights got cut off, he did justice on the bills," the young guy replied, speaking from the heart.

"I swear on my life, I wouldn't lie about something like this," he added after he saw the question mark in Jason's eyes.

"What you say this white boy's name was?"

"All I know is that they call him White Boy Danny and he be trying to act like he's a black nigga from the hood," the guy responded.

"Good looking out," Jason replied, giving him a pound.

"Fuck da clothes. You feel like talking?" Pumpkin asked when Jason returned to her side, feeling the vibe that something was wrong.

"Not really. I just got to find out about somebody called White Boy Danny," he said, deep in thought.

"I know him! He got da best weed around," Pumpkin replied.

"Tell me everything you know about this dude," Jason stated sternly as they walked into a hip-hop clothing store.

CHAPTER
FORTY-FIVE

"I've been thinking about you a lot since the last time we were together," the girl said into the phone.

"Yeah, what was you thinking about?" Reese asked.

"You know, how the dick was mad good," she said with a shy smile.

"Oh, you want this big piece of wood in your fat ass again?" he asked with a voice full of ego.

"Of course. Could you come by? Nobody gonna be home all night," the girl said in her best slutty voice.

"I wanna lay my shit down, but I gotta handle something important for the next couple of days," Reese stated, the wheels turning in his scheming head.

The girl felt that her pussy tactic wasn't working, so she tried a different approach.

"Baby, I really wanted to surprise you, but I guess I might as well go ahead and tell you. You remember how you was saying how my friend had the banging body, like she should be stripping or something?"

"Yeah, what about it?" Reese asked.

"Well at first she didn't want to say something, but then

she told me when she heard all the details on how you fucked me so good, she been thinking about having a three-some with us," the girl said, smiling through the phone.

"Tell her I'm with it. When do she wanna get down with the program?" Reese asked, imagining doing her friend doggy style while the other girl licked his balls.

"She said tonight would be perfect because her man had to make a run out of town, and he won't be back until tomorrow afternoon," the girl said.

"Fuck it. I'll be by tonight around one. You be ready for this monster," Reese said quickly before the freaky girl had a chance to change her mind.

"Don't worry. You just make sure you're not too tired. Oh, and bring by some smokes," she threw in before hanging up.

Much later, Reese was ringing the doorbell, thinking both women were going to come to the door butt naked, wearing nothing but high heels.

"Damn, I like a nigga that's right on time," the girl said, smiling seductively at Reese, who already had a thick Philly blunt in his mouth, puffing on the pungent smelling weed. Reese stepped inside, taking a good look at the girl who had on a long, white, see-through silk robe with red pumps.

"Sit down and relax. Tonight it's all about you, player," she said, throwing on an X-rated porno DVD.

"Where's Shorty at?" Reese asked as he took a big, frosty bottle of Grey Goose out of a paper bag and placed it on a table next to him.

"Oh, her boyfriend called at the last minute and wanted her to make a quick run for him. She said she was on her way," the girl stated as she sat on Reese's lap and began playing with Daquan's diamond and platinum chain, that Reese now wore.

After ten minutes of bullshit chatter, she felt Reese's

hand creeping toward her crotch, so she quickly interrupted him.

"Let me go call her again and see where exactly she's at," the girl said. Reese told her to hurry up as he opened the bottle of vodka. "She's about five minutes away," the girl said as she walked back into the living room with her robe now fully open, revealing a well-made push-up bra and showing an enticing flat stomach that had a tattoo of two light blue dolphins circling each other around her belly button.

"That's what I'm talking about," he said, pulling the girl toward him.

Reese was so into the horny girl sucking on his neck and watching the X-rated movie, that he didn't even see the two men slowly walk into the living room until they were already there.

"Who the hell—" was all Reese could say before a hard blow to his ear knocked him and the girl completely off the couch and onto the floor. The girl quickly jumped up and covered herself.

"Get your bitch ass up!" Head yelled. Reese did as he was told, holding onto his ear that was slightly hanging off from the force of the blow.

"You want my chain? Here, take it," Reese said, hoping this was about jewelry.

"Nigga, you think this is about some lame chain? It's not, but I'll take it anyway," Head said as he took the chain from around his victim's neck while still pointing the gun directly at him. "Go get something to tie him up," Head said to his partner.

Minutes later they had Reese tied up with some thin clothesline rope from the kitchen that the girl had provided for them. Head looked at the blood that soaked the back of the girl's sofa and then back at the bottle of Grey

Goose. He then took the bottle and took a drink. Reese glanced over and saw the big, black guy doing something like preparing some weapon.

"So Knowledge wanted shit to be on again? Well it's on again, starting with your little ass," Head said, smiling down at the shivering Reese. Then the other guy turned toward Reese with a lead pipe wrapped in black tape, with prison razor wire wound tightly around it. "Now I'm gonna only ask you one time, and one time only: Where that nigga Knowledge lay his head at?" Head asked.

"Come on, why shit gotta go down like this?" The next thing Reese knew, the lead pipe hit him squarely on the right side of his face, causing soft flesh and blood to fly across the room.

Just as Reese started screaming, the girl came out of the bedroom fully dressed and stood shocked at all the blood.

"What's going on? I thought you said you was only gonna talk to him, or at least take him somewhere else to do your thing," she said, thinking of how she was going to explain all the blood to her mother.

"Bitch, sit your ass down and shut the fuck up!" Head yelled. Reese was so shook about what the men were planning on doing to him that he completely forgot about the girl.

"OK, I'm cool. Can I at least have my money now?" she asked, not wanting to be any part of what was going down.

"You got some weed. Ain't that what you said you wanted?" Head replied, laughing and knowing she wasn't going to get anything else.

"You set me up for some fucking weed? I'm gonna kill your fucking ho ass," Reese shouted, still holding on to his damaged face.

"Ha, ha, ha, you best be trying to keep these niggas from digging any deeper into your ass, you punk wannabe thug," she said, looking directly at him.

"You really thought you was gonna get off on some freak shit tonight, huh? Well, shorty had other plans for you," Head said, smacking Reese with the gun again.

"OK, OK, don't hit me again. It was all Knowledge's idea. I tried to tell him, let's just get paper and forget about this beef, but he wouldn't listen." Head just laughed, telling his boy to hit Reese again with the razor-studded pipe. The pipe slashed across his stomach, causing pink, bloody meat to appear. Reese screamed and lunged toward Head, clawing his face. A middle finger dug into Head's bad eye, causing him to yell out in pain as both men fell to the floor.

"Get him off me! Get him off me!" Head screamed as the finger felt like it was tearing its way toward his brain. Reese was growling like an animal right before a .45 slug tore away half of the back of his head.

Head stayed on the floor, holding his eye, as his partner told the girl to get some towels. The girl came back with the towels as Head placed one on his eye and then started kicking the already dead Reese.

"I wasn't done with you yet, nigga," he yelled.

"Let's get the fuck out of here before some nosey neighbor calls the police," Head stated, regaining his composure.

"What about her?" the other guy asked Head.

"Fuck her! She's not gonna get the chance to tell on me for some petty drugs," Head responded.

The guy raised his weapon as the girl instantly raised her hands in a self-defense posture. The bullet shot straight through her hands and tore into the soft flesh just above her lip. Both men then walked back toward the car, with Head guzzling liquor to quiet his pain.

CHAPTER
FORTY-SIX

Goldmine was listening to her new Alpine system blow-ing Lil John and the East Side Boyz. Since her new drug venture, she had added expensive wood trim through-out the Mustang, which now sat on twenty-inch Asanti Gator rims. Very soon, she planned to upgrade her whip to a Benz or the same kind of Beemer Doc used to have. She had to admit that she was sold on the BMW seven se-ries, even though she had only pushed it for a couple days.

"Fuck dat white bitch!" Goldmine said out loud as she blew weed smoke out the window. She had just come back from a real-estate office, trying to put down on a house in a quiet neighborhood.

"I'm sorry, miss. There's nothing we can do. You have no type of collateral to help secure the loan, nor do you have a feasible way to pay the monthly mortgage note," the sunburned woman stated.

"I can put $60,000 down within the month," Goldmine stated.

"That just won't do. You have a good day," the woman coldly replied.

As Goldmine was leaving she overheard the forty-something woman talking to one of her coworkers.

"She has some nerve coming up in here. Her pimp probably sent her." Goldmine spun around on her heels at that comment.

"You got something to say, den be a woman and say it to my face," Goldmine yelled.

"We don't want no trouble. Could you please just leave?" the other woman asked, placing her hand on the telephone, ready to dial 911.

"You prune-faced bitches wish you could get it like me, and look as good," Goldmine said in an icy tone.

"Hello, we have an African American woman here who's threatening us," the lady said into the phone after calling 911.

"Fuck you and da police," Goldmine replied, throwing a Luis Colmen pure python bag over her shoulder and storming out like a true female from the hood who knows where she stands.

Goldmine made it back to Ronnie's house, which she had practically turned into a dope house with reinforced five-inch thick steel doors in the front and back. She knew it was dangerous for any person to be selling some good-ass dope at cut-rate prices, but for a woman it was practically suicide. Goldmine wasn't in the game for the long run, though. She just wanted to make as much money in the shortest time possible. She knew without a doubt that soon, somebody from Doc's camp would be paying her a visit, looking for the missing heroin and maybe questioning her about the MIA bodyguard.

"So how's business?" Goldmine asked Dallisha, who was counting small packs of dope. The dope was packaged in plastic bags with a red stamp reading BLUE NILE.

"Shit is sweet. The fiends can't get enough, but you know niggas are starting to hate," she said.

"Fuck dem jealous motherfuckers. They do more yap-ping den da bitches," Goldmine said with a twisted-up face. Just then, Ronnie came in from the back door after serving a couple customers. They had built two slots into the steel door: one just small enough for money and dope to exchange hands, and the other for them to see who was at the door.

"So, Anne been asking for more weight, or what?" Gold-mine asked Ronnie.

"Last time I spoke to her, she said her man knew a guy from outta town who might be interested in a few keys, if you could swing it," Ronnie answered while lighting up a cigarette.

Goldmine looked at Ronnie, knowing she had to get out the game like yesterday. She suspected Ronnie was using the product herself, and not only that, Ronnie was also using the heroin as a powerful tool to act out her sick-est fantasies.

Goldmine had walked in the house one night to pick up some money and found Ronnie kneeling between some girl's thighs. Ronnie only had on a pair of oversized boxer shorts and six-inch Timberland boots. The girl in-volved had her knees almost to her ears and had a couple of old-fashioned, wooden clothespins attached to her nip-ples. Ronnie, meanwhile, was slowly pushing what looked like a steroid-induced cucumber in and out of the girl's hairy vagina. And the middle finger on Ronnie's other hand was deeply embedded in the wiggling girl's butt hole.

When Ronnie saw Goldmine standing there with a sur-prised expression, she purposely jammed the vegetable in the girl to the fullest extent possible, causing the mildly at-tractive girl to bite her lip. And a millisecond later, Ronnie withdrew her middle finger, licking the feces-smeared ap-

pendage as she winked at Goldmine with her green contact lenses.

Goldmine mostly put up with the woman's freaky, out-
landish ways for the dough. She wished Anne Sprinkles'
peoples would buy more weight, so she could get rid of
the dope and bounce out the hood for good. Selling the
heroin piece by piece would inevitably bring trouble at a
much faster pace than if she could sell the drugs by the
bulk.

"Tell her to set something up. Whatever her peoples
need, I can work it," Goldmine said now to Ronnie. Goldmine then took the stack of money her sister had waiting
for her and left just as a carload of up-to-no-good dope
fiends was pulling up.

"Hey, I hope you still got some more of that Blue Nile,"
a slim, greasy-faced man said from the backseat as he
wiped his runny nose with the back of his hand. Goldmine
just jumped in her car, not bothering to answer. She had a
habit of not having or wanting contact with any type of
fiends unless she really had no choice in the matter.

CHAPTER
FORTY-SEVEN

White Boy Danny sat on his tattered, worn-out sofa chair, drinking tallboy cans of Budweiser, one after the next. He was thinking about the meeting tomorrow night with some guy who called himself Knowledge. His father, who was still an active detective, had told him that Little Vietnam was heating up something fierce, probably due to the high-powered guns Danny had sold to a group of drug dealers.

"The blacks are dropping faster than cockroaches. But don't worry. We in the department consider niggas' deaths misdemeanor homicides," his father said with a mocking laugh. He went on to tell his son that other drug dealers were going to be knocking at his door, wishing to purchase even more weapons to try to keep up with their rivals.

Sure enough, Pops was right, as he usually was. Knowledge soon found out that White Boy Danny was the person who sold his enemies the guns that took out a couple of his boys. Knowledge told Danny that there were no hard feelings—business was business and money was money, no matter where it came from. Danny agreed, and so they arranged a meeting.

The money was rolling in, but more important things plagued Danny's mind. He couldn't stop thinking about the beautiful black little girl whose lifeless body he had tossed away like an old newspaper. His only souvenir from the incident was her small panties, which were losing their sex appeal for him. At night, when he put the garment to his face, he noticed that a lot of its softness was gone, plus a horde of hungry ants had attacked the crotch area, eating away most of the natural discharge.

People still dropped by his house to cop some of his weed, bringing with them the news of the young girl's shocking death.

"You remember shorty Tiffany, who came through a couple of times? Well the police found her naked and dead," one of Tiffany's female friends told Danny when buying some good chronic.

"Oh, I think I do remember her. That's some fucked up shit," he replied, secretly fingering the panties in his pocket.

White Boy Danny had fought back the huge, irresistible urge to lock the door after the girl came over by herself for some Chronic. He knew it would be a dangerous move because he never knew who she could have told where she was going. When the urge became too strong, he smoked a dank and headed down to the Greyhound bus station. He had heard stories on how pimps often frequented the station, looking for girls who were down on their luck, or straight-up confused runaways looking for a new start in Atlanta. Almost all the women got more than what they bargained for when the smooth talking guys promised them things—food, clothing, shelter, and fame with no strings attached. That was usually how the Red Light District got populated with fresh new faces.

If they could snatch up a girl by just talking, then why can't I? Danny wondered as he parked his car down the block.

Danny spotted a woman of about twenty standing off to the side by the front entrance. She was pretty, but a little old for his taste. There wasn't much of a selection, so he walked slowly past her to feel her out.

"What's up? I got some eighteen-karat-gold chains. Shit is real. I'll even let you test them right here on the spot," the woman said, flinging out a few thick, gold, herring-bone chains from out of her jacket.

Damn, that bitch is a hustler. Someone's probably watching her, or somebody down with her is looking out for the cops, Danny thought as he told her that he was straight.

Danny went back to his car and drank a couple more cans of beer before he decided to try his luck again.

"How you doing? Is everything all right?" Danny asked a black girl of about sixteen who was carrying a backpack and another bag in her hand. The girl turned slightly and looked into Danny's innocent blue eyes, instantly feeling relaxed.

"Oh, I'm fine. I'm just waiting for some friends of mine. They should have been here by now," she answered.

"I hope they come soon, because it can be dangerous out here at night. A lot of guys try to prey on young, beau-tiful girls like yourself," he stated in a flattering voice.

"Are you a cop or something?" she asked. Danny took the opening and struck.

"Yeah, I work the undercover division in this area, mak-ing sure nothing happens to anybody, especially pretty girls like you." The girl blushed and threw him her widest smile.

"Thank you," she said.

"Oh, I forgot to tell you. I just found out a little while ago that there was a major accident on the highway, so your friends might not be here for a couple of hours due to the traffic problems," Danny said.

"For real?" she asked, looking at her watch.

"I know it's getting late, but I can drop you off. I'll feel better knowing that you made it safely to your people's house," he said.

"I don't know. What if they come and I'm not here?" the girl asked, still thinking about what to do.

"I could radio one of my partners to give your friends a message that you're with me, and that you should be arriving back at their place soon," Danny said. Just as the girl was reaching in her pocket to give Danny a piece of paper with the address on it, a four-door sedan pulled up and a passenger called out the young girl's name. The girl ran up to the full car, laughing as one of her girlfriends got out and took her bag.

"This is my cop friend," she said, turning around to introduce Danny. "Where did he go? He was just standing here a second ago," she said in a puzzled tone.

Meanwhile, Danny was back in his '66 Impala, driving away and cursing himself for acting too slowly.

CHAPTER
FORTY-EIGHT

"Where da fuck is dat nigga Reese at? He's probably laid up with some chickenhead getting smoked out, instead of taking care of dis here business," Knowledge said, not talking to anyone in particular. Little did he know that he was mostly right about Reese being with some girl, but they were both laid up attracting flies, with slugs imbedded in their skulls.

Knowledge was pacing the floor looking stressed, something he rarely was. His motto and attitude toward life's unsuspected surprises was: for every problem, there were at least a hundred different ways to solve it.

"Yo, guys, in a minute I'm gonna have dis bullshit little stretch of town locked down tighter than fish pussy, and den we can move on to bigger and better things," Knowledge said in an arrogant tone of voice.

Knowledge was talking to two of his boys from New York, who had just arrived in Atlanta late the previous night. He specifically handpicked these guys because they were wicked with the gun and they didn't ask too many questions.

"I know you niggas are tired from da long ride and need a little relaxing. We gonna hit up dis spot where da thick-ass shorties just be throwing da pussy if they know you a NYC nigga," Knowledge said with a smile, ready to relieve a little stress himself.

They all jumped in a dark blue Ford Taurus with the extra dark tints, that Knowledge had just bought to be incognito until he finished the beef with the small-time locals. He drove, thinking about how Reese's story concerning Daquan's death didn't add up.

Why would Head and his crew take da chain and leave the bag full of dope behind? And how did da dope get back inside da spot without Reese knowing anything about it? Knowledge wondered.

As soon as Knowledge parked the car down the block from the Warehouse, he made up his mind that Reese had to go.

After being searched, all three men grabbed a table inside the club. Minutes later a long-legged waitress brought them a bottle of Hennessy Reserve, which Knowledge immediately attacked. He wasn't in the mood for no weak-ass champagne. He wanted the straight, hard shit all night. The men then turned their attention toward the stage where a well-put-together woman, wearing some kind of jungle outfit was crawling on all fours, tooting her ass up at the crowd. She had a face like a warm bucket of mud, but her body and energetic stage performance made up for what she lacked in the looks department.

"Any one of you fellows want a lap dance?" a girl asked, shouting over the music.

"Do my men over here," Knowledge replied, lifting up her short skirt to get a full view of her assets.

Knowledge was on the verge of being totally drunk as he held a full glass of Henny in one hand and a handful of the dancer's ass in the other. She grinded to the beat of the music on the crotch of the guy closest to Knowledge, while Knowledge slipped his fingers in her pussy a few times. She kept quiet, knowing Knowledge's rep in the streets as a man whose temper could explode at any given second.

"Dat's enough. Go on, get," Knowledge said, throwing some money on the floor after spotting some new strippers just coming in from the back room, shaking their asses like it was going out of style. His boys laughed as the girl picked up her skirt with the money and trotted off, still trying to hold her head up.

Knowledge rose from his seat to get some more ice for their drinks when he bumped into a guy.

"Yo, money, you need to watch where da fuck you going," Knowledge growled into the guy's face.

"You're the one who ran into me. Oh, I see that you a little tore up, so I'm gonna let it go," the guy said after he noticed Knowledge wobbling a little on his feet.

"Let it go? Do you know who I am, you country-bama, lame-dressing nigga," Knowledge shot back.

"Oh, you're one of them up-north niggas who think that everybody down south is soft. So what's up?" the guy asked after hearing Knowledge's New York accent. Knowledge tensed up for the showdown, but then a hand lightly grabbed his arm.

"I thought I recognized your voice. Forget about dat bullshit drama." Knowledge turned around and was looking directly at Pumpkin, who wore a stunning black bodysuit that hugged every feminine curve and crevice.

"What's up, Shorty? Where you been at?" he asked, completely ignoring the guy like he was a bothersome fly.

"I'm just trying to stay up," Pumpkin responded, glad the altercation had been squashed. Soon they were seated at the table with Knowledge ordering a tall Electric Candy for Pumpkin and another bottle of Hennessy for his boys.

"Yo, Knowledge, who's that guy over there peeping you?" one of the guys asked after about fifteen minutes had passed. Knowledge looked across the room, screwed his face, and responded in a slurred voice.

"Dat's the country motherfucker who tried to test my steez a little while ago."

"So whatcha wanna do?" he asked, trying to hype the situation up even more. The more Knowledge stared at the guy and his friends, the more his hatred grew for Atlanta-born guys, especially since the killing of his peoples in Little Vietnam.

"I should go over there and push his shit back right now," Knowledge spat out as he reached down in his boot and pulled out a concealed silver .25 automatic gun. He knew that most clubs in Atlanta never checked guys' footwear for weapons, whereas in New York they routinely made everyone take their shoes off. Knowledge cocked a round into the chamber, placing the gun on his lap.

"Come on now, forget about him," Pumpkin said. "He's a nobody. Remember you always telling me it's all about dat paper."

"What! What you defending dat clown for? You saw how he tried to play a live wire like me," Knowledge said, turning his attention to Pumpkin. The more Knowledge thought about his drug beef, the more his rage grew against all Georgia people. "Dem Atlanta boys are pure faggots and fuck da bitches, too. They could suck a dick, too," Knowledge shouted, causing a couple of heads to turn.

Pumpkin knew the situation was starting to turn sour, so she got up and quickly tried to leave.

"Who da fuck you think you are, turning your back on me?" Knowledge asked, grabbing Pumpkin by her ponytail and yanking her down.

"What da fuck you doing?" Pumpkin yelled, surprised

that a guy she considered cool would flip the script on her like that.

"You probably riding some Atlanta nigga's dick with dat stank ass of yours. Dat's why you haven't had time for a real motherfucker," Knowledge said.

"Fuck her and them niggas. I say we set it," Knowledge's boy said, standing up ready for some excitement. Just then a bouncer rushed over wearing a tight black T-shirt, trying to make his arms seem bigger than they actually were. The same instant the bouncer was about to grab Knowledge in a chokehold, Knowledge turned to the side and stuck the gun in the surprised man's face.

"What da fuck you was gonna do, huh, big boy? What!" Knowledge asked, letting Pumpkin go. Pumpkin scrambled out of harm's way as Knowledge backed the bouncer against the table.

"Come on, man, I was just doing my job," the bouncer said, holding his hands up and feeling weak in the knees.

"Dat's da same shit da COs say when niggas catch their soft ass up in da hood." Then Knowledge crashed a hard Hennessy bottle on the bouncer's head, causing him to drop like a ton of bricks.

"Yo, Knowledge, let's roll. I see bitches on the phone," his boy said, quickly finishing up the last of his drink.

All three men soon exited the club and sped away.

"I'm gonna see dat little bitch again," Knowledge said out loud, meaning every word and thinking about how Pumpkin had tried to play him.

CHAPTER FORTY-NINE

Doc was staring out the window of his cell, smoking a Newport and thinking about how it all came to this. He was in a special part of the jail labeled MO for mental observation. He was placed there since a CO captain discovered him on the cold floor, nude and shaking uncontrollably. When pressed on how he got there, Doc couldn't remember. All he kept saying over and over again was that he wanted to go home.

"Hey, Doc, when I get out of here, me and my ol lady are planning on having a baby. We're not going to a white hospital so some cracker doctor can tell us our baby died, and then sell it to some rich folks across the waters. We gonna have what you call a good, ol-fashioned natural childbirth at home. Could you give me a few pointers?" a guy from the next cell over called out.

"I told you before I'm not a real doctor. It's just a nickname that was given to me," Doc responded.

"So how the hell you get into medical school," the guy asked, sounding more confused by the minute.

"Yo, Doc, if I got bitten by a dangerous snake on my dick, would you suck the poison out to save my life?" another MO inmate yelled out, causing the whole cellblock to be filled with laughter.

An hour later one male and one female guard told Doc to get ready to go. Doc then turned around and stuck his hands through the metal slot where his meals were placed, so the CO could handcuff him, which was standard procedure in that particular unit because of the unpredictable violence that often occurred. Walking between the guards, Doc had a fearful sense of apprehension, thinking he was going to relive his nightmare all over again.

"I heard you was the big man on the streets. Why you sweating and shaking so much like we walking you to the electric chair?" the fat female corrections officer, who looked like she might deliver twins at any moment, asked Doc with a mocking snicker.

They soon led Doc to a room on the upper floor, where two straight-faced white men wearing neatly starched, dark suits were waiting for him. Once they had Doc's handcuffs off, the strange men introduced themselves as Agent Carter and Agent Finley.

"OK, Simmons, I'm gonna cut through all the bullshit. I'm not going to sit here and yank your chain, telling you that I'm going to offer you a sweetheart deal, because I'm not. I think you're trash, human scum," Agent Carter said, taking off his jacket and placing it on the back of the chair. "And the crazy routine? You might have these other uneducated clowns fooled, but it doesn't fly with us," he added, invading Doc's private space.

"We know Mooka is planning on expanding his network throughout the Atlanta area," Agent Finley explained.

"We also know that you owe him a large sum of money, which you can't possibly pay back because we seized all of your assets. We found your driver chopped up like fucking minced meat. That's just the African's style to send out a gruesome message to you and everybody else who has plans different from Mooka's," Finley finished, sliding some eight-by-ten glossy pictures of the dead body across the table to Doc.

"Things happen. If you know so much, what you need me for?" Doc asked, not bothering to look at the pictures.

"Listen, asshole, for all I care, you can rot in jail until you have gray hair around your nuts. Mooka wants his money and since you obviously don't have it, he'll settle for his dope. Me personally, I don't give a fuck if all you animals tear each other's throats out. I live in a nice house in the country away from niggers like you, who prey on good, hardworking blacks, but I have a job to do, and so does my boss, who answers to somebody higher up. It's all bullshit when the black politicians start hollering about all the violence, guns, and drugs in their communities, even though they don't live there. Every once in a while we got to throw them something and that something happens to be you," Carter said as a thick vein popped out on the middle of his forehead.

"When we catch this sick fuck, which we will, we want you to testify in court about the heroin he gave you and other deals you made throughout the years," Finley said with a wink.

Doc looked at Finley in a puzzled way, knowing there had only been one time when he bought drugs from Mooka, and even then he never even met the man.

"Don't worry. We supply you with all the necessary

dates, times, that sort of thing," Finley explained, talking as if Doc was slow to catch on.

"So what do I get out of everything?" Doc asked.

"You and your family get to live," Agent Carter answered with a hearty laugh.

CHAPTER FIFTY

Goldmine, Dallisha, and Ronnie were riding in the Mustang, on their way to meet with some guy that Anne Sprinkles said wanted four kilos of their Blue Nile heroin.

"Is dis nigga on some real shit or what?" Goldmine had asked yesterday.

"My man has been knowing him all his life. He put all his money together for this deal so he could come up again," Anne answered. But Goldmine had never trusted the dope fiend white girl, who acted as if black people were the most gullible and trusting race on earth.

Halfway to the meeting with the mysterious buyer, Goldmine felt something wasn't quite right with the whole setup.

"Oh, shit! How could I be so stupid? I forgot I was supposed to see dis nigga I know from da club about the rest of the dope," Goldmine said, not wanting to reveal her true feelings and alarm the other women.

If something were to go wrong, she would hope they would know how to handle themselves, being that crazy-ass Ronnie had a snub-nosed .38 hidden in the back of her waistband. If everything went according to plan, with the money she was going to make from this deal Goldmine planned to retire from the drug game. She had already let Dallisha know that she could handle the rest of the dope herself, breaking Goldmine off with a piece of the profit since it was hers in the first place.

"Come on. We need you. You know you have a way of talking to a motherfucker," her sister pleaded.

"I'm sorry. I completely forgot. But you can't walk by a knot of dough while trying to stack your other paper. Dat's just like a pimp strolling by a potential whore on his way to cop another bitch," Goldmine replied.

"Go ahead and do you. We'll be all right," Ronnie said, taking her pistol out like she was aiming it at some-body.

"Cool. Pull over by dat cab stand. You have my number. Call me if he tries to lower da price or some other bull-shit," Goldmine said, jumping out the driver's side as Dall-isha took over at the wheel.

"Here's the place," Dallisha said while trying to peer through the darkness. She parked in back of an old, destitute-looking former furniture warehouse, and they both got out.

"Watcha doing?" Dallisha asked when she saw Ronnie take three of the packages out of the shopping bag and hide them in some thick bushes.

"I'm not taking any chances of getting ripped off. We don't know this nigga from a hole in the wall," Ronnie an-swered.

They walked to a door where they could see a light from inside through the dust-covered window. Ronnie knocked on the door and an extremely tall man with a custom-made suit appeared, motioning for the girls to step inside.

"For your safety and ours," he said while a much shorter man searched the girls.

"Shit! I don't know you motherfuckers," Ronnie said after they found the hidden gun on her.

Both Dallisha and Ronnie felt a little more at ease, assuming these guys weren't stickup kids because of the expensive suits they wore and the large, sparkling diamonds that danced in the light from their wrists and fingers.

"Please, over here," one of the men said, leading the group to a table. "Can we inspect the heroin?" he asked, wanting to get down to business right away. Ronnie took the package out as Dallisha looked around for any surprises. Once they finished testing the heroin and were satisfied with the product, he asked where the rest of the kilos were.

"We got it. Let's see some money," Ronnie said, glad they hadn't also found the stainless steel carbon knife she still had on her person.

"Fair enough," the tall guy responded, producing a briefcase filled with neatly stacked, crisp money.

Shortly thereafter, Ronnie was back with the remaining three packages, smiling to herself as she thought about all the money she was about to have in her possession. Ronnie had already planned on robbing Goldmine and Dallisha once they were back in the car with the cash. Things couldn't have worked out more perfectly when Goldmine said she had something else to do.

"OK, now where's the rest of the remaining heroin?" the African asked, his voice taking on a much colder tone.

"The deal was for only four kilos. If you want more, we can set something up for later on," Dallisha stated, getting into the mix of things.

"We want the rest of the heroin right now," he barked, his accent as strong as ever. Then out of nowhere another man came into view, holding some type of small, compact machine gun. He ordered the women to sit down.

"Ain't this some shit. They are some stickup boys. Wait till I get into Anne's ass," Ronnie mumbled to herself, but did as she was told.

Another man came out from the shadows carrying a large silver platter. He was eating raw condor eggs dipped in spicy Maltese sauce, and on the side was a hard piece of ostrich meat peppered with rosemary seeds. The girls stared at the man, who appeared to be in his late sixties, stood about five foot four, and had dark, wrinkled skin that hung from his bony frame like the loosely fitted silk shirt he wore. He said something to the other three men in a language neither woman understood, and then he sat down on another table and continued with his meal.

"It seems that he wants us to talk to the tough, black, American girl first," the shorter guy said with a smirk. Two of the Africans led Ronnie away, with the last one closely guarding Dallisha, who knew that this was something more than just a simple robbery.

Within minutes Dallisha heard an ear-piercing scream echoing from the back room, which she knew to be Ronnie's voice. The shattering screams continued for ten minutes straight and then there was a stifling silence. Dallisha was visibly shaking now as the African holding her at gunpoint was smiling, his eyes saying, *you're next.* Dallisha started thinking about running toward the door, but she knew she was so scared her legs would fail her, plus she suspected the guy would shoot her in the back without a second hesitation. The screams soon started again, followed by some intense moaning. The men then emerged from the room just as the old man was finishing up his exotic, late-night dinner. He pointed a pure ivory cane carved with the face of the ancient god of vengeance at

Dallisha, who peed on herself when the Africans started walking toward her.

"It seems that your friend wasn't as tough as she wanted everyone to believe," he said, staring straight at the terrified girl.

"What you want?" Dallisha managed to say.

"We want the rest of the heroin you stole. I don't want you to go through what went on with your friend, but I can't speak for him," the tall guy stated, looking over at his friend who was wiping down a pair of steel pliers.

"Sometimes the simplest tools can be the most effective," the second man said, blowing on the pliers and then wiping them down again.

"Call Goldmine and tell her you want her to bring the remaining heroin down right away," the guy ordered, handing Dallisha a cell phone.

Without having to be told a second time, Dallisha took the phone and quickly dialed her sister's number.

"Stacey, this is Dallisha. These guys say you have their dope. All they want is the rest of it back and they'll let me go," she frantically said into the phone. Goldmine paused for a minute before she spoke.

"Hold up. I'll be right there," she said and then hung up the phone. Dallisha couldn't believe her ears as she repeatedly dialed the number again, only getting the voicemail.

Before she could dial her sister's number again, the phone was roughly snatched from her hands. The short African started talking to the old man in their native tongue with the old man raising his voice at all three men. In a blinding instant, the old man rose from his seated position. As he walked toward Dallisha he swiftly transformed his cane into a sword. Without any emotion, he swung the sword with his frail arm, slicing off the young woman's head. Rich blood spurted up toward the ceiling for a few seconds before the recently decapitated head landed on the table, with Dallisha's eyes still looking up at the African drug lord Mooka, wondering what the shriveled-up old man was going to do.

CHAPTER FIFTY-ONE

Jason was on his way to see Head to straighten some things out. Chase had died at the hands of his brother, and now Free was facing murder charges for the fucked-up lie that Head had told him. He wasn't sure how the confrontation was going to go down with Head, but he was prepared for whatever jumped off. To make the situation even more tense, he'd been hearing rumors of some wild-ass Africans that were trying to move in on Little Vietnam.

Jason slowed his Jeep to a crawl because the block was thick with fire trucks, ambulances, and police cars.

"What the fuck is going on now?" Jason asked out loud as he got out of his vehicle and walked toward the crowd of loud people. As he walked closer to the busy scene, there was a foul odor in the chilly night air, somewhat similar to burnt eggs and diseased, rotting meat. Jason dropped the Newport right out of his mouth, not prepared for what his eyes were seeing. There was an unidentifiable body lying on a front lawn with a still-smoldering car tire tied around the unfortunate victim's neck. The face was a mass of twisted, fused, burned flesh with both eye sockets completely hollowed out, as if a hungry vulture had picked them clean.

The intense heat had caused the tire's rubber to grotesquely mesh together with the victim's neck and chest area, making the man resemble something out of a science fiction horror movie.

"Damn! Who's that?" Jason asked a young woman of about eighteen while he covered his nose with his doorag.

"That's Head. Niggas are going crazy around here. That's why I'm getting my baby and getting the fuck outta here because . . ." Jason wasn't paying the talkative girl any mind anymore. All he heard was the name Head and knew from the jump that no Americans would kill somebody in such a brutal fashion. He knew the Africans were somehow involved. He then looked across the other side of the yellow caution tape. There was a chubby woman in a flowered housecoat lying in back of the ambulance with an oxygen mask on her face. She was flailing her arms wildly as the attendants tried to calm down the hysterical woman. Jason knew that must be Head's mother as he spotted one of Head's girlfriends, crying as she talked to a couple of detectives. Their eyes met as the girl pointed a finger at him, causing the police to look over in his direction.

Jason wasn't sure, but he could have sworn he heard someone call out his name as he hurriedly walked away toward his Jeep. He didn't know what the police wanted with him, but he wasn't sticking around to find out, plus he was rolling dirty.

Jason made it home and called Pumpkin as he started throwing clothes in a big duffel bag.

"Pumpkin, what's up? This is Jason. You remember how you said you wanted to get outta Atlanta because there was nothing here for you? Well let's do it," he said into the phone.

"Yeah, when?" she asked.

"Right now. No, I'm dead serious. I'll be by in a few to scoop you up," Jason said as he finished putting all his sneakers in a big trash bag. Since his sister's funeral, some of his relatives thought it would be in the best interest of his grandmother if she stayed with them for a while. Jason took one last look around to make sure he didn't forget anything, and then he headed out the front door.

Beep, beep, beep.

Pumpkin came down the stairs after hearing the horn. She threw her things in the trunk, slid in next to Jason, and gave him a peck on the cheek.

"So we really gonna bounce?" Pumpkin asked excitedly.

"Yeah, but we gotta make one quick stop before we leave," he said, pulling off.

"You know what to do," Jason stated twenty minutes later as he left the engine running and the couple got out.

"Who is it?" a voice asked after Pumpkin knocked on the door of the house in front of which they had stopped.

"Hi, it's me, Pumpkin. I want to cop an ounce of dat hydro," she answered.

"Yo, it's not a good time right now. Come back tomorrow," White Boy Danny shouted from behind the still closed door.

"Come on. It'll only take a minute," she replied.

"I said I'm motherfucking busy. What are you, deaf or something?" Danny yelled as he cracked open the door. Jason then kicked the door in with full force, sending the stunned Danny flying onto the floor.

Jason and Pumpkin rushed into the house, with Jason holding two guns in each hand. There, sitting around a table filled with an assorted variety of pistols and machine guns, were Detective Summerset and Knowledge, plus one of Knowledge's boys from New York.

"Don't nobody fucking move," Jason ordered, waving his Glock for Danny to go over by the other three men.

"What the fuck you think you doing? Boy, do you know who I am?" Detective Summerset asked with an air of authority.

"Yeah, you're a fat piece-of-shit cop whose the one bringing all these gats into the black neighborhoods," Jason replied, now fully understanding what had been going on. Jason also remembered this detective as the same detective who had tried to tell him that his sister's death might have occurred because she was out whoring and caught a bad trick.

"What? You're a stinking pig? What's dis, a setup?" Knowledge shouted, standing up and looking at both of the white men.

"Shut up and sit the fuck down 'fore I blast your punk ass," Jason said, aiming his gun directly at Knowledge.

"Everybody calm down before things get out of control," the detective said, his hand inching its way toward his service revolver.

"Fuck you and dat bitch," Knowledge yelled, pulling out his gun.

Summerset, thinking Knowledge was directing the comment toward him, snatched his weapon out and started firing wildly in Knowledge's direction. Two shots caught Knowledge's boy in the stomach as he fell forward, clutching his midsection. Knowledge and Jason began exchanging wild shots, with Knowledge trying to kill Pumpkin in the process. She had already dropped to the floor, covering her head. Jason started backing out of the front door, yelling for Pumpkin to come on as Knowledge, who had ducked behind the couch, was frantically trying to throw another clip into his gun.

Knowledge ran out of the house just as Jason was pulling

off. He began firing at the back of the Infiniti truck, breaking the stillness of the night. Then Knowledge quickly went back into the house and saw White Boy Danny kneeling down over the detective, who had a large, gaping hole in the side of his neck.

"Pop, Pop, look what the niggers done. I told you to let me handle them," Danny was saying to his dead father.

"I hate all you motherfucking cops," Knowledge said just as Danny turned to the side to look up at him. No less than six bullets ripped into Danny's face, leaving his family to prepare for a double funeral with closed caskets.

Knowledge then grabbed a couple of the more expensive, high-powered machine guns, wrapped them in his butter-soft, Avirex leather jacket, and walked back to his car as if he was just out taking a late night stroll.

CHAPTER FIFTY-TWO

"Oh shit, you're hit!" Pumpkin shouted when she noticed blood dripping down Jason's arm and forming a puddle on the car's seat.

"I'm cool. I got to make one more stop," he said.

"What! Are you crazy? Let's just get da fuck outta dis town. I can go back to dancing wherever we go and you could just chill," Pumpkin said with urgency in her voice.

"I want to pick up my nephew. You know his mother is a fucking crack head. I just can't leave him," Jason said, feeling a little dizzy from the slug that was still lodged in the meaty part of his shoulder.

"We can come back later. Please, let's just spread out right now. A cop is probably dead back there, along with everyone else," she replied, almost begging him.

Jason pulled to a stop sign and was about to say something when an old van rammed them on Pumpkin's side, sending the jeep flying onto the sidewalk.

"Jason, you all right?" Pumpkin asked, looking at Jason, who was on the verge of passing out. Before another word could be said, a set of strong hands snatched Pumpkin out of the Jeep and threw her to the ground. Pumpkin was head-butted on the bridge of her nose, causing her eyes to water.

"Yeah, I bet you thought you would never see me again!" And there stood Storm, smiling at the shocked Pumpkin. "I'm gonna cut that pretty young face of yours so bad that when I'm through, it's gonna look like a goddamn jigsaw puzzle," Storm said wickedly, holding a military type of knife under Pumpkin's nostrils.

"Oh, God, I never did anything to you," Pumpkin said, trying to shield her face.

"God can't save your stuck up ass now," Storm said, ready to carve up the young girl.

Suddenly Pumpkin heard a click and saw Jason standing behind Storm with his gun in his hand. The weapon had misfired, so Jason rushed the woman, grabbing her in a headlock and pushing her off Pumpkin. Pumpkin then heard police sirens sounding closer and closer as Jason struggled for the large combat knife. Pumpkin jumped up to help her man just as Storm broke free of the weakened Jason. Storm swung the knife upward toward his groin, severing major arteries. Jason let out a low grunt as he grabbed his privates, trying to prevent any more damage as he fell to his knees. The front of his jeans quickly became saturated with dark, sticky blood as Storm stabbed the dying man in the chest.

Pumpkin knew there wasn't anything she or anybody else could do for Jason as she hopped in the driver's side of the Infiniti Jeep, thinking about how they had almost made it out of this madness.

As Pumpkin was driving off Storm violently plugged the knife into Jason's slowly pumping heart. Before the out-of-control Storm could stab the man again, police cars pulled up and officers hopped out with their guns drawn. Pump-kin couldn't hear exactly what the police were telling Storm, but she knew that they asked the madwoman to drop her weapon.

Pumpkin looked in the rearview mirror just as Storm began charging the police. As she turned away she heard a rapid succession of gunfire. Already tired of being in the face of death, Pumpkin drove off, crying and not knowing exactly where she was heading, but she knew without a doubt that she was leaving Atlanta.

* * *

Goldmine boarded a Greyhound bus headed for Balti-more. She wore a pale pink, baggy J. Lo sweat suit and a pair of slightly tinted Gucci shades. She chose the first bus that was leaving the station and brought a one-way ticket. Since her sister had called her saying some guys wanted their dope back, she knew she would never see Dallisha alive again. She threw away her cell phone, grabbing the remaining heroin and money, not bothering to even pack a few items.

"Fuck dat shit. Niggas probably on their way to my place right now. I'll buy some new shit later," Goldmine said, walking to the back of the bus.

"Do you mind if I sit here?" Goldmine asked an older woman, who looked like the grandmotherly type who would bake oatmeal cookies for all her grandchildren.

"No, child, I don't mind. Please have a seat. It be good to have somebody nice to talk to," she said.

Hours later Goldmine felt as if her brain would burst out of her skull from the endless chatter the old woman heaped on her. She talked about everything from how her grandson would love to meet a nice, decent girl like Gold-mine, to describing in detail how each one of her ten cats had a certain cute habit.

"Could you watch my bag for me while I go get something to eat?" Goldmine asked, standing up as the bus made a scheduled stop.

"Go right ahead, dear. Could you bring me back a soda?" the old lady asked, digging in her pocketbook for some loose change.

"Don't worry about it. I got it," Goldmine said.

"God bless your soul," Goldmine heard the old woman say as she walked down the aisle.

Goldmine didn't want to take the chance of walking around with a bag filled with dope and forty thousand dollars in cash. She bought a candy bar and Pepsi from the vending machine and was halfway through her cigarette when the driver made an announcement that it was time to board the bus again. Goldmine crushed her Newport and jumped back on the bus, not wanting to be left behind.

"I got your drink," Goldmine said, looking at an empty seat. She quickly looked under the seat for her bag and found only empty space.

"You seen the old lady that was sitting right here?" Goldmine began frantically asking the other passengers, who shook their heads, and looked at Goldmine like she was crazy. She then ran up to the bus driver, who was just sitting down.

"You seen da old lady from da back who I was talking to?" she asked.

"The one with a gray overcoat?" he asked.

"Yeah, you seen her?" Goldmine asked.

"Oh, she left about ten minutes ago. This was her stop. Someone picked her up. I think it was her sister or somebody," the bus driver replied, starting the engine.

Goldmine stood there dumbfounded, not believing her

ears. She had just got beat by what she took to be a sweet old lady. The only thing she had to her name now was three dollars and a warm soda.

"Easy come, easy motherfucking go," Goldmine said as she walked slowly back to her seat.

Sneak Peek

GET MONEY CHICKS

BY ANNA J.

A Hustle Gone Dead Wrong

"Bitch, what is you whispering for? I can't hear a thang you sayin'," my girl Karen yelled into the phone over the loud music in the background.

My heart was beating in my throat, and even if I tried I couldn't speak no louder than I was at the moment. I collected my thoughts as best as I could, but all I could hear were sirens, the clink of handcuffs, and bars shutting behind me. I had to get out of there and quick.

"Girl, you gotta go get Shanna and get over here quick. I think I killed him, girl." By now tears were rolling from the corners of my eyes like a run in a pair of stockings. I couldn't breathe, and my vision was blurring as we spoke.

"Over where? Black Ron's house? I thought you was in there pulling a caper?"

"Karen, listen to me. You have to go get Shanna and come over here now! I need y'all. I don't know what to do."

"No problem. I think I just saw her pull up to the building. We'll be there in like three minutes."

Instead of responding I hung up. Snatching my clothes from behind the chair, I slid into my gear quickly and went downstairs to wait for my friends. In my heart I hoped this nigga was just playing a cruel joke, and was just trying to scare me. I couldn't go to jail for murder. I didn't have time to be fighting no bitches off me 'cause I was fresh meat, and as sexy as I am there's no doubt they'd be trying to get at me.

Not even four minutes passed, and my girls were pulling up to Black Ron's door. I breathed a temporary sigh of relief as I opened the door to let them in, but the moment the door was closed I busted into tears and fell into Shanna's arms. If my morning didn't start out bad, my night was ending in the worst way.

"Mina, pull yourself together and talk to me. Where is Ron, and what happened?" Shanna said, making me stand up on my own two feet and wipe my face. I sniffled a few times in an attempt to catch my breath. We took seats around the living room, and I ran the entire day down to my girls.

"I met Ron at the club last night and we came here to handle our business. He was already drunker then a mu'fucka, so I knew getting ends from him was going to be a piece of cake," I said to them as I wiped snot and tears from my face.

I went on to tell them how Black Ron, the largest dealer in all of this side of Yeadon, was popping Xani's like they were lifesavers. He had already been drinking way before I saw him at Heat, a local night spot in Sharon Hill over there on Hook Road where all the ballers hung out. He was up in that piece flashing money like he had just won the damn Power Ball, and I was on his ass before any of those other smut bitches could take advantage of his weak state of mind.

We left there around two in the morning, and I ended up having to help him to his car and drive to his crib so he wouldn't kill me and any other unsuspecting motorist behind the wheel. By the time we got to the crib he was able to walk a little straighter, and he made it upstairs just fine.

My plan was to fuck him to sleep and help myself to a little bit of that money when he was out like a light. I would then ask him for money in the morning because I knew he didn't know how much money he was throwing around the night before. I mean, the late great Notorious B.I.G. said it best, "Never get high on your own supply." A chick like me will catch you slippin' and then the next thing you know, it's curtains.

By the time I got finished taking a shower and came back into the bedroom, this nigga was lying back in the bed with his dick in his hand, watching *My Baby Got Back* on the television. Silly me thought he would be out for the night, but I guessed I would have to work for my money this evening.

"You feeling better?" I asked him, inching closer to the bed. He turned his attention my way for a split second before looking back at the television.

"Yeah, my head pounding a little, but I'm cool. Thanks for seeing that I got home. Out of all the tricks I fuck with, you are the only one I truly trust."

I didn't say anything; instead I toweled my body dry and began to apply some of the lotion he had on his dresser. I pretended not to pay him any mind, but I saw him go from watching me to watching the porn movie out of the corner of my eye. I made a display of massaging my breasts and spreading my legs, acting the entire time like he wasn't in the room.

"Girl, get over here and ride this dick. What you puttin'

all that damn lotion on for anyway? You just gonna be ashy in the morning all over again."

I continued to lotion my body like I didn't hear what he said. He was stroking his dick in a long, slow motion, and I'd be damned if I didn't want some of it. Black Ron was definitely working with some shit. I figured I might as well make it a two-for-one deal—get the best nut of my life, and the cash to go with it.

Walking over to the bed, I waited until I got to the side to drop the towel. Through half-closed eyelids, Ron watched me give him head while he finger fucked my pussy and smacked me on my ass.

Now, this nigga had been drinking Henny all night, so I knew this was gonna be forever. My head skills were impeccable, and in no time flat I was swallowing all of his babies. But his dick was still standing at attention.

"Damn, girl. If you used your head for anything else you'd be a genius. Get up and ride Daddy's dick."

Ignoring the comment he made, I did what I was told, riding him like I'd been taking horse riding lessons my entire life. I guess my momma's dreams of me being a ballerina were crushed, because the woman I am now is nothing like the girl I was back in the day.

I was on his dick hard, knowing the payout at the end of the night would be marvelous. He stretched my long legs out in all kinds of directions, and I could have sworn I heard him saying something about loving me before he pulled his dick out and busted yet another nut in my face. I pretended like I enjoyed it while he panted all hard in an effort to catch his breath beside me.

Reaching over to the side of the bed, I grabbed the towel to remove his children from my face. This dude was a beast, and although I could see him falling asleep, I knew it would be on again in the morning. I took that moment to take eight one hundred dollar bills from his pants pocket and put it in my wallet before lying in the bed next to him. He snuggled up close to me, and before I knew it I was sleep, too.

In the morning I woke up to him sliding his already hard dick into me from the back, and I had to clear the cold out of my eyes so I could focus. This nut was a little quicker than last night, and I was grateful. I laid back in the bed and watched him stumble around the room, and almost fall into the hallway over one of his Timberland boots. I laughed, but not out loud, because Black Ron is crazy and has been known to knock a chick upside the head for less. When he came back into the room, his eyes looked bloodshot, and he damn near crawled to the bed to get in it.

"You gonna be okay, BR?" I asked, noticing his breathing was getting heavier and he was breaking out in a sweat. I didn't know what was wrong with him, but I wouldn't just leave him like this. I still had to get paid for my services.

"Yeah, I'm cool. Those damn pills got me trippin'," he said in a slurred tone as his eyes closed, and his head fell to the side.

"How many did you take?" I asked, scared as hell. I didn't know what was happening, but I couldn't call the cops because I knew this nigga had drugs or something up in this camp, and I'd be damned if I was going to jail for conspiracy.

"Like four of 'em this morning, but I'm cool. I just need to sleep it off."

I didn't answer; I just moved closer to him and let him put his head on my stomach. Not too long after that he was snoring and I was able to turn him on his back. I watched him for a little while, but before I knew it I was asleep, too.

"And when I woke up he wasn't breathing and was foaming at the mouth. I concluded my story in a loud wail. "Lord, please, if you get me out of this one I promise I'll stop being a ho!"

"Girl, he prolly just thirsty. Let's go see what's crackin," Karen said, and we all got up and followed her upstairs. When we got into the bedroom, he was the same way I left him: sprawled out on the bed, ass naked, with his dick pointing to the ceiling.

"Damn, that nigga working with that? I had no idea," Karen said as she got closer to the bed. I stayed my ass by the door because I didn't know if he was going to jump up or what.

"Damn girl, I know you said you had a killer pussy, but I didn't know you was for real about that shit," Shanna said.

While Karen and Shanna stood there laughing and high-fiving each other I was a nervous wreck standing in the doorway. I killed a man—I think. And I didn't know what to do. How was I going to get my hot ass out of this mess?

"OK, I gota plan." Karen's loud-ass mouth brought me out of my trance. At that point I was open to anything, as long as no one pointed the finger at me.

"OK, what is it?" Shanna said while scoping the room out. I'm sure she was looking for something to take, and I could care less. I just wanted to leave.

"Mina, wash him and dry his body off. Fix the sheets around him when you're done. Shanna, go get a trash bag out of the kitchen. It's clean-up time."

"I ain't touchin' his dead ass. You do it!" I yelled at her, still stuck in the doorway. I wasn't about to go nowhere near Black Ron. The next time I would see his ass was at his funeral.

"Bitch, that's your pussy juice all over him. You want the feds to come and get your ass?"

I stood there for a second more before I ran to the

bathroom to throw up. I couldn't believe the turn my day had taken, and I knew if nothing else I had to walk away clean. Taking the rag from the sink I used the night before, I soaped it up and went to the room to handle my business. It was hard for me to clean up Ron's dead body, but what else could I do?

I didn't want to get caught, so I had to handle my business. In the meantime, Karen had found his stash, along with his jewels and a couple of brand new button-down shirts with the tags still on them. We cleaned as best we could and was out of there in no time.

Back at Karen's crib, she counted the money we took from Ron's while Shanna rolled one of five Dutches and I stared out of the window watching the world pass me by. I couldn't believe the life I was living, and I knew after today things had to change.

I got up and changed into a pair of Karen's sweats, taking the club outfit I wore the night before and throwing it in the garbage. I didn't want anything to remind me of that horrible day. I came back in the living room just in time to get the blunt passed to me. Inhaling deeply, I hoped the effects of the illegal drug would cloud my mind long enough for me to make some sense of what happened. I was scared to death, and even though my girls told me I would be cool, I knew I was waiting for what happened to come around to me.

"So, what do we do now?" I asked Karen and Shanna. The weed started to take effect, and I wanted to enjoy my high as long as possible.

"We wait. I'm sure someone will find his body soon. We just act like we don't know nothing and keep it moving. We got a couple of thousand to spend, so we focus on that."

I knew Karen was right, but I couldn't help but think

about it. I was now sure that it was the Xanex pills that killed Black Ron, but I was the last one seen with him, and that was my biggest fear. For right now, I would do my best not to worry, but like they always say . . . what you do in the dark always comes out in the light.

About the Author

DeJon was born in California, but raised in Queens, NY, where he started writing short stories for various school newspapers. Dejon is in the process of producing a documentary film, which is titled *Rules Of Engagement For The Inner City*. Currently, he is working on *Ice Cold Vengeance* (the sequel to *Ice Cream For Freaks*).

LOOK FOR MORE HOT TITLES FROM

Q-BORO BOOKS

DARK KARMA - JUNE 2007
$14.95
ISBN 1-933967-12-9

What if the criminal was forced to live the horror that they caused? The drug dealer finds himself in the body of the drug addict and he suffers through the withdrawals, living on the street, the beatings, the rapes and the hunger. The thief steals the rent money and becomes the victim that finds herself living on the street and running for her life and the murderer becomes the victim's father and he deals with the death of a son and a grieving mother.

GET MONEY CHICKS - SEPTEMBER 2007
$14.95
ISBN 1-933967-17-X

For Mina, Shanna, and Karen, using what they had to get what they wanted was always an option. Best friends since day one, they always had a thing for the hottest gear, luxurious lifestyles, and the ballers who made it all possible. All of this changes for Mina when a tragedy makes her open her eyes to the way she's living. Peer pressure and loyalty to her girls collide with her own morality, sending Mina into a no-win situation.

AFTER-HOURS GIRLS - AUGUST 2007
$14.95
ISBN 1-933967-16-1

Take part in this tale of two best friends, Lisa and Tosha, as they stalk the nightclubs and after-hours joints of Detroit searching for excitement, money, and temporary companionship. These two divas stand tall until the unforgivable Motown streets catch up to them. One must fall. You, the reader, decide which.

THE LAST CHANCE - OCTOBER 2007
$14.95
ISBN 1-933967-22-6

Running their L.A. casino has been rewarding for Luke Chance and his three brothers. But recently it seems like everyone is trying to get a piece of the pie. An impending hostile takeover of their casino could leave them penniless and possibly dead. That is, until their sister Keilah Chance comes home for a short visit. Keilah is not only beautiful, but she also can be ruthless. Will the Chance family be able to protect their family dynasty?

Traci must find a way to complete her journey out of her first and only failed

LOOK FOR MORE HOT TITLES FROM

Q-BORO
BOOKS

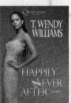

LOOK FOR MORE HOT TITLES FROM

Q-BORO
B O O K S

OBSESSION 101
$6.99
ISBN 0977733548
After a horrendous trauma. Rashawn Ams is left pregnant and flees town to give birth to her son and repair her life after confiding in her psychiatrist. After her return to her life, her town, and her classroom, she finds herself the target of an intrusive secret admirer who has plans for her.

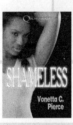

SHAMELESS- OCTOBER 2006
$6.99
ISBN 0977733513
Kyle is sexy, single, and smart; Jasmyn is a hot and sassy drama queen. These two complete opposites find love - or something real close to it - while away at college. Jasmyn is busy wreaking havoc on every man she meets. Kyle, on the other hand, is trying to walk the line between his faith and all the guilty pleasures being thrown his way. When the partying college days end and Jasmyn tests HIV positive, reality sets in.

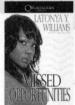

MISSED OPPORTUNITIES - MARCH 2007
$14.95
ISBN 1933967013
Missed Opportunities illustrates how true-to-life characters must face the consequences of their poor choices. Was each decision worth the opportune cost? LaTonya Y. Williams delivers yet another account of love, lies, and deceit all wrapped up into one powerful novel.

ONE DEAD PREACHER - MARCH 2007
$14.95
ISBN 1933967021
Smooth operator and security CEO David Price sets out to protect the sexy, smart, and saucy Sugar Owens from her husband, who happens to be a powerful religious leader. Sugar isn't as sweet as she appears, however, and in a twisted turn of events, the preacher man turns up dead and Price becomes the prime suspect.

Attention Writers:

Writers looking to get their books published can view our submission guidelines by visiting our website at: *www.QBOROBOOKS.com*

What we're looking for: Contemporary fiction in the tradition of Darrien Lee, Carl Weber, Anna J., Zane, Mary B. Morrison, Noire, Lolita Files, etc; groundbreaking mainstream contemporary fiction.

We prefer email submissions to: candace@qborobooks.com in MS Word, PDF, or rtf format only. However, if you wish to send the submission via snail mail, you can send it to:

Q-BORO BOOKS Acquisitions Department
165-41A Baisley Blvd., Suite 4. Mall #1
Jamaica, New York 11434

*** By submitting your work to Q-Boro Books, you agree to hold Q-Boro books harmless and not liable for publishing similar works as yours that we may already be considering or may consider in the future. ***

1. Submissions will not be returned.
2. Do not contact us for status updates. If we are interested in receiving your full manuscript, we will contact you via email or telephone.
3. Do not submit if the entire manuscript is not complete.

Due to the heavy volume of submissions, if these requirements are not followed, we will not be able to process your submission.